BOOKS BY MIMI STRONG

For a current listing of books and
series, visit www.mimistrong.com

CHAPTER 1

My heart got slammed pretty hard, but it wasn't broken. When you've got as much sass as me, you don't crumble easily.

However, nothing knocks you over quite like having a complete stranger notice your pain. For me, it was the photographer's assistant, a very nice, very gay young man named Mitchell.

(Not Mitch. *Mitchell.*)

I was getting ready to mainline three espresso shots when *Not-Mitch* Mitchell came up to me, tipped his immaculately-groomed face to the side, and said, "Two things: may I call you Peaches, and may I offer you a hug?"

I held him back with a raised palm. "Don't you dare be nice to me. I am just barely hanging on by a thread."

We were alone in the swanky kitchen at the photography studio. Mitchell, compact and blond with an angelic face that made his age difficult to guess, looked around furtively, then whispered, "Did you have a fight with your boyfriend? With Dalton Deangelo? We've never met, but of course I love him to pieces. That face. Those green eyes." He fanned himself with one hand. "But if you want me to, I'll start hating him immediately."

I wrapped the pristine white terry cloth robe tighter around myself, keenly aware that the bits of fabric I was modeling that day were underwear and not the parts of a swimsuit. I'd said to my father it was basically the same thing—underwear, bikini, whatever. But it was NOT basically the same thing.

Just like how dating someone because you like them is NOT basically the same thing as dating them as research for an acting role.

I'd been up past four o'clock that morning wrestling with the horrifying realization that Dalton Deangelo, the super-hot actor you know and love as vampire Drake Cheshire, had been dating me the last two weeks as *research*.

He'd been in my hometown shooting an indie movie in which his good-looking, successful character dates a chubby girl. I happen to *be* a chubby girl (just one of my many awesome attributes), so you can see how I made that leap of logic.

I tossed back three tiny cups of espresso and tightened my robe again.

Mitchell swatted my hand. "Not too tight, or you'll give yourself red wrinkle lines on your skin."

"So? Won't they just airbrush that out?"

Mitchell laughed. "My boss doesn't allow airbrushing of his photos."

"No airbrushing?"

He gave me a sympathetic look. "The lighting is very bright."

"That's what I'm afraid of!"

Another sympathetic look. "Do you want that hug now? It will help. I give excellent hugs."

"Fine, but stop being so damn nice to me. Treat me bad. I think a little abuse brings out my strength."

"I can be butch," he said, frowning.

"You're wearing a lavender turtleneck and what smells like Chanel No. 5."

He frowned and joked, "Shut up. I'm going to be all forceful and hug you now and you're going to like it."

Mitchell was already blushing with embarrassment as he came in to give me a hug, so I squished my chest against him harder, then murmured in his ear, "Pull my hair."

Bless his heart, he reached up and gingerly gave my teased-out blond locks a tug.

"You animal!" I howled, laughing.

He stepped back from the embrace, grinning. "My hugs are good, right?"

I kept laughing, and then I remembered the words I'd read in Dalton's movie script the night before. His character told a friend that *maybe being with a fat girl wasn't so bad after all. That if he closed his eyes, there was so much of her, it was like having a threesome.*

It was the meanest thing I'd ever seen, and I've seen cruel things.

And then I wasn't laughing anymore. I was sniffing back tears, barely hanging on, and poor Mitchell scurried around apologizing and handing me tissues.

~

Thanks to Mitchell, I got through the morning's photo shoot. The photographer seemed both disgusted and fascinated by me, if that makes sense.

He'd say things like, "Interesting," as he looked at one of my curves or creases, and I didn't want to know what he meant. I had two days of photographs, and I just had to get through it, one minute at a time, the same way you get over heartbreak.

Whenever I got flustered, mixing up my right arm with my left arm and nearly knocking over lights instead of looking fetching, Mitchell caught my eye.

"Don't make me pull your hair," he'd whisper in his trying-to-be-butch voice.

I wanted to fold him up and take him back home to Beaverdale in my luggage.

I told him about my souvenir plans when we took a lunch break, and he looked me straight in the eye and said, "Your town is called Beaverdale? Oh, no. That's all wrong. In case you haven't guessed by the summer-weight cashmere mock-turtleneck, I'm not into beaver."

We were standing under the awning of a food truck, eating salad wraps with rice noodles, prawns, and peanut sauce. The day was overcast just enough that Washington didn't seem so far away from LA.

"Oh, no," Mitchell moaned, staring past me.

I turned and followed his gaze.

"Hold me back before I embarrass myself," I muttered under my breath.

The shirtless man approaching us was all meat, no filler. His six-pack was so defined, he made Dalton Deangelo look like the *Before* picture in a gym advertisement. Oh, and he had a face of some sort, too. Not that I saw it for the first minute or so when he came up to us and greeted Mitchell by name.

They talked while I jammed the noodle wrap into my mouth to keep myself from saying something ridiculous. I don't think of myself as being a very fun or outgoing person, but my mouth thinks it's fun. My mouth says a lot of things, not necessarily endorsed by me or my brain.

"I'm Keith," he said, offering me his hand. "We'll be shooting together this afternoon."

I shook his hand gingerly. "Nope. You couldn't be more wrong."

He laughed. "You're Peaches Monroe, right? Yes, I assure you. We are shooting together this afternoon."

I turned to Mitchell. "It's true," he said, offering me another of his sympathetic looks.

Keith ordered a salad wrap and leaned back against the food truck, his shirtless torso on display. My gaze drifted up to his face. I'd already had a gander at everything around, above, and below his gray jogging shorts, but my eyes had saved the best for last. His face had a sexy Clark Kent vibe, with a square jaw, smirking lips, and a swirl of curly dark hair falling down over his forehead. The only flaw keeping him from being SuperMan's alter ego was that his eyes were a golden brown, not blue. He wore nerdy black-framed glasses, which, combined with his bare chest, caused a few circuits in my brain to over-fire and burn out. The result was a shocking five seconds of silence before my mouth got moving again.

"Nice glasses," I said. "Are you a part-time model and a part-time accountant? Do you get changed in a phone booth?"

Keith leaned back against the food truck, his abdominal muscles gleaming like six tiny little glazed hams. "Sure. Give me your number, and I'll do your taxes." He took a bite of his wrap and chewed slowly. "What are you doing after the shoot?"

"Hands off, Mr. Greedyfingers," Mitchell said with sharp authority. "She's Dalton Deangelo's girlfriend, and if anything of

4

yours touches her inappropriately this afternoon, I'll use my taser on the offending appendage."

Keith held his hands up, chuckling. "Easy, Mitch."

"Mitchell."

Keith turned to me, his dazzling, rich mahogany brown eyes gently removing the zip-up hoodie I was wearing over my fancy-pants bra.

"So," he said. "This your first shoot working with another model. Don't be scared. I'm big and strong. Find something you like and grab on."

Mitchell rolled his eyes. "Peaches, just ignore him. He's disgusting. They're *all* disgusting."

My eyes wandered over to Keith's nipples and skipped around those pink circles like they were merry-go-rounds at the Model Keith Amusement Park. My brain dug up something I'd read somewhere about male models: *they ice the nipples during the photo shoot, so they aren't puffy*. Keith's nips looked great exactly how they were.

"Come on," Mitchell said, tugging my hand.

I wanted to stay and gaze at the scenery, but Mitchell led us back to the crosswalk to return to the photo studio.

Once we'd left the cute model boy behind, I asked, "What makes you say that cute guy is disgusting?"

"I don't like how they flirt with the girl models. But if I'm being perfectly honest, it works. He's going to be a big star soon."

"He's kind of a big deal?"

"Keith Raven? Oh, I guess you wouldn't have heard of him, since you're new to the business." We stood for a few minutes in silence, waiting for the light to change and stop the endless flow of LA cars. "Keith Raven is up and coming. Today's shoot can make or break a modeling career, for both of you."

"No pressure," I said with a snort.

"He likes you."

"Sure, he does," I said sarcastically. "All the hottest guys just can't get enough of my peaches. I'm the luckiest girl in the world."

"Sweetie." Mitchell reached out to grab my hand in his to give it a squeeze. "You've got something people want. You have a spark. You know who you are. People will always be attracted to that."

"Plus there's my awesome personality."

"Mmm." He looked down at the pavement, then we both cracked up laughing.

"Flirt with Keith Raven," Mitchell said. "Let him *think* he's getting somewhere with you. The magic will come out on the film. Don't worry, because you're in a safe space. I won't let things get too far on the set."

"You mean suck in my gut, take all the complicated posing directions, and grope some hot male model, all at the same time?"

"It's like you've done this before!"

~

We got back into the studio, where they touched up my hair and makeup again. They actually put makeup on way more than my face and neck. The makeup girl went through a full tube. My pale Washington skin had never looked better.*

*There was one time I'd gotten into self-tanning products, but the change had been too transfixing. I was working in a clothing store at the time, and the manager pulled me aside to have an intervention about the amount of time I was spending admiring myself in the shop's many mirrors. I was so humiliated, I never self-tanned again.

Because my skin looked so radiant once more, I thought to myself, *Hey, maybe this underwear photo shoot with flirty Keith Raven won't be so bad.*

Never before has someone tempted fate so flagrantly.

My round bits got shoveled/nestled into a sky-blue bra and panties set, and I was under the hot lights on set once again. I think I know why movie stars are called stars. The constant bright lights are so intense, the rays burrow their way into your skin and make you glow in the dark.

Mitchell put on the music, which wasn't so much music as it was a curious soundscape, from wind chimes to people whispering, plus what sounded like hair being cut—that *shirr-shirr* sound. The sounds rolled up into my brain and set off little starbursts of pleasure, making me feel calm and relaxed for the shots.

The photographer, a scrawny, bearded fellow who had a weird name I can neither pronounce nor spell, said, "Like this, yes. Just like this. Yes. Gaze down. Gently up. Softness. Softness. Gaze up. Softness. Stargaze. Like this, yes."

It had taken me all morning to figure out when he said "Like this" he didn't mean for me to stop and stare dumbly at him for an example of what to do. What he meant was "Like that," and someone needed to correct his grammar, but he was the professional and I was the amateur, so I didn't say anything. Being in LA had shushed me, in a way.

Keith walked onto the set wearing nothing but a shiny pair of sky-blue pocket briefs, slung extremely low—so low I could see curly-yet-trimmed pubes popping out.

He gave me a toss of his hair as greeting and said, "Hey Peaches, how do you like these apples?" He twirled around to reveal round, tanned butt cleavage. Then he made his butt cleavage dance with a series of muscle pulses.

Mitchell leaped into action, jumping between us with a towel held up to cover the dancing butt cleavage.

"Too late," I said, giggling. "That image will never scrub out of my brain."

The photographer smiled for the first time that day, and the half-dozen other people on the set also perked up. Keith brought an earthy, feel-good energy with him. Even the air had a zing to it, like a summer night right before lightning strikes.

Keith adjusted the only things he could, his black-rimmed accountant glasses and his underwear, pulling them up to the nearly-decent level, and we got started.

"Just relax," he murmured to me as he moved in closer.

"I'm totally relaxed."

He looked down, his gaze licking all over my bare skin like a giant tongue. "Then why are your knuckles white?"

I unclenched my hands and shook them out. "Just practicing my grip for when I grab onto you. You did invite me to grab onto whatever I like, right?"

He raised his dark eyebrows high over the plastic-framed glasses that made him look nerdy-cute. "Be my guest."

I reached up. I was going to *pretend* to tweak his nipple between my bent fingers, but he leaned in at the last second, and I grabbed the pink button of flesh.

He closed his eyes and grinned.

As the flash bulbs pulsed with bursts of light, I stood there with his nipple pinched between my fingers.

"Yes," the photographer said. "Just like this. Sensual. Demure. So cheeky."

Keith leaned forward and whispered in my ear, "Chin up. Keep going. Now wrap your right arm around my back. No, not the left, the right. The left one blocks our bodies to the camera. Now look up at me like you want to kiss me."

At regular volume, I said, "I'm not an actress."

"All beautiful women are actresses," he said smoothly. "And there are few as beautiful as you."

I released the nipple, draped my right arm around his hot, nearly-naked body, and gazed up at him. He'd tricked me with flattery, because now I *did* actually want to kiss him for being so sweet.

The photographer called for some adjustments to the lighting, but instructed us to keep going, so we did.

I gazed up longingly at Keith, drinking in his beautiful face. Mitchell swooped in and took the nerdy glasses off Keith's nose, and suddenly he looked so dangerous. I trembled. Just one knee. Just one tremble. But Keith noticed.

He knelt down and swept his fingertips behind my knee. I lifted my leg reflexively, and Keith placed the sole of my foot on top of his thigh. I gulped, the sound of my hard swallow audible over the sibilant soundscape. He brushed his lips across the tip of my knee, and he gazed at Miss Kitty like he was heading there next, diving in lips first.

"Eep!" I exclaimed, which made me feel ever-so professional.

There were people all around us, and cameras, and still he was devouring me with his eyes.

He gazed up through dark eyelashes while the corners of his mouth twitched up in a wicked grin. I remembered what Mitchell had said about flirting with Keith to make sure we got great photos. Dimly, I was aware of photos being taken. I needed to play along, so I lifted one hand up to the corner of my mouth and pretended to nibble my finger.

The soundscape playing over the speakers whispered like wind in willow trees, like secrets being told. Inspired, I moved my finger to the center of my lips, making a shushing gesture.

Keith gazed up with an innocent expression. At the photographer's suggestion, he stood again. He surprised me by grabbing me roughly by both shoulders.

Naturally, I slapped him across the face.

MIMI STRONG

CHAPTER 2

I'd just slapped the dangerously-cute model after he grabbed my shoulders.

"Sorry," he stammered, stepping back and looking confused.

Mitchell called out, "Water! Water now!"

I flinched, feeling ashamed of my overreaction and expecting to be hosed down for my bad behavior, but then the hot lights turned off and one of the junior assistants hustled up with a bottle of water.

Keith took the bottle in his hand, hunching over and leaning on Mitchell. With a wince, he cracked the seal to remove the cap. He tipped up the bottle and guzzled a third of the water, then scowled at the bottle as he put the cap back on.

Mitchell asked if he needed a chair or a break, but Keith said he'd be fine in a minute.

"You let yourself get dehydrated," I said, partly admonishing him and partly soothing him.

Mitchell snapped his fingers and instructed one of the girls to bring a chair.

Keith's eyebrows knitted together, and he sat down in a folding chair being quickly set up behind him.

"Is this normal?" I asked Mitchell.

Mitchell nodded, then signaled that he had to do something, but would be back in a few minutes.

Keith looked up at me from where he sat recovering in the chair. "I scared you."

"Pfft. I don't scare that easy. Sorry I slapped you."

"I took the usual diuretics, but last night's party put me over. I had one beer, and it tasted like another. You know how that is."

A tiny female assistant whispered something in his ear.

"No, thank you. I don't take drugs," he said.

She ran off, red-cheeked and looking scolded.

He gazed up at me, his helplessness doing a number on my emotions. "But I wouldn't mind a square of chocolate. Is there a vending machine nearby?"

I started walking toward the dressing room. "Yes, there is a candy supply nearby, and it's called My Purse."

~

A moment later, we'd both enjoyed a few squares of dark chocolate heaven, he'd sipped more water (but not so much that he'd lose the definition lines on his abdominal muscles), and we got back to shooting.

"Would you feel more comfortable with your glasses?" I asked.

"They're just props. I have perfect eyesight."

"Aren't you Mr. Perfect."

"I bet you say that to all the guys."

"Just the ones I model underwear with."

"I feel special. Did you ever tell me what your plans are for tonight?"

Mitchell interrupted us with a subtle cough, then said, "Feel free to talk through the shoot, but without moving your mouths."

"Don't get me in trouble," I whispered, trying not to move my mouth.

"My middle name is Trouble."

I held my finger to his lips and warned him with a flash of my eyes. I didn't want to get fired on my first day as a model, not even for a boy as cute as him.

I turned my back to him and gave him a coy over-the-shoulder look. The photographer approved of this, and we kept going.

Keith's sexy stare and his touch still made me nervous, but his mini dehydration crisis had made him more life-size to me. Plus, like the beginning of so many great relationships, we'd bonded over some high-quality chocolate.

By the close of the session, we were both dressed in the most outrageous of the outfits yet, and the poses were getting equally creative. I wore stretchy, black booty shorts that were stitched to mimic leather shorts, plus a red patent-leather bustier. On my skin, everything felt about as sexy as those plastic zip-up bags duvet sets come in, but I knew I *looked* hot. My peaches had never looked fresher.

I stood on set waiting for Dalton—whoops! I meant Keith. Not Dalton. Nope, Dalton was barely even on my mind, except for a brief thought once every hour or so, tinged with guilt and sadness, plus a bit of rage.

I pushed away those thoughts like a bad dream.

Keith Raven, sexy and mildly-dehydrated underwear model with a bad reputation, walked onto the set in a pair of red pouch briefs. The most notable thing about the briefs was that they were not... shall we say... opaque.

I could see right through the taut fabric. Peen and peen's best friends, the round lads. Stick and berries.

As discreetly as is possible for a big-mouthed, free-spirited gal such as myself, I surreptitiously alerted Keith to his nudity.

"Dude, I can see your mancandy."

"Really?"

"That banana hammock does not conceal your banana."

He leaned in and whispered in my ear, "That's why I'm getting paid triple my rate."

He'd whispered to me plenty during the shoot, mostly posing instructions, but this time, his lips touched my ear. His whisper spiraled into my ear like a swirling whistle, and set off fireworks in my brain. Before he pulled his face away, he let out one hot exhalation across my ear. My woowoo did a happy dance.

Mitchell clapped his hands, breaking the spell.

"One last shot, everyone," Mitchell announced. "It's going great, people, so let's jump up and knock this last one out of the ballpark. Let's knock the old pigskin. Wait, is that a football?"

The photographer scowled at Mitchell. "I've asked you not to mangle sports metaphors."

Mitchell shook his fists in a pretend cheer. "Rah, rah, go Tigers! Spank the competition!"

Everyone giggled, and the photographer called for a wooden chair to be brought in to the otherwise-plain set. He called Mitchell to him, then Mitchell ran to the quiet lady who was there on behalf of the underwear line, then she came up to me and pulled me aside.

She said, "We'd like to take a few shots of you pretending to get spanked, but only if you feel comfortable with that."

"I should call my dad," I said. "He's sort of my manager. Wait, that might be an awkward conversation. 'Hey, Dad, do you mind if a sexy male model in see-through underpants pretends to spank me? It's just pretend spanking, not real spanking. Oh, it's for the photo session, not recreation. Hello? Dad?'"

She looked pointedly at the big clock on the wall.

Part of me knew I ought to say no. Time pressure is a classic manipulation technique, and I knew that.

"You don't need to call him," she said. "We probably won't even use the shots, but they'd be good to have."

I'd barely slept the night before, and it had been such a long day, but the photographer seemed more excited than ever. He and Keith were talking over the shot, and they both looked so stoked.

"What the hell," I said with a shrug as I walked back to the camera. "Let's do this. Spank me, baby. I've been a bad girl."

"I like this side of you," Keith said, giving me an admiring look.

With my hand on my hip, I said, "You like all the sides of me, especially the front side."

"I don't know. Your front side's got some serious competition from your back side."

"I bet you say that to all the girls."

Everyone else returned to their positions for some lighting discussion, leaving us to talk in semi-private.

"You're a big flirt," I said. "Is that why they hired you?"

"Nah. I'm just lucky I look enough like your boyfriend, Dalton Deangelo. I'm the cheap knock-off version of him, but I don't mind. My contract just expired for another line, and I worried I wasn't going to get picked up. Then I'd be back to doing headless shots for smaller lines, and that's no fun."

"Wait, you got picked for this because you look like Dalton?"

"Peaches, I'm good, but I'm not that good. Of course it's because I look like him." He tilted his head to the side and gave me a dramatic look. "See it now?"

I did see the resemblance, and I got an unsettled feeling, like I was in the midst of doing something wrong. Was I? This whole underwear modeling thing had only happened because of a chain of events that began with me dating Dalton Deangelo while he was in my hometown shooting a movie. Was I... riding his coattails? And was appearing in sexy magazine spreads being spanked by someone who resembled him... taking advantage of that connection?

Someone was giving instructions, and I shuffled around aimlessly, hoping I was getting closer to where they wanted me.

WHACK!

Keith's hand landed on my ass. I hadn't been expecting it, so naturally my reflexes kicked in and I went to slap him.

This time, though, he dodged and caught my hand by the wrist.

More clicks. More photos were being taken, whether I was confused or not.

"You won't fool me twice," he growled playfully.

"Keith, I'm the fool."

"That's not sexy talk," he whispered, his eyes on the photographer.

"I don't feel sexy."

"Bend over my knee. I'll make you feel sexy."

I looked into his warm, gold-brown eyes, searching for guidance, or strength, or wisdom. What the hell was I doing? Everything was wrong.

Keith took my hand and leaned in so his face was close to mine, my palm on his chest. The world kept spinning around me, my thoughts and fears swirling. The clicking had stopped, and now assistants were buzzing all around us as the photographer changed his lens.

Keith's eyes were steady. He alone was the stillness amidst the storm. My palm rested on his chest.

"Can you feel my heart?" he asked.

"No."

"Do you ever meditate?"

"No."

"Close your eyes."

I swallowed hard and shut my eyes. Without my vision, I noticed what hadn't been clear before. The weird whispering-chirping soundscape had stopped playing on the stereo, replaced by normal music. A piano. The song was beautiful, and hauntingly familiar. I couldn't feel Keith's heartbeat through the muscle of his chest, but I could feel his chest rising and falling with his breathing. I deepened my breaths to match his.

After a moment, I felt a rhythm, though I couldn't tell if it was the pulse from my hand or from his chest. Either way, the beating soothed me. I could hear traffic on the other side of the studio's windows, and it sounded almost like water. The air felt moister now, like rain was about to fall.

I opened my eyes to find Keith's face in beautiful relaxation, his eyes closed. I could see thin red lines on his eyelids. He had the tiniest scar running through one eyebrow. You wouldn't see it unless you were right up close, like this, and his dazzling eyes were closed.

This is what he looks like when he's sleeping, I thought.

He murmured, "Are you staring at me?"

I didn't say anything, just grinned.

"I can feel you looking at me," he said, his thick, dark lashes still resting on the tops of his impressive cheekbones.

"Are you wearing mascara?" I asked.

His eyes flashed open.

"None of your business," he said, pretending to be embarrassed.

The photographer interrupted us to say the lens was changed and it was time to shoot.

Mitchell brought by more water and concerned looks. I assured him I was fine.

For the next hour, I felt like I was outside of my body, watching myself as I bent and knelt and stood and bent some more. I was a marionette on invisible strings.

What was that expression? What awful name had that hoochie reporter woman who'd invaded my bookstore referred to actors by? *Meat puppets*. That was it. I felt like a meat puppet.

The meat puppet purses her lips as she gets spanked.

She looks demure. *Yes, like this*. Like this.

Spank, spank.

The meat puppet does as she is told.

Then she slinks off at the end of the shoot, to visit the washroom and discreetly remove the rivers of sweat from her private cracks.

~

As I put on my own underwear and clothes, I wondered how I was going to survive more shooting. Today was Sunday, which seemed like an odd day for a photo session, but what did I know?

I had tomorrow, Monday, free to unwind, but was due back at the studio Tuesday. I'd planned to hang out at Dalton's house on my own, relaxing by his backyard pool and sending him flirty text messages urging him to return to LA sooner, but now I never wanted to see him again. I didn't even want to walk into his house and smell his scent in the air.

Someone knocked on my door. "It's me, Mitchell," he called out.

"Come on in. There's nothing out that you haven't already seen today, from a variety of angles."

Mitchell came in and parked his compact, gym-hard body on a bench. He ran one hand through his close-cropped angelic blond curls as he said, "You should be proud of how well you did today. I know I am."

"I'm such an amateur. Just admit you were all laughing behind my back when I was getting changed."

"Not at all. The truth is, everyone was terrified, but that was before."

"Terrified? Of what?"

His cheeks reddened.

17

"Great," I said, reading between the lines. "You all thought I was going to be terrible and ruin all your reputations with my fatness."

His eyes bulged.

"My curvaceousness," I said.

"This is brave new ground for us, but I saw some of the shots and they are phenomenal." He held up one finger to keep me from arguing with him. "I have been known to stretch the truth to make models more comfortable, but I swear on a stack of *In Style* magazines, I'm not lying. The shots were great, and this whole thing is going to be huge."

"Huge?"

"I can't say anything right, can I?"

"Fine, I believe you. Thank you for saying that, and thank you for being so nice to me. If you're ever in my part of Washington, you have a place to stay. I'm serious. It's just a fold-out couch, but it's all yours."

He laughed and looked up for a moment like he was considering a visit.

"But won't you be moving to LA?" he asked. "To be closer to Dalton?"

I could sense that he was digging for information, but I'd been practically naked in front of the guy all day, and being secretive about my feelings seemed ridiculous.

"He hurt me," I said. "I'm confused and I don't know what to do."

He nodded.

I added, "Easy come, easy go."

"Let's get some sushi and talk."

What was my other option? I thought about returning to Dalton's modern house, all alone. That didn't seem fun. I should have been exhausted, given my lack of sleep, but I wasn't. My nerves were still tingling from the photo shoot, and I didn't feel like slowing down at all.

Mitchell said, "I could use some fun, actually. I've barely done anything but work and sleep for months now. We don't even need to talk about your personal stuff. I'm sorry if I was being nosy."

"At least you care," I said. "I can't talk to my roommate-slash-best friend, because she'll rub it in that she warned me."

He squealed. "My roommate-slash-best friend is the exact same way! And he gets cra-a-azy jealous, too."

"Shayla's really nice, though."

"So's my roommate."

I shook my head. "Roommates."

"Can't live with 'em, can't manage the rent without 'em."

I finished getting my hoodie jacket zipped up. "Sure, let's get some sushi."

Keith walked into the room without knocking. "I love sushi. Come on, I'll drive."

Mitchell gave him a dirty look, but underneath the glare was some amusement. He didn't love the guy, but he didn't hate him, either.

Mitchell said, "I'll drive, but my Miada's only a two-seater. Peaches will come with me."

Keith said, "We'll flip for her." He pulled a coin from his pocket, tossed it high in the air, and caught it on his palm. "Heads, she's coming with me."

Mitchell said, "I didn't call it. You're a cheat."

I pulled out my phone and held it up, recording video. "Guys, could you start over? Try to make it really clear you're both fighting over me, Peaches Monroe. Maybe say my full name."

They both looked sheepish, then Keith tousled his black hair with one hand and said, "Peaches, drive with me. I'm a very safe driver."

Mitchell crossed his arms over his compact body. "It's not his driving I'm concerned about," he said to me.

"I'm twenty-two," I said to Mitchell, still recording with my phone. "How about I drive to the restaurant with Keith, then you can give me a lift home? Seems a lot safer than the other way 'round."

They both agreed to that, which cut my little video short, but at least I had something fun to show Shayla when I got home.

~

When Keith led me to his vehicle, I thought he was playing a joke on me. It was an old van, painted a vivid sea green.

19

"Is this thing a movie prop?" I asked. "Does it actually run?"

"Don't laugh, it's paid for," he said, holding open the passenger door. An earthy scent wafted out.

"I wasn't laughing," I said as I stepped in. "This funky green van is better than what I drive, which is nothing."

As he circled around to the driver's side, I glanced into the back, which held plants in green plastic pots along one side, and bags of soil along the other side. No wonder the van had an earthy, yet pleasant, scent.

"I've been running a landscaping business with my sister," Keith explained as he got settled into his side and started the engine.

"In addition to being an underwear model."

He flashed me a grin. "Modeling is nice work when you can get it. In between the days spent in see-through briefs, playing make-believe with luscious women, I muck around in the dirt." He pulled the van out of the parking lot, following Mitchell's blue Miada. "What about you? When you're not shaking your fruit for the camera, what do you do?"

"I manage a bookstore called Peachtree Books." I stared out the window at the billboards and passing traffic. "That's where everything started. I met Dalton Deangelo when he came running in, looking for a place to hide. Then we talked for a bit, and he said he wanted to get to know me. Little did I know—"

My throat started to close off, stopping my anecdote short of where I'd thought it was going. Dalton had only wanted to know me so he could use the research for his movie role. His sudden interest had seemed so romantic at the time, like the foolish notion of love at first sight, but now all I felt was the shame of being so naïve.

Keith didn't need to know the details, and he didn't seem to be asking.

"I'm just having fun now," I said. "That's the most important thing."

"If I saw you fully clothed in a bookstore, I wouldn't have looked twice at you," Keith said, staring straight ahead at the road.

"Um. Thanks? Thanks for your honesty, I guess."

"No, I'm sorry about how that sounded. I meant it as an admission of my shallowness."

"Okay."

We drove in silence for a few minutes, until finally it became so awkward, I reached for my phone. No new messages from Dalton, which was a relief. I wanted to confront him in person when he came back to LA on Wednesday, and I didn't want lovey-dovey text messages to weaken my stance. He had strung me along, using lines cribbed directly from his indie film script, and I deserved an explanation. I would officially end the relationship with him, but first I wanted to see him squirm.

Keith broke the silence, saying, "You scare me. My confidence is all an act. Even after hours and hours of meditation and self-reflection, I'm as insecure as hell. But you're just… you. And even when I tried to intimidate you on the set, you never backed down. What's your secret?"

"I've got nothing to lose."

"Explain."

"Nobody expects me to be good at any of this. I know I'm a colossal joke, a publicity stunt. I've got nowhere to go but up."

"The *whole thing* is a publicity stunt. I knew it."

"At least I'm getting paid," I said.

"What's the going rate for something like that? For being someone's pretend girlfriend?"

"You tell me," I said with a laugh, pretending to know what was going on.

What the hell was Keith talking about? Not that it really mattered what he thought. His job was to stand next to me and fill out underwear, and he was more than qualified for that. Perhaps a little overqualified. My cheeks reddened as I realized I'd been glancing over at his package.

We stopped at a red light, and Mitchell jumped out of his Miada up ahead of us and dashed back. "Roommate disaster unfolding. Custom dress, wrong sequins, giant tantrum. Sorry, but I have to bail on sushi." He handed a business card to Keith to pass to me. "Call

21

me if you need anything. Please forgive me for bailing. See you Tuesday!"

The light changed and people were already honking as he dashed back up to his car.

Keith turned his head and gave me a deliciously naughty look, his brown eyes twinkling under a wavy lock of black hair. "I think we can do better than sushi."

CHAPTER 3

I chuckled nervously and crossed my legs, feeling younger and much stupider than twenty-two. A good-looking man with a muscular torso and a sizable flotation device will do that to you, even if he *says* his confidence is all an act.

Keith crossed three lanes and turned right, looping back the way we'd come.

He wouldn't give me any hints, then he took me to a cozy steak and seafood restaurant where everybody seemed to know him.

A man I assumed was the owner came by with a bottle of chilled vodka and tiny glasses. "My man," he said to Keith as he poured us all drinks. "I decided on the Alfa Romeo. You'll have to take it on the PCH sometime, trade me your wheels for the day."

I accepted the glass of vodka and shot it back, as I didn't want to be rude. "Smooth," I said, smacking my lips. "You do know he drives a green van straight out of a *Scooby-Doo* movie, don't you?"

The man laughed, partly distracted by another group of people waving him over. "You make sure my man takes good care of you," he said. "Because if he doesn't, you know where to find me." He winked twice, then waved at the other table and headed their way with the bottle of vodka.

"I met Edgar when I started to do the landscaping," Keith explained. "Don't get your hopes up. Edgar winks at all the girls, but he goes home to his wife, Vanessa."

"She's a lucky woman."

A waitress with long, dark hair came by our table with a tasting plate, on the house.

I noticed Keith wasn't checking out the hot waitress, but gazing at me, a look of adoration on his face.

"Why are you being so nice to me?" I asked.

He seemed surprised by the question, and didn't answer.

I continued, "I'm sure you have a dozen girls on your phone who'd be here with you tonight in a heartbeat. Scrawny girls with big, round boobs up to their chins."

"I've decided not to date models or actresses anymore. I want a real girl, who's honest."

"I should introduce you to my roommate."

"Maybe I'll have to come visit your town. Foxworth? Farmville? No, that's not a real town, is it?"

"Beaverdale." I watched as he drained a tall glass of water. "Did you really take diuretics before today's shoot?"

"You have to, as a male model. The world may accept a voluptuous girl in her underwear, but it's a total double standard. We men have to be hard. Rock hard."

"Speaking of which, did you have a sock stuffed in there? Underneath your goodies?"

He grinned and took the prop glasses out of his blazer pocket and put them on, turning into Clark Kent.

"I know those glasses are fake," I said.

"But I still like wearing them to read menus."

"You're crazy," I said. "But at least it's a cute kind of crazy."

He perused the menu, avoiding my question about stuffing his shorts. Oh, that faux-nerdy look was doing a number on me. He made the room feel warm and my clothes feel restrictive with the simple addition of fake glasses.

That single shot of vodka had gone straight to my head, loosening my inhibitions.

I kicked his foot under the table. "Hey, so what else about today was fake? You gonna tell me or do I have to pat you down?"

He flipped over the menu as he said, "This is a trade secret, so keep it under your hat, but we underwear models use a loop with Velcro. It goes under and over and fluffs everything up."

"Like a ring sort of thing?"

He flipped the menu page, looking studious. "Yes. Over and under and all the way around." He looked up at me, catching my breath with his brown eyes, still dazzling in the dim candle light of the steak house. "Don't be worried about my circulation. I took everything off right after the shoot."

The waitress returned and we were silent as she set down our drinks—vodka and soda, Keith's choice. It was also my mother's favorite drink, and I didn't mind it sometimes, though I prefer sweeter drinks, usually, like sangria.

I took the smallest sip, my body loosening up just from the smell and the idea of more booze.

Some other ideas floated through my head, including me playing nurse and checking on Keith's circulation.

Booze always makes me horny.

I felt my cheeks flush, remembering the interesting shapes that had been visible in the pouch front of Keith's underwear that day. There'd been a lot there for a girl to hang onto.

We placed our food order, and after the waitress was gone, I said, "I wasn't worried about your circulation, not until now. Are you sure that's safe?"

"Why don't you reach under the table and feel for yourself?"

I snorted and sat upright. "I have a boyfriend."

"How long is the charade set to last?"

"What? You're weird. I don't know if I can even talk about Dalton. I signed a Non-Disclosure Agreement. Which is too bad, because I know some pretty interesting things about the guy."

"Figures," he said, nodding. "Forget him, then. Tell me about your favorite books. Your top five deserted island picks."

How did he do that? Switch from being an incorrigible tease to being a gracious dining companion? Was it the fake glasses?

"Only if you tell me yours," I said.

He began counting them off on his fingers, as if he'd been waiting for someone to ask this question. "First of all, *Swiss Family Robinson.* Classic story, plus appropriate to the situation, I think."

I took a sip of my drink—a little bland for my taste, but refreshing —and leaned in with interest as he talked about his favorite books, which were mostly from his childhood.

Our food arrived, and we still weren't through the list, because I had to keep arguing with him and lobbying for my own favorite books.

We ate and laughed, and I forgot about everything in the world that existed outside of the warm glow of the candle on our table.

"And last, but not least," he said, "*Call of the Wild.*"

I gasped. "That book always made me cry. You wouldn't think a story told from the perspective of a dog would be so heart-rending, would you?"

"I know! It seems so silly. I love dogs, but I wouldn't expect great art from them."

I grinned, feeling a pleasant buzz from the drinks, good food, and bookish conversation. "Not every dog has it in him to write an epic tale like that."

Keith tossed back his drink and crunched the ice cubes, keeping eye contact with me the whole time. "This is a great song." He nodded toward the small, checkerboard dance floor. "Come on, let's dance off some of this meal."

The music did have a hypnotic, trippy quality, but no one else was dancing.

"I don't think you can handle my moves," I said, shaking my head.

He was already up, offering his hand.

"Oh, hell." I got up and followed him onto the dance floor.

Keith was doing an admirable job keeping my mind off my imminent break-up, so the least I could do was provide him with a laugh or two at my goofball attempt to move my body to music.

The song changed as soon as we got to the dance floor (doesn't it always?) and he caught me in his arms.

"Grab onto me," he said.

"You sure like to say that."

"And you sure like to peer at me through those pale eyelashes like a flirt, and make me want to kiss you."

"Stop being so flirty. We have a professional relationship, and I'm not available to you."

He pulled me in closer, our bodies swaying together easily.

His lips next to my ear, he murmured, "I have those soft bags of topsoil in the back of my van. We don't even need to drive anywhere. I could be all yours." His hands traveled down past the small of my back, over my buttocks.

I grabbed his hands and moved them back up again. "Mitchell warned me about you male models, and I should have listened. Now I'm pressed up against all your bumps, and I'm not sure it's even legal for you to have all these bumps."

"Bumps," he said, chuckling.

As we danced some more, he gazed down at me like he couldn't understand why I was resisting his advances.

And why was I resisting? My affair with Dalton Deangelo had been brief and exciting, but was now as good as over. Did I really care if brown-eyed and charm-oozing Keith had a dozen girlfriends? The attention was nice. The dancing was sexy. He put me at ease, except when his hands traveled down to my ass and I thought about riding him like the twenty-five-cent horsie-ride machine at the grocery store.

Ride A Champion, the horsie-ride machine proclaimed.

Keith Raven certainly was… a champion. As we danced, I imagined him murmuring stage directions to me in bed the way he had during the shoot.

He leaned down and whispered near my ear, "Those photos of us are going to be so hot."

"I'm worried about the lack of airbrushing."

He laughed, loud enough to turn heads in the restaurant around us.

I pinched his butt. "Don't make fun. I've eaten a few more cookies than you, and I assumed there'd be some digital sculpting. Mitchell told me the photographer doesn't do that."

Keith swept a lock of my hair behind my ear.

"You know how magazines have spreads on the no-makeup looks? And really it's just natural shades and as much makeup as any other look? That photographer does the no-retouching look, but trust me, there's retouching."

"I'm so relieved I could kiss you!"

His eyebrows quirked up, and then he was kissing me, his hot lips on... my cheek. It ended as quickly as it began, and he said, "You're welcome."

I looked around, feeling guilty about a silly cheek kiss. If a paparazzi saw us together, and Dalton saw the photos—and he might even see them instantly, thanks to the magic of the internet—he'd be hurt. I was through with him, but I was no monster.

"I should get going," I said, pulling away.

"Has anyone taken you to get a great night view of the Hollywood sign yet?"

I shook my head, no. I'd been in LA only one night. My sense of time stretched out like gooey taffy. Had it really been just one night? The lack of sleep was playing tricks with my sense of reality. I wanted to climb into bed. With Keith. His body had been next to mine for most of the day, and I ached to press myself against him. I didn't want anything from him emotionally. Just his sweet, sweet skin. And his hands. And maybe a little taste of his money maker. The poor thing had been fluffed up, collared, and stuffed into so many underpants that day. He could probably use a massage after all that hard work, filling out pouches.

"Sure, let's see the Hollywood sign," I said.

He held his arm out like a gentleman to escort me back to our table. He took care of the bill quickly, then whisked me out of the restaurant.

The inside of his van smelled even earthier now, in the dark of night. The scent of the dirt drove me crazy in a way that surprised me.

My tongue was awake and calling my attention. My tongue wanted to be inside Keith's mouth. I kept my mouth shut, wondering how my tongue had gotten so randy all of a sudden. My mouth watered, and my tongue swirled around like a hamster on an exercise wheel, going nowhere fast.

I should have stopped drinking after the first vodka and soda, like Keith.

"How did you get into modeling?" I asked.

We were driving through a neighborhood that would have alarmed me if we'd been in a fancy car. The green van blended right in, though, and nobody even batted an eyelash our way.

"Officially, I was scouted after appearing in a charity calendar."

"What do you mean, *officially*? Is that not true?"

"True enough," he said. "As true as anyone's story around here. A word of advice? Don't ever go peeling back the onion layers. You'll only find more of the same onion."

I gazed over at his profile in admiration. "You're more than just a pretty face and a full underwear pouch, Keith Raven."

He grinned and fiddled with the buttons of the radio on the van's dash. "Raven's actually my middle name. My real last name is Lipschitz."

"Not as marketable." I zipped up my jacket.

Keith noticed this and wordlessly turned on the van's heater.

"Cool night," he said.

I inhaled the rich, loamy scent in the van and settled into my seat. Finally, I was starting to come down from the action of the day, but I had a new problem. Finding out Keith's last name was Lipschitz had only made me want to kiss him more.

After a few more minutes of driving, Keith pulled the van to the side of the road and stopped the engine.

He jumped out and was at my side to help me step down before I even had my seat belt off.

We were in an area with few street lamps, and the night was inky black around us. I took Keith's hand so I wouldn't stumble in the dark, and followed as he led me up a hill.

When we crested the rise, there was the sign.

"Wow," I said. "I've seen it so many times in movies and on TV, that I have to remind myself this is the first time I'm seeing it for real."

"For real?" he asked.

"Yeah. I've never been to LA before."

We were still holding hands from the climb, and he turned to look down at me. In the darkness, his brown eyes looked black and dangerous, his cheeks gaunt.

"We think we know what's real and what isn't," he said. "Who's to say you haven't seen this sign a thousand times for real? Who's to say that when you close your eyes and imagine something happening, like kissing a beautiful stranger, that it isn't just as real as whatever happens when your eyes are open?"

"My eyes are wide open now. This is real."

"Is the sky above us real?"

I gazed up at the night sky. Because of the city light and the smog in the valley, I couldn't see any stars. The city itself, with its twinkling lights, made its own starlight.

Keith was so close to me, I could feel his body heat radiating my way. He murmured, "*We are all in the gutter, but some of us are looking at the stars.*"

I pulled away, a bitter taste in my mouth. "That's Oscar Wilde. You're using someone else's words."

"That's from *Lady Windermere's Fan*. You work in a bookstore, so I assumed you knew that quote." He pulled me back toward him. "I'm not trying to pull one over on you, Peaches. I'm a gardener with the last name of Lipschitz, and I brought you to see this beautiful view because I was hoping to kiss you."

I turned and took in the Hollywood sign again. If the letters were all in a perfectly-aligned row, it wouldn't look as real. The flaws, including some of the sections not being as brightly-lit, were what made me believe I was seeing the sign and not imagining it.

Keith wrapped his arms around me from behind, scooping me in close to him. How good it felt to be embraced. On a cool summer night, there is no feeling greater than this. I trembled at his touch.

He murmured near my ear, "The only thing more adorable than you looking up at the sky for stars is you looking at that sign with stars in your eyes."

I snorted. "Stars in my eyes? You're so corny."

"How about some more Oscar Wilde? *To live is the rarest thing in the world. Most people exist, that is all.*"

"That one makes me sad."

He kissed the top of my head from behind. "Don't be sad. Tell me what makes you happy, and I'll do it."

"Keep holding me like this forever."

He leaned down and nibbled the edge of my ear. A fierce desire shot through my body like a shot of ice-cold vodka.

For the second time in less than a month, a way-too-hot man was touching me. Actually, it was the third time, if you counted play-wrestling with my former high school crush, Adrian Storm. I was becoming quite the squeeze toy for hot dudes. The downside to being a boy toy was that the boys would get bored and move on. The upside was the squeezing.

Oh, yes. The squeezing.

"I feel so safe in your arms," I said.

"You shouldn't feel safe at all," he growled sexily. "I know we just had dinner, but I could eat you up in one bite. I took the last name Raven because it's short for Ravenous."

I shuddered at the rasp in his voice. "You were really helpful during the photo shoot today. All your coaching was so practical."

"Practical?" He made a sound that was a cross between purring and growling, and licked the crevice behind my ear. "I had to say something to take my mind off all the dirty things I wanted to do to you."

"You should have done those things for the photos."

"It's not underwear modeling if the underwear's on the floor."

"Right. That would be porn, I suppose."

He purred and licked my ear again, which made my eyes roll up into my head with pleasure.

When I finally caught my breath again, I said, "Have you ever done any... nude stuff?"

"Not on film," he replied with a chuckle. "Why? Do you want to make a sex tape with me and leak it on the internet?"

"Not tonight," I said jokingly. "My hair's a bit messy."

"I wouldn't make that video," he said. "If I ever got lucky enough to be with you, it would be very private and very personal."

I looked down at his forearms, covered by his blazer jacket, wrapped around me and framing my breasts. The jacket was pushed up enough I could see the dark hair on his arms. The hair was very short, like it had been trimmed, which seemed probable.

He continued, "As for tonight, though, all I want is a kiss."

"That's all you want?"

"All I want for tonight."

In the silence that followed, I had a little argument with myself. *He's lying, and he wants to brag about having you as a conquest,* howled the suspicious detective part of me. *He's lying, and he's a filthy sex addict,* said the part of me who wears librarian glasses and her hair in a bun. Then my randy tongue jumped into the argument and started yelling incoherently: MOUTH! KISS! TONGUE-KISS! TONGUE WANT MOUTH!

I have never been in the situation of being involved with two men at once, but I was keenly aware of the wrongness of my desires. Sure, I had broken up with Dalton in my heart, but I hadn't uttered the magic words, so I technically wasn't a free agent. I wasn't free to drill my tongue into a sexy model's face like I was trying to get the last of the Nutella out of a jar.

But then, despite my reservations, I was turning, turning clockwise, turning in Keith's arms, away from the glowing Hollywood sign and toward his glowing Hollywood face.

CHAPTER 4

His mouth came down and met my lips hesitantly. His skin smelled like sunshine, even in the dark.

I didn't know if it was an act, or what, but he kissed me exactly like someone who doesn't kiss someone new very often. He paused, waiting for me to move before he parted his lips. My tongue charged ahead, into his mouth. He moaned in surprise, but then inhaled deeply and relaxed his jaw, his mouth welcoming.

His saliva was sweet and clean, and I wanted to crawl inside his gorgeous mouth, decorate it with throw pillows, and live there forever.

Then his hands were on my back, rubbing up and down as we kissed, keeping me from floating away. I reached down and did something I'd wanted to do since the minute I'd seen him—I slipped my hands into the back pockets of his jeans and clutched his remarkable ass.

Oh, what an ass it was. Not skinny, but pleasant and round. I dug my fingertips in, pulling my body in tighter to his.

To my surprise, Keith's hands didn't stray from my back. We stood and kissed under the night sky, both of us fully clothed, for what must have been close to an hour. My body ached for more, but I was also relieved to be enjoying this moment, this kissing.

I didn't want to compare, but Keith was one of the better kissers I'd experienced, if not *the* very best. He mostly kept his eyes closed, except he seemed to sense when I opened mine, and then he opened his and gave me a shy look before going back to kissing.

His face had been closely shaved earlier that day, and his chin was only faintly raspy against mine. He kissed his way down my cheek and onto my neck. His touch was gentle and maddening, because I wanted more. Or did I? Being kissed gently on the neck was less overwhelming than having my neck sucked on, but the sensation still tingled all through my body.

I wanted to stay there and kiss him until the sun came up, but the day caught up to me, and one of my kisses turned into a yawn.

He pulled back and looked at me sideways. "I'm boring you?"

"Not at all." With his eyes on me, my tiredness disappeared instantly. "I didn't sleep last night. I was nervous about the shoot." That last part was only part of the truth, but it was all I wanted to think about.

"You're probably at some sad hotel, right? Do you want to stay over at my place tonight? My sister just moved out, but she left her bed, so I have a spare room. We both have the day off tomorrow, so I can be your tour guide."

"I don't know."

"I live not far from here. I swear, there's an entire bedroom for you. You can even lock the door if you're worried."

I poked him in the chest. "You'd better lock *your* door, mister."

His eyebrow quirked up. "Or what?"

"Or I'll find the drawer where you keep your felt pens and I'll draw boobs on your forehead while you're sleeping."

"I've never known a girl from Washington before. Are they all as fun as you?"

"Don't be silly. I'm not that fun. My roommate is the fun one." I yawned again. "See?" I pointed to my mouth. "It's not even that late, and I'm ready for my tuck-in."

He started toward the path leading to the van, his elbow out again like a gentleman. "Come on, then. I'll fold down the blankets and give you your tuck-in."

~

As we drove to Keith's apartment, I savored the sensation of stepping into someone else's life, like a tourist.

Something occurred to me.

As I smelled the soil bags in the van and looked around at Keith's neighborhood, I realized this was how Dalton must have felt when he saw me working in the bookstore, and then tagged along to my cousin Marita's wedding. Like a tourist. There to take some photos and make some memories. But wasn't that also the whole point of life?

My thoughts circled and bit their own tails.

I don't know about you, but I get terribly philosophical when I'm overly tired to the point of hallucinating.

The underwear model driving the van turned to smile at me. Maybe I was hallucinating? That would certainly explain a few things.

We pulled up to Keith's apartment building, which was the color of my terra cotta pots back home, and cheerily accented by landscape lighting. Great curb appeal.

The building had a central courtyard, with a shimmering pool, and not another soul in sight. Everything looked about sixty years old and worn from use, but taken care of.

Keith was all apologies as he opened the door of his apartment, explaining that he'd been meaning to clean and decorate, but wasn't sure how long he'd be staying.

Besides a few dirty dishes in the kitchen, the place looked fine to me.

I stumbled around, feeling clumsy and bleary-eyed.

Keith loaned me a shirt to sleep in, I used the toiletries I'd taken with me to the shoot in my purse, and I crashed hard on the comfortable spare room bed, face down. I jerked awake five seconds after falling asleep—one of those feeling-like-you're-falling sensations —and opened my eyes to see a photograph on the nightstand of two beautiful, dark-haired girls staring down at me.

"Never you mind," I muttered, flipping the photo over and then myself. Sleep came to me, as welcome as buttered muffins, hot from the oven, only to be interrupted by...

The sound of my telephone ringing.

Brightness. Morning already?

"Hi Dad," I grumbled sleepily, because I knew his ring—or at least I thought I did.

The room was bright, but if there was an alarm clock, it was hiding from me.

"That's kinky," came the voice on the other line.

"Who's this?"

"Your pony, Lionheart."

Oops. It was not my father.

It was Dalton Deangelo, that lying devil.

"You remember Lionheart," he said.

I grunted, unsure of how to inform him I wasn't speaking to him, now that he had me on the phone.

He continued, "You didn't sleep at my house last night, and I got worried. Did you go to a hotel close to the photographer's studio?"

"Who wants to know?"

"Where are you?" he replied.

"Wait. How do you know I'm not at your house? Do you have creepy spy cams all over that place?"

"Not spy cams, but I can log in remotely to the security system. I can tell that everything's armed now and the house has been empty all night."

"You're not wrong."

A pause. "Something's wrong with you, though."

"I'll say."

"What did you hear?" he asked, sounding less than innocent.

"I didn't *hear* anything, unless you count the stuff I heard in my head—the stuff I can't get *out* of my head. I read your script, Dalton. Your little game is up, because I know all about you now. I know what a lying, deceiving twatweasel you are."

"Did you just call me a twatweasel?"

"Don't change the subject. Just level with me, one adult to another. Admit you were stringing me along using lines from the script for your movie with the dumb name, *We're all Stardust* or whatever."

"*We are Made of Stardust.* That's the title."

"Is that all you have to say? No explanation? Well, I hope you got in a lot of awesome research about what it's like to nail a chubbo, because the next one you get won't be me."

"Peaches."

"Furthermore, I hope the next chubbo you bang for sport is really big and smothers you past the point of enjoyment, until you're gasping for breath and afraid for your life."

"What are you talking about?" Heavy sigh. "Okay, I'm remembering some lines that may have bothered you. You do realize that was a movie script you read? It's not exactly a true account of how I feel. Plus whatever copy was lying around my house is an older one. It's not even the current version."

"Oh, really? So when you said that line to me, *Join me in the darkness, walk through my dreams, and hold my hand in the morning light*, did you mean that?"

"Sure. Who wouldn't? It's a great line."

I held the phone away from my head and shook it. The door to the bedroom was closed, but I had no sense of where in the apartment Keith was at the moment, or how thin the walls were.

Slowly and calmly, so I wasn't yelling, I asked Dalton what I really wanted to know: "When you ran into me at the bookstore and asked me out on a date, was that research for your role?"

I heard a smacking sound in the silence, like the sound of someone's mouth opening and closing because they're nervous.

Finally, he said, "I really like you. Everything I said to you, I meant."

"That doesn't sound like an apology, or the answer I wanted to hear."

"I'll be in LA in two days. Let's talk then, and I promise I'll make it up to you."

"There were some very hurtful things in that script."

Sounding annoyed now, he said, "Don't be ridiculous. A script is just words on a page. There's no nuance. It's bare bones without the actor giving it life."

"I don't want anything to do with actors, and I don't want anything to do with you, Dalton Deangelo. We are over."

"I don't get any say in the matter?"

"Sure. Let's take a vote. I vote we're broken up. What's your opinion?"

And then I ended the call before he started talking. That wasn't quite enough, though, so I threw the phone on the bed a couple of times, just to really show him.

What would he have said? That he'd started off dating me as an experiment, then found out I was an actual human being? Ugh. Where do you go from there? A relationship built on lies is like a bra with no underwire. *Useless.*

The floor creaked on the other side of the door, then Keith said, "I wasn't listening in. Not at first, but then it got interesting."

I jumped out of the bed and flung open the door.

Keith flinched, his arms up over his head for protection. "Not the face," he howled, grinning wildly. "Not the abs either. Those are my payday. Just kick me in the shins."

"Listening in is rude."

"So's yelling so loud you wake up your host and rouse his curiosity."

Still holding his hands up protectively, he said, "You look really cute in my jersey."

I stared at him, standing in his burgundy bath robe, looking just like a regular person in a regular apartment.

He breathed.

I breathed.

After a few seconds, I managed to get my bitch dialed down from eleven to about five.

"I'm sorry* I woke you up," I said. "I'm sorry I'm not being a very good house guest."

*See? I can apologize. It's very easy. You just say one little word, and mean it. Why is it so hard for some guys to do the same?

He said, "I'm sorry I was eavesdropping, and I'm sorry that you broke up with some guy."

"Not just *some guy*. Dalton Deangelo. You knew that. Everyone knows that. But we're through now."

"Oh." His thick, black eyebrows rose and stayed quite high for a while, as he moved into the corner of the apartment with the kitchen and started moving things around. "There's been a huge misunderstanding on my part. I'm just a dumb model. I thought you

38

and Dalton were just pretending to be dating, for the publicity. Wow." He stared down at his fancy coffee maker like he'd forgotten where to put the water. "Wow," he repeated.

"I'm glad we're through," I said, taking a seat on one of the stools next to the counter. The chrome chair was more comfortable than it looked, thank goodness. "It was only a few weeks, but I was already sick of the disbelief on everyone's faces when they found out their perfect hero was dating a chubby commoner."

Keith ran his hand through his near-black hair, looking embarrassed. "I meant that... I wouldn't have kissed you last night if I'd known you were actually with someone else. I don't approve of cheating."

"Me, neither! Keith, you have to know... I was really pissed at Dalton. In my heart, it was over."

"Okay," he murmured.

"We're cool, right?"

He rummaged through the cupboards and pulled down a silver container and a measuring spoon.

I put my face in my hands and rubbed my eyes. I felt horrible. Keith had been so kind to me, and I'd violated his mouth with my cheating mouth, and now he hated me.

I held up my hands and tried to find the words to apologize again, but nothing came to me.

Keith measured out the coffee grounds, the smell a pleasant distraction.

The kitchen looked renovated, much newer than the building itself, with cabinets in a light-hued wood, and unusual, oval-shaped handles. My mother used to have oval-shaped handles in her kitchen, and they drove her nuts. She's not OCD or anything, but they wiggled around and she could never get them straight. Even when they *were* straight, they felt crooked to the fingers during casual use. She wasn't crazy; I felt the wrongness, too.

The oval handles in Keith's little kitchen filled me with a sad, desperate feeling—homesickness. I would see my mother again, but I would never *live* with her again, never hear her day-to-day run-downs of things she couldn't get quite straight. Every time I saw Kyle, he'd

39

be noticeably bigger, because I didn't see him every day. My father rarely got to see me do some casually stupid thing and mention that I was "prone to whimsy." Okay, I didn't miss that last thing.

Keith got the coffee perking, and finally said, "Yeah, I guess we're cool. I wish I hadn't made such a jackass out of myself last night."

"Don't say that. I really enjoyed kissing you."

"Stolen kisses," he said, giving me a hungry look with his dark brown eyes.

"You do look a bit like a raven," I said. "Your last name that you upgraded from your middle name is perfect."

"And you, my fair maiden, look like a peach."

I glowered at him, crossing my arms over my chest, still wearing nothing but his jersey and my underwear, yet strangely comfortable.

"Thanks a lot," I said, my voice flat with sarcasm. "I'm round and fuzzy to you?"

He laughed. "I meant sweet and delicious. Your round parts are nice, as well, but I haven't seen anything that's fuzzy."

"My mother says I'll get the family chin-fuzz when I turn forty."

"And you're how old now?"

"Over half-way there."

He put his elbows on the counter—tiles, light brown—and leaned in close to me, examining my chin. "Nothing yet." He put his hands on either side of my jaw, gently tilting my face up. His touch was warm and reassuring, and I didn't want him to stop holding my face, so I rested my hands on top of his.

His voice low and quiet, he murmured, "How many more days are you in LA?"

I swallowed. "Nine days," I whispered.

He leaned in closer, nearly touching his lips to mine.

"I just got out of a relationship," he said.

"What a coincidence. Me, too."

"My wounds are nearly as fresh as yours. Do you know what animals do in the wild when they're wounded?"

"They die."

He smirked, then relaxed his mouth into a solemn expression.

"I have a proposition for you."

"Does it include coffee?"

"I'm suggesting that you and I make like wild animals and lick each other's… emotional wounds."

"Interesting." I gazed up into his model-pretty eyes, rimmed with thick, black eyelashes. No wonder he was in demand as an underwear model. That face could sell seawater to sailors.

"The next nine days could be *very* interesting," he said.

"Keith, what you need to know about me is I'm a very smart girl. Top of my class when I make the effort. When I put together furniture, there are never any leftover pieces."

He was still holding my face, and staring at me with an amused expression.

"Are you trying to let me down easy? I can handle the truth. At casting calls, they don't mince words. I've been told to my face I'm not attractive enough. That hurts. Also, too old, too young, too tall, too short. I've heard everything. So, lay it on me. Are you turning me down because I drive a crappy green van, live in a run-down apartment, and I'm not as rich and famous as your last boyfriend?"

"What I mean is that I'm the kind of smart girl who does extremely stupid things. Like walk around shirtless with the blinds open. And go running through the woods at night. Or, come to think of it, naked trespassing by day. I do a lot of stupid things, but that stops now."

"So you don't want to use me as your emotional Band-Aid and personal play toy for nine days?"

I bit my lip. "No?"

"Sounds like a question."

He closed the distance and rubbed the tip of his nose against mine.

"I should go back to Dalton's house," I said. "That's where I was staying. Let's have a cup of coffee, and let's keep everything between us professional from now on. We can heal each other's emotional wounds as friends. That could work."

He withdrew his hands from the sides of my face and pulled back to stand up straight.

"One cup of coffee," he said. "Then I'll drive you wherever you want."

I nodded, proud yet disappointed by my good decision-making.

Keith pulled the full carafe from the coffee maker, grabbed two mugs from the cupboard, then turned and left the kitchen. He walked into the bedroom—his bedroom—without a word.

I sat at the counter for a moment, my chin on my hands.

His bedroom was where he kept his bed. Beds are not where friends hang out. *A friend should not go in there*, argued the sensible part of me.

But he has the coffee in there, said another part of me.

And he's probably naked, said yet another part of me. (That would be our friend, Miss Kitty.)

CHAPTER 5

Despite the urging of some body parts, I wasn't falling into this new trap of Keith's. Nope. Not going into his bedroom, even if he did have all the coffee.

I wandered over to the washroom, where I freshened up with a quick shower and gave my teeth a brushing. I came out in a towel and sat on the sofa. I expected Keith to come out of the bedroom, fully dressed and laughing about his hilarious joke, but he didn't.

The door was mostly closed.

I went to the doorway, pushed open the door, and stood there in my towel. The curtains were drawn, and the room was dark and still.

"How's that coffee?" I called out.

"Drop the towel and get your sweet ass in here, Miss Smarty Pants Class Valedictorian."

"I was never a valedictorian. That honor went to an evil wench named Brie. She always had the best clothes, and her family was mega-rich." I had more to say about Brie, but stopped myself. I'm stupid at times, but I do realize high-school girl grudges are of very little interest to men, unless there's hair-pulling or pillow fights.

The curtains were really thick in Keith's room, and my eyes hadn't adjusted yet, so all I could see was shapes. One shape in particular stood out. Oh, yes, he was naked.

"Why don't you get in here," he called gently. "Pretend I'm that wench Brie's boyfriend."

"She went out with a few different guys."

"Pretend I'm all of them. Or pretend I'm her daddy."

43

I squealed. "Mr. Harrison? He owns the big grocery store in town. I still see him all the time."

"And?"

"And I'm dropping my towel. Now I'm coming in. Don't laugh, and don't look at my butt."

I slipped into the dark room and closed the door behind me. It was cooler in here than in the rest of the apartment, with the air conditioner whirring steadily.

With his voice deeper than usual, he said, "Why, Peaches. You've certainly grown into a fine young woman. I'm so glad you and my daughter are friends."

"No role-playing," I said. "You're an underwear model and I'm a girl who packs chocolate in her purse at all times. This, right here, is the full fantasy."

I got onto the bed on my hands and knees and crept forward for a kiss.

"We'll take it slow," he said, gently caressing my lips with his.

I glanced around the room, stopping when I spotted the packets that were at the ready on his bedside table. We were good to go.

"Good to see you have prophylactics standing by at the ready," I said. "All the better for licking each other like wild animals."

"Do you think a dozen is enough?" he asked innocently.

"Sure. If things go sideways, at least we can make a balloon animal zoo." I kissed him again, enjoying the sense of calm I got when we touched. My pulse wasn't racing at all. Either I was getting better at staying cool around incredibly hot guys, or there was something different—better—about Keith, compared to he-whose-name-shall-not-be-invoked.

"Your hair is dripping on me," Keith said.

"Sorry." I pulled away.

"Shh, don't be."

Did he just shush me? Shushing usually makes me angry, but this time, I just sat there quietly as he pulled his robe from a hook near the bed and patted my hair to remove water.

"Nearly done," he said, and then he did something curious.

I was sitting in the center of the bed with my legs out in front of me. He climbed over my legs, straddling them while facing me. When his butt came down on my thighs, my legs parted to let him sit on the bed. He kept reaching around my head, patting my hair dry, with his money makers nuzzling up against Miss Kitty. Casually. Like, *Oh, didn't see you there, m'lady.*

His balls rubbed against my mound as though we were sharing a pair of Fundies*, and I breathed in the scent of his body and ran my hands over the fascinating terrain of his chest.

*Fundies are novelty underwear for two people, often given as a gag gift by people who've never actually had sex. This mention of Fundies was in no way sponsored or suggested to me by the wacky pervs who make Fundies.

Keith's chest was beautiful, rippling under my fingertips as he finished towel-drying my hair. I tried not to think of how I looked to him. Surely after posing together in our underwear the previous day, there were very few surprises for either of us.

Keith tossed the robe aside and pressed both of his cool palms against my back, pulling me in for a hug. The hug lasted a long time. Like, I thought we were done hugging and began kissing his tanned shoulder, but the hug kept happening. Finally, I just gave into the hug, going limp. I think that's what you're supposed to do when a bear attacks you.

After a moment, I became aware of my breathing, and how it had fallen in rhythm to match Keith's. I wondered if our hearts were beating together as well, because it sure seemed like it. He was still straddling my lap, our parts commingling like overly-friendly co-workers at an open-bar staff Christmas party, and the whole thing felt intense, but good.

An energy was climbing up my backbone, like a fast-growing vine, made of fire. The energy was sexual, but also more than that. What was Keith doing to me with this hug? Was he some sort of new-age earth muffin type? Honestly, if he'd started chanting next, I wouldn't have been surprised.

More notably, he was at least as turned on as I was. His modeling talent—the part that filled out the underwear pouch—was straining upward to see the world, or at least my nipples. The velvety pink skin stroked softly against my stomach, and I realized we were swaying, albeit gently.

Oh, his gorgeous thing was almost as pretty as his face. I wanted him in me—in my mouth to begin with. Keith was hugging me so tightly, though, that I couldn't make any moves. Despite the coolness in the room, our bodies were hot against each other, and any moment I was going to start sweating.

"This is perfect," he said with a calm voice.

Were we still hugging? Yes, apparently we were.

"I'm not sure what I'm supposed to be doing."

"Being here with me is more than enough." His hands started moving, stroking up and down my back. After being held in one spot for so long, the sensation was incredible. My back felt like it was made of light, and every spot Keith pressed or squeezed emitted new colors.

I moaned and leaned my head back, arching my upper body. He kissed my neck, his mouth hot and wet against my skin.

Gasping at the ecstasy of his touch, I moaned for him not to stop. This was so much better than the hugging.

When he reached my jaw, I tilted my head up again and we kissed passionately, our tongues caressing. It was rubbing up and down against my stomach now, the base of it getting wet from me.

"Trade spots?" he asked as he reached behind him for a condom.

"How?" I asked, but then I saw what he meant. Still facing him, both of us seated, I moved my legs to extend over top his thighs. He got the condom in place and used his hand to bend himself down enough to enter me. With a wiggle and a slight lift from me, bracing my palms behind me, he slid in. His whole incredible length and girth filled me gently. I gasped again at the sensation, fireworks sparking throughout my nerves and behind my eyelids.

This was happening. For real.

He caressed my breasts, moving in and out slowly, rhythmically.

Everything felt so good.

He took the next part as slowly as the beginning, and the more I let go and stopped worrying about getting somewhere, the more the divine pleasure built up. We swayed together, not moving very far in either direction, but still building heat.

"Lift your pelvis," he whispered. "A little more muscle tension increases the blood flow."

I leaned back again, using my palms for support, arching my back. Whatever was happening, the magic was working. I whimpered as I ground myself against his firm muscles, my sensitive nub mashing into his damp skin and short curls.

Keith fondled my breasts and craned his neck down, palming them upward so he could taste my nipples and run his teeth over the taut tissue. He sucked on one, then the other, making my eyes roll up in my head with pleasure.

His hips were rolling, moving in rhythm with and then against mine. I couldn't get enough of him, moving gently back and forth inside me. I started to come, and I could tell it was going to be a big one, after all that buildup. He wrapped his arms around my back and pulled me close to him, then used his upper body strength to drive me up and down atop his hardness. My legs wrapped around him.

I cried out and buried my hands in his hair, hanging on for dear life as my orgasm shuddered through both of us. My wails quieted down until they were just raspy breaths. One final aftershock made me squeak with surprise.

We stopped moving, and all was still. He was hard inside me, neither coming nor going, from what I could tell.

"That was fantastic," I said, giving him a kiss. The skin around his mouth was moist with sweat. "Now what? How shall we finish you off?"

"I'm good," he said.

"I'll say you're good! Forget modeling, you should get paid to do that!"

He chuckled. "I don't like to release every time, if that's what you mean. I'm more about the journey than the destination."

With that, he shifted back on the bed, withdrawing. One at a time, he pulled his legs out from under mine and swung around to lie on his side, gazing up at me.

"You're really done?" I asked.

He pulled the sheet to cover himself from my curious eyes. I'd never heard of a regular guy choosing to not orgasm. Naturally, I was worried I had scared him, or that something was wrong with his twig and berries, perhaps permanent damage from wearing the wrap-around rings for underwear shoots.

"Everything works just fine," he said, as though he knew exactly what I'd been thinking. "What I really wanted was to hold you, kiss you, smell you, and taste your skin. I got all that, plus hearing you the sound of you coming. As for my preference, I find my senses are sharper when I'm not... *finishing* every day."

He reached for my hand and pulled me to lie alongside him, my back against his front, our lower halves separated by a sheet.

"I'm not complaining," I said. "Just curious."

"And suspicious."

"Not suspicious." I brought his hand up to my mouth and gently gnawed on one of his knuckles. He had lovely hands for chewing on. "A little hungry is all."

He combed through my damp hair with his fingers. "The sex was hot, but now our coffee is cold. Life always has a way of ensuring balance."

I wriggled, feeling comfortable nestled against this man who'd been a stranger not twenty-four hours earlier. What surprised me most was I had no desire to run away, to flee the scene.

He nuzzled my ear and asked, "Remind me, how long do I have you?"

"Nine days," I said. "Only nine days, and then I'm leaving LA."

"I like this arrangement. You're exactly what I needed to get my mind off Tabitha."

My leg twitched. At the mention of some other woman's name, the urge to flee had surfaced. What was that all about?

"Tabitha broke your heart?"

"She took my heart out of my chest, rented a moving truck, filled the moving truck with pianos, and ran forward and back over my heart repeatedly."

I stifled a giggle.

He continued, "It gets better. She rented the moving truck using my credit card, too."

"Wait, are we still talking in metaphor? This is getting complicated."

His fingers caught in my hair tangles and yanked at my scalp, making me yelp and grab his hand.

"Easy there, wild beast."

"Tabitha's fault," he growled.

Her name again. The urge to get away was almost unbearable.

I rolled away from him, off the bed, and out of the bedroom. I hustled, butt-naked, around the apartment gathering my stuff and getting dressed.

I could just leave! *Good idea, Peaches!*

I'd thrown on my clothes and was hopping on one foot, trying to get my shoe on for a getaway, when keys jingled on the other side of the apartment door. A second later, someone was opening the door. Scratch that. Two someones. Tall, leggy, brunettes—a matching set.

One of them scowled at me and said, "Who the hell is this whore?"

The other one smiled and tucked her brown hair behind her ear, then extended a hand to me. "Hello!"

I just wanted to slip out, without a weird confrontation, so I had to think fast. Glancing around the apartment, I spotted a red broom and dustpan.

"I am *cleaning* lady," I said, using a (probably offensive) accent I made up on the spot.

The two girls stared at me, one looking as amused as the other looked irritated.

I continued, waving my hand in a swirl, "Out of Lemon Pledge. Have to go… store. Buy more. He no buy, tsk tsk." I shook my head, really getting into character. "Bachelor. Always messy. With the beard hairs on the sink."

The mean girl turned to the nice one, saying, "Seriously, Tabitha. Now he's banging the cleaning lady? This has got to be rock bottom."

"No rock bottom," I growled. "No banging cleaning lady."

I resisted the urge to cram my shoe up her butt and slipped it on my foot instead. What confused me most was that the nice girl was Tabitha, Keith's ex-girlfriend. Who was the mean girl, and what pooped on her Pop Tart?

Miss Nasty said, "Your hair's wet. You just had a shower, so stop lying."

I put on a huge, stupid grin. "I clean shower real good. I get right in and scrub, scrub, scrub."

"Ladies!" Keith called out, drawing our attention. He was dressed and looking every bit the model in a tight-fitting gray, V-neck shirt and light brown chinos. My jaw actually dropped at the sight of him. Damn, he was sexy.

Miss Nasty demanded to know who I was, where he'd been, what he was doing, and about a million other things, all peppered with swear words and spewing out of her nasty mouth like a volcano of ugly.

Keith came around to my side and draped his arm over my shoulders. "My housekeeper and I are in love," he said.

My jaw dropped again. Now, despite what had just happened in the minutes leading up to here, I'm not big on lying, even for the purposes of a hilarious farce, but the look on Miss Nasty's face was all it took to bring me over to the dark side.

"So in luff," I said, still in my pretend-broken English. "I no resist big, handsome man. So sexy, like horse."

Miss Nasty snorted. "Like horse! Keith! This is what rock bottom looks like. Here you are. I hope you're happy, wallowing in your filth."

I nearly cracked up. "No filth. I clean real good."

Tabitha had already ducked away, into the kitchen. Some dishes clattered, and she returned to the area by the front door where we were standing, holding a popcorn-sized green glass bowl. "Got what I came for," she said cheerily.

"Nice to meet you," she said to me. "I'm Tabitha, by the way."

"You break heart," I said, hugging my arms around Keith protectively and putting on an exaggerated frown. It was surprisingly easy to play this role of Keith's cleaning lady. The broken English forced me to slow down and think about what I was saying more than I usually did.

Keith squeezed me tight against him and kissed me affectionately on the side of my forehead. "And then you fixed my heart," he said to me.

"I did? Oh! I did."

To the other girls, he said, "Yeah, this has been going on ever since you both moved out. I didn't tell you, because we weren't sure where it was going until now." He leaned down and rubbed his nose against mine, then gave me a quick kiss on the lips. "Ursula is moving in with me," he announced.

In unison, the brunettes said, "Ursula?"

I nodded. "Family name. You no like?"

They seemed skeptical, but there were so many lies being flung around, they didn't know what to disbelieve first.

Keith said, "Ursula, this is Tabitha, my former girlfriend, as you've figured out. And this other charming young woman, who seems to have forgotten the manners we were raised with, and needs a dose of cayenne to remind her, is my sister, Katy."

I pointed to him, then Miss Personality, aka Katy. "Keith, Katy. Brother, sister. I get. Keith is nice." I gave her a dirty look, my eyes nearly squinted shut, like I was putting a curse on her—a curse I would have learned back in my homeland, wherever that was. "Katy is like kitty-cat who is not so nice." I held my hands up in a clawing gesture and hissed.

Katy's mouth knitted up, erasing her lips entirely from her face.

Tabitha edged closer to the door. Considering she was the ex-girlfriend, she was taking everything rather well. "Come on, let's go already," she said to her friend.

"Not yet," Katy said, her lips still thin with tension. "Ursula, you're invited to dinner tonight, with our parents, at their house."

"No, no. Too much," I said, which wasn't a lie at all.

"Sounds great," Keith said, squeezing me tight against him. "I've been meaning to introduce her to Mom."

"Hah!" yelled Katy, making me jump.

She opened the door and the two of them were off, without another word.

The door closed, and Keith held his finger to his lips for a moment, then went to watch them leave via the peephole.

After a moment, he turned around and gave me a sheepish look.

"You're crazy," I said.

"Me? You're the one who pretended to be my cleaning lady."

"I had to protect myself. I can take down one mouthy bag of hair extensions, but not two at once."

"That's my sister you're talking about."

"News flash! Your sister's a mouthy bag of hair extensions. I'm surprised she doesn't have a reality TV show."

"She got a callback for Big Brother."

"Color me anything but surprised."

"You'll warm up to her, I promise."

"No, I won't, because I'll never see her again."

In response, he gave me a pouty look.

"Forget dinner," I said. "Family drama is not what I signed up for."

"If I take you out today on the best date you've ever been on, then will you come with me to dinner?"

I rolled my eyes. "Now I know why Mitchell warned me about you boy models. Those gorgeous brown eyes of yours are very difficult to say no to."

He put his fingers under the edge of my jaw and tilted my head to face him. Tenderly, he kissed me on the lips. His gentle touch took my breath away, and with it, my resistance.

As he pulled away, he said, "Let's unbreak these hearts. For the next nine days, let's practice saying yes to each other, and saying yes to life."

Another kiss.

"Say yes to me, Peaches," he said. "Let's experience utter happiness together, no strings and no baggage, for nine days. Just say yes."

CHAPTER 6

Keith gave me another kiss, this one weakening my knees and softening my legs to the consistency of over-cooked carrots.

He said, "I'm all yours, body and spirit, if you say yes."

"Yes," I whispered.

"Good." He kissed me again.

Muffled by his mouth on mine, I mumbled something about breakfast.

He pulled away and said, "Let's go to this great pancake place I know of."

"I don't know," I said with a sigh. "First you make coffee that we don't drink. Then you have sex but don't come. Please promise me we're not going to order breakfast, then leave as soon as the food hits the table."

"I wouldn't do that to you."

"If I get a forkful of pancakes and you knock it on the ground, that would be very Keith Raven of you."

He chuckled and leaned down to pull on a pair of shoes. "And if you took off running when I was in the other room, that would be very Peaches Monroe of you, wouldn't it?"

I gave him an innocent look. "I don't know what you're talking about."

"You were scrambling to get out of here when my ex and my sister showed up. I bet you do that a lot—run away when things get intense. We should work on that."

To change the topic, I grabbed the red broom and started sweeping around the entryway. "I clean house real good."

"More pancakes for me." With a shrug, he opened the door and started to leave. "C'mon, Ursula."

I let the broom clatter to the floor and put my hands on my hips. "What the hell was that about, with that name? Ursula is the fat, ugly sea witch from *The Little Mermaid*. Thanks a lot."

"Ursula is a beautiful name, and I've never seen that movie. I never liked cartoons."

I grabbed my purse and followed him out, muttering that he was the weirdest guy I'd ever met. Who doesn't like cartoons?

~

We had breakfast at a diner, where the ridiculous waiter acted like he didn't know what a mocha was, so I had to order a coffee plus a hot chocolate, then make a dribbling mess as Keith laughed at my dumb ass.

"You're making fun of me," I said. "Which makes this more of an average or typical date for me, and *not* the *best date ever*. I guess I won't have the pleasure of seeing your bag-of-hair sister again."

He reached under the table of the booth and squeezed my thighs just above my knees. "You're going to have many pleasures today."

I pulled some napkins from the silver dispenser on the table and sopped up the mess I'd made. Which reminded me… that morning's bedroom sporting hadn't turned me into a water feature. Perhaps that squirt-o-rama had been a one-time event, just to clear the ol' peri-urethral ducts.

Looking across the table at Keith, I had the urge to ask him what he knew about the phenomenon. He seemed like the kind of guy who read books about sex. On second thought, he also seemed like the kind of guy who'd be obsessed with making the squirting happen again, just for the experience. Nope, this secret was going into the vault with the others.

"Where to after breakfast?" I asked. "Cruising Mulholland Drive in the green van?"

Keith smirked. "The van does have a sun roof. I have a few ideas in mind. How do you feel about roller coasters?"

"How do you feel about getting barfed on?"

"No Knott's Berry Farm, then. Okay, Plan B it is." He pulled out his phone and mumbled about making arrangements.

The waiter brought our food, and at the same time, the music cranked up a few levels. *Free Fallin'* by Tom Petty was playing, and I could hear the faint sound of people back in the kitchen of the restaurant singing along like it was their favorite tune.

Hearing *Free Fallin'* like this, I experienced something not unlike *déjà vu*. My mother loved the song, and the video played in my mind as Tom Petty sang about places in LA, including Ventura Boulevard, which had always sounded so magical to me, a girl in small-town Washington. He sang about good girls, bad boys, and broken hearts.

As I looked over at Keith, a chill went through me, giving me goose bumps all over. I was a good girl with a broken heart. Had I simply jumped from one bad boy to another?

"Yum," Keith declared as he dug into his low-carb breakfast. With his young-looking face, he didn't seem that dangerous, but I would have to be careful around him and guard my heart.

~

After breakfast, we drove to world-famous* Rodeo Drive.

*Their marketing and branding efforts must be working, because I can't say or even think about Rodeo Drive without the *world-famous* modifier in front.

As we drove past Gucci, Prada, and stores I'd never heard of but imagined were equally pricey, I said, "Keith, I don't know how much they're paying you to stand around looking sexy in your underpants, but I'm sure not getting Gucci money."

He laughed. "Don't you want to go in and have a look?"

"Just to look? I'm not like you, all restraint and denial of pleasurable release. I don't go to bakeries to sniff the icing, you know?"

He chuckled and kept driving. I continued to stare out the windows like the hick tourist I was. The palm trees and blue sky made every angle of Beverly Hills look like a postcard. Although I'd never been to the city before, so many buildings and streets looked familiar—I guess from all the TV shows and movies shot there. We drove past a brick building that looked like the nightclub Drake

Cheshire—Dalton Deangelo's vampire character—owned. Thinking about him didn't feel good. The hurt around my heart extended so far, even my armpits ached when I imagined his lying face.

Keith parked the van, shaking me out of my funk.

"I'm not dressed for fancy shopping," I said, feeling self-conscious about my casual clothes, which I was now spending the second day in.

"That's why I brought you here, to my friend's boutique. He has a fashion line, and he's on the verge of moving to New York and making it big. I'll move there and do the runway shows, of course." The way he was grinning, I was pretty sure he was being sarcastic. From what I'd gathered during my short time in LA, *everyone* was on the verge of making it big and going somewhere.

"What's your friend's name?" I asked. "Something fashion-y, like Sergio? Or Mutt? Or... Jean-Ralphio?"

"Guy," he said, pronouncing it like the Indian word for clarified butter: *ghee.*

Keith ran around to my side and opened my door, then helped me step down. The air outside the van didn't smell as nice as the inside, so I asked, "What's that smell?"

"LA."

"No, it's like... rotten eggs."

"Maybe the Salton Sea is to blame. It's a hundred and fifty miles from the city, but there are seasonal fish die-offs, and with shifting weather patterns, sometimes the anaerobic layers get oxygen, which causes the hydrogen sulfide gas to form, and... that's more than you wanted to know, isn't it?"

"You really are an earth muffin type, aren't you?"

We started walking up the sidewalk. Keith looked troubled by what I'd said, so I corrected myself, saying, "Not in a bad way. I think it's amazing you know about soil and stuff. My neighbor back home, Mr. Galloway, is always talking to me about the pH levels in soil. It's always egg shells and coffee grounds, or something. I have no clue, despite working in a bookstore with a substantial gardening section."

"Egg shells for calcium, and coffee grounds for nitrogen," he said. "Now you know."

"What about talking to plants. Does that do any good?"

"Plants are like people. Some benefit from conversation, and others continue to act like idiots, no matter how much you yell at them."

"Excuse me?"

He chuckled. "I meant me, not you."

He opened the door to a narrow store that looked like it had been built in the leftover space between two larger buildings, and we went into his friend's clothing boutique.

If this were a movie, there'd be a montage here of me trying on the most amazing assortment of clothes, many of them flattering wrap style dresses. The prices were a little YIKES, but Guy took a shine to me and said if I bought one, he'd give me three more. I bought two dresses, and he kept stuffing more things into the bags until I begged him to stop. Keith tried to pay for everything, but I wouldn't allow it, saying he was doing more than enough by giving me somewhere to stay and being my personal tour guide.

I walked out of the boutique feeling like I was in a fairy tale. Specifically, I felt like the side character who somehow cons her way into getting the makeover and goodies that were supposed to be for the main character, the skinny, big-lipped girl who weighs under a hundred pounds, in shoes.

With my shopping loot on one arm and my underwear model on the other arm, I wondered if there wasn't an Anne Hathaway type somewhere wondering where her life-swag went.

When we got back to the van, Keith gave me a knowing look, like he *knew* I was having the best date ever, and he didn't need to ask. He looked so smug. Why is smug so sexy? I swear, it's like catnip for Miss Kitty when a cute guy looks so self-satisfied.

"Off to the second and best part," he said. "Why don't you change into one of those dresses?"

"Sure, I'll just flash all of California with my body and get changed right here in the van."

"They're going to see everything on billboards soon enough."

My voice small and squeaky, I said, "Billboards?" Had there been billboards in the agreement? Classic smart-girl move: I had my father read the modeling contract and didn't pay that much attention. So much whimsy.

I muttered something about horses and barn doors, then wrestled out of my clothes quickly, while we drove along a quieter street. I slid into one of my new wrap dresses, a purple creation with leopard-print highlight details. The combination of purple and leopard-print sounds tacky, but I assure you, the dress was pure class. The knock-off version sold at K-Mart would have been tacky, but this was the original. A designer original, by Guy Weird-last-name.*

*Not his actual name. I'd happily give him full credit, if the logo on the labels wasn't indistinguishable swirls.

For the next stop, we drove out of the city.

Keith could go ahead and look smug, because I was having a good time.

"How do you feel about gardening?" he asked.

"I've got a few potted plants, but sometimes I can't tell weeds from plants."

"I meant today."

As the van pulled into the parking lot of a garden with an admission gate, I glanced back at the bags of dirt in the van and said, "You're kidding me. We're here on a landscaping job?"

He jumped out of the van and opened the back door instead of coming around to my side.

I wandered back with a confused scowl on my face.

"Catch." He tossed a plastic bag of potting soil at me.

"I'm wearing a dress," I wailed as I caught the bag. "I'll help you plant some daisies or whatever, but let me get changed!"

With a bag of dirt on his shoulder, he stepped up to me and leaned down to whisper in my ear, "Follow my lead. We're about to skip the long admission line."

I looked behind him, at the chain of people snaking from the entry and through the parking lot.

"You're a bad boy," I whispered back.

58

"You should have taken Mitchell's warning." He gave me a peck on the lips, then turned and started walking confidently toward the entrance.

Why do I always get myself into these predicaments? I stared after his adorable butt, which was so cute. *How cute was his butt, Peaches?* Cuter than a basket of baby bunnies at a carrot buffet.

I followed Mr. Cute Buns in, and was not at all surprised to be waved through by friendly, yet not-that-bright staff. To save someone a reprimand, I'm not going to name the park, and to keep you all from hating Keith Raven for the wrong reasons, I have to let you know he made a generous cash donation to the donation box in lieu of paying admission.

Okay, I lied. There was no donation made.

Keith is a bad boy with a cute butt. Sue me!

We dropped the soil off just inside the gates and started walking along the tour path, passing through a tunnel of tree branches that reminded me of The Arch of Swords, that old tradition of military weddings.

As we walked, Keith held my hand and named off every flower, shrub, and tree we passed.

"Enough with the Latin," I said after twenty minutes of what sounded like a bunch of *Harry Potter* spells. "What's the deal with you and Tabitha?"

He frowned, which I interpreted as his desire to have someone badger him until he cracked. Like what a therapist might do. If that therapist had no training and was me.

"She seemed so nice," I said, impressing myself with the soothing, therapeutic tone of my voice. "You're a little complicated, with the extreme gardening boner you have for shrubbery, plus the nearly-nude modeling, but you seem like a real catch. Why couldn't you two crazy kids make it work?"

"I don't want to talk about it," he said, which I had a hard time creatively misinterpreting, though I did try—for several silent moments of walking.

The garden was beautiful—all lush and tidy, with just the right number of chubby bumblebees flying around from blossom to blossom.

We walked by a wedding party having their photos taken. We stopped to watch as the photographer set the camera on a timer, then tossed it up in the air to take an aerial photo of the group, looking up.

As we left and continued our tour, Keith and I both said in unison, "I wonder how often he has to buy a new camera."

We didn't jinx each other, but laughed and laughed.

Keith pulled me with him to hide on the other side of a big tree, where he kissed me with vigor and grabbed my ass with even more vigor. We kept kissing, and he brought one hand around to the front of my knee, then up my skirt and down my panties. I gasped in shock as his fingers nudged my hot crease. People were all around us, even though we were hidden behind the tree.

He growled near my ear as he rocked his fingers back and forth, gliding across me.

"Mercy!" I moaned.

He whispered in my ear, "Don't worry, you're not going to come. Just relax. Let it build, but don't come."

"You are the worst," I breathed.

"Is this good?" He swirled his fingertips in a circle.

CHAPTER 7

"Is this good?" he repeated.

I whimpered that his fingers on my sensitive spot felt *very* good, and he rotated us around so my back was against the rough tree bark, my hair getting tangled in small branches as I rocked in rhythm with his hand.

He kissed me, licking my lips slowly with his tongue, then swirling it in my mouth, but just the tip, just a tease.

The first sparks started between my legs, and I lunged for his mouth, wanting to inhale him, tongue first, but still he held back. My muscles clenched in anticipation, and then he slowly dragged his fingers up, out of my panties.

I opened my eyes and stared at him in disbelief as he put his fingers in his mouth and sucked them, relishing in my taste and my frustration—mostly my frustration.

I whisper-scolded, "Keith Raven, you are a tease!"

He laughed and smoothed down the front of my purple wrap skirt, then pulled me forward and smoothed the back of my hair.

"You're so fun to tease," he replied.

"Oh, so this is all my fault? Right. Blame the victim."

He leaned back, his arms wrapped around my lower back so our hips and legs were touching. After a studying look, he said, "Admit you're having a great time today."

Playing coy, I said, "I like my new dress."

"So do all the men in this park. They're all checking out your peachy curves, and the wives and girlfriends are all pissed about it."

"You're mistaken. The girls are all checking YOU out and wondering what the hell you're doing with a regular girl like me."

With a growl, he pushed me back against the rough bark of the tree again, his hands on either side of me and his torso pinning me. As he kissed my neck and earlobe, he said, "There is nothing regular about you or the way you make me feel. If there weren't so many people around, I'd throw you down in a bed of daisies and bury my face between your sweet thighs."

I gasped for air. "And then what?" I was so turned on, I felt like what he was describing was actually happening.

"You'd discover underwear modeling is one of my side talents, but tongue-work is my real specialty."

"Oh?" My heart was pounding, my whole body quivering.

He licked the side of my neck roughly, then gently, flicking my earlobe, then giving it a hard suck, his breath hot and ticklish in my ear.

"Excuse me," came a high, thin voice.

I opened my eyes to see a well-dressed elderly woman in a sunbonnet standing nearby.

Keith pulled back and wagged his finger at me. "Enough of that, miss! This is a family park."

The woman didn't walk away, but stayed there, staring with a big grin on her face. "You're Keith Raven," she said.

"Yes, Ma'am," he said. "Would you like to take a picture with me?"

She waved her hand. "No, no, darling. I don't want to take up any more of your time. I just wanted to say I have your calendar photo on my fridge at home."

Keith turned and walked up to her, ready for more conversation. I watched in awe as he turned on the charm, and the lady—who must have been at least eighty, if a day—melted like a girl under his attention.

"That calendar's out of date now," he said. "I'll have to send you a new picture to display for your friends."

"My daughter has epilepsy," she said. "We appreciate all the fund-raising you and those other nice boys do."

"You're welcome. I only wish I could do more." He pulled out his phone and said, "If you don't mind giving me your mailing address, I'll put something in the mail for you."

She fanned her face with one white-gloved hand. "If I give you my house number, you won't show up unexpectedly, will you?"

He got a sly grin. "That depends. When's your birthday?"

Her eyes got big and she took in a big gasp, then let out a torrent of girlish giggles. Once she calmed down a little, she was able to give her address. The woman didn't have anything to take a photo with, but Keith insisted on getting one with his phone, for *his* collection. "On the tough days, I look at pictures like this to feel the support of my fans," he said to her.

I used the camera on his phone and took the photo of them. The woman's son and family came to retrieve her, and Keith insisted the son take a photo of the three of us, including me.

As I stood on one side of him, smiling for the picture, I fought down an overwhelming sense of pride. For Keith, getting a picture with me in it may have been a casual impulse, but being included meant so much to me. I remembered vividly how shut-out I'd felt by Dalton goofing around with his fangirl. This was the opposite feeling.

Once we were on our own again, in the fragrant rose garden, Keith put his arm around my shoulders and said, "Not one of these roses is as lovely as you in that purple dress."

I pointed to some enormous, peach-pink blossoms. "Not even this one?"

"Not even. So, are you coming to dinner with my family tonight?"

"Of course," I said. "I need to eat dinner anyway. I came to LA like so many other small-town blondes before me, hoping to catch my big break, and I think impersonating your cleaning lady is the opportunity of a lifetime."

"When you put it like that, it does sound glamorous."

"Then tomorrow, it's back to the old grind of putting on fancy underwear and having my picture taken."

"What a coincidence! Me, too."

We stopped to admire some unusual rust-hued roses with streaks of yellow. They were labeled *Dragon's Blood*, and my sexy gardener/model was transfixed for a moment.

In the stillness, I heard my phone tremble in my purse with another text message. I was in no mood to check messages and ruin what had become a fun day, so I quickly switched it off.

Had it only been that morning that I broke up with Dalton? Had it only been three days ago I was in Beaverdale, helping bookstore customers pick out great summer beach reads? Who was this gorgeous girl in a knockout designer dress? As Keith had noted, this girl actually *was* getting checked out by other men, including sunhat-wearing dads pushing strollers. Whoever she was, I loved being her.

~

Keith's parents lived in a neighborhood on the west side of LA called Mar Vista. As we drove along, I saw kids running through sprinklers, and tree-lined streets with modest, post-war bungalows.

"Except for the palm trees, this could be Washington," I said.

"It's a good place to grow up. We lived on the grittier side until I was ten, then we moved over, to north of Venice, which is much nicer."

"Venice Beach?"

"I meant Venice Boulevard, but the beach is west of here. Look at you, knowing all about LA. Soon you'll be telling me shortcuts."

"Don't be so sure of that. I keep getting turned around and thinking the sun's in the wrong spot in the sky."

Keith pulled the van over and parked on a street that looked like a nice place to call home.

"Are you ready for the Lipschitz experience?" he asked.

"I keep forgetting that's your real last name."

He didn't move from his seat. "My parents worry too much about their kids. Especially about me. Can I tell you something personal?"

Uh-oh, here it comes. "Sure."

"I got mixed up in drugs when I was younger. I'm clean now, but working in the fashion industry isn't without its temptations. When I started modeling, my parents acted like I was going off to war."

Looking over at the ordinary brown house we'd parked next to, I could understand how the people who lived in such a house would be scared. You make a nice life for your family, then your kids go off in search of things that terrify you.

He continued, "They've been so sad lately—my parents. We've had some death and illness in the extended family, and when Tabitha and I split up, my mother took it even harder than me."

"I'm sorry to hear that."

"So, I dragged you here tonight, kicking and screaming—"

"No! Fair and square, you took me on the best date today."

He smiled, his expressive brown eyes lively. "As I was saying... I invited you here tonight because you're the most fun person I've met in a long time."

"Hah!"

"And I think seeing me with someone as warm and giving as you will make them stop worrying about me so much."

Putting on my fake accent, I said, "I clean house real good."

"About the housekeeper thing... my sister's gullible, but my parents aren't. They'll have you figured out in five minutes."

"Challenge accepted."

"Okay then," he said cheerily, jumping out of the van and running around to my side.

I was already nervous enough, but my hands started to sweat as we slowly made our way up to the front door, stopping to admire all the various shrubs and flowers in the front yard.

Some of the tall flowers were held upright with green gardener's tape, looking tidy in a way that bordered on ridiculous, but who am I to judge? One time, I threw out a whole batch of geraniums that were purchased for my terra cotta pots, because they were pink, not red, and I really had my heart set on red.

The world is a chaotic place, our destinies shaped by chance meetings and the rash decisions of others. We are helpless against fate, so is it any wonder we stomp our feet over getting our choice of pizza toppings, and spend our free time mulching coffee grounds into our gardens, our own miniature planet earth over which we have control?

The door to the house opened, and Keith's parents stepped out onto the front step, father and mother, handsome and beautiful, respectively.

Under my breath, I muttered, "This confirms you're not adopted."

We walked up to Keith's black-haired, brown-eyed donors of photogenic traits, and I shook both of their hands.

"Mr. Lipsch—"

"Call me Ken, and this is Kendra."

The woman gave me a friendly hug, squeezing her small chest against my D-cups. As she pulled away, she said, "We're Kenny Squared, Ken and Kendra. And what's your name, sweetheart?"

"Ursula?" I looked to Keith for guidance, but he only raised his eyebrows. "I clean house," I said.

Kendra gave me a sidelong look. "What accent would you say that is, Ursula?"

"Polish?" I bit my lip.

"My Keith would never hire a cleaning lady," she said. "Too much of a control freak. So, what's the real story, you two little jokers?"

Keith ruffled my hair and pulled me in close to his chest. We hadn't even made it in the door and his mother had already figured me out. I made a note to watch myself around her.

"This is Peaches Monroe," Keith said proudly. "She designed the clothing line I'm modeling this week."

Kendra wrinkled her nose. "Oh. You're still doing that?"

"He's an incredible model," I said. "He helped me out on set so much yesterday."

Keith's father waved us into the house. "Everybody, get in the house. Our business is not the street's business."

We all went in, and were shown to the dining room, which was around the corner from the kitchen and separated from the front room by a rounded archway.

My least favorite new acquaintance, Keith's sister Katy, sat at the table, drinking what appeared to be white wine with ice cubes in it. She gave me a look that was so acidic, it could probably remove stubborn bathtub mildew.

"Why'd you say you were the cleaning lady?" Katy spat at me.

"So you wouldn't be jealous of my awesome career and act like a jealous twat. Oops, I guess it didn't work."

Keith's father exclaimed, "Peaches! Katy! Such language. Keith, go and fetch the cayenne."

"I'm sorry," I said, holding my hands in the air. "I come into your home and immediately insult your daughter. My bad. Even though the bag of hair deserved it."

Keith had already gone to the kitchen and returned with the cayenne pepper.

"You don't have to do this," Keith said to me.

"Do what?"

Keith explained that punishment for swearing in the house was holding cayenne pepper on your tongue for thirty seconds. The rule was for everyone, all ages.

"Oh, please. Twat isn't a swear word. In England, I hear it's as common as toast, but heaven help you if you say fanny."

Ken said, "That's two and a half now."

"Hit me," I said, and I stuck my tongue out to be seasoned. *What a ridiculous punishment.*

Keith's mother administered the cayenne to both me and Katy, as kindly and lovingly as if she was giving cold medicine.

As I held the cayenne on my tongue, I had the following thoughts:

I wonder what's for dinner.

Keith's parents look exactly like the wholesome types who buy books about kinky BDSM.

Do me three times and never call, but this pepper is hot as hell.

I wonder what Dalton's doing. Not that I care.

Did I ever finish reading the final Harry Potter book?

Ow, pepper is hot.

Keith's dad is a fox.

Is something burning?

I will not cry. I will not cry.

Oh, no, my eyes are leaking.

"Time," said Ken.

I didn't move, didn't close my mouth.

A dish of sour cream and nachos was placed on the table, between me and Katy. Cooling, soothing sour cream.

Katy didn't move. Tears of pain were also streaming down her cheeks.

Still refusing to swallow first, I gestured with a jerk of my chin for Katy to go ahead and take the first cooling bite.

She returned the gesture, not budging.

No, you.

She glared back at me. What was up her fanny, anyway? Was she just born pretty and never had to develop a personality like the rest of us? Keith was gorgeous, and he still had tons of character and goodness, but maybe it was different for girls.

The burning of the pepper didn't bother me anymore. I was floating, my emotions free and ecstatic. The discomfort was there, but solely in my mouth, and it was only temporary, because all things are transient. I'd transcended the sensation, distracting myself with higher thoughts, and—

Oh, to hell with it.

I grabbed a fist full of chips, scooped a wide swath through the sour cream, and gobbled it down. Never before have I had such delicious sour cream. My whole body tingled, the endorphins flowing from the pepper. Keith took a seat next to me and squeezed my knee casually, and I melted from his touch.

Everything around me came into focus, sharper and brighter. The silverware picked up light from the chandelier overhead, the tines of my fork tipped in diamonds.

His mother brought in some covered dishes, wearing oven mitts, and then a green salad in a giant wood bowl.

"We're a little odd," she said apologetically. "We like to eat our salad alongside the dinner instead of before."

Right. Having salad with dinner is odd, but the cayenne punishment isn't. Interesting family you have here, Keith.

"That's a beautiful dress," his mother said to me, admiring the purple dress with the leopard print accents. "I'd like my Katy to wear something pretty like that, instead of those little shorts that show her bum cheeks for the whole world to see."

"Mom!" Katy howled, sounding fifteen, though she looked about my age.

We passed the wood bowl around the table, all helping ourselves. The greenery looked suspiciously like either kale or the plastic stuff Christmas wreaths are made of, so I didn't take much, obviously.

Keith leaned over and rubbed his chin on my shoulder affectionately. "You doing okay?" he whispered.

I nodded, yes. I hadn't called anyone a twat or a bag of hair for several minutes, so things were going better than expected.

Keith's mother started to tell us about the farmer's market where she bought the greenery, but Keith cut her off, sternly saying to his sister, "All right, Katy. That's more than enough."

Katy smirked and widened her eyes, trying to look innocent, but failing. "What was I doing?"

"Stop glaring at Peaches like you're a nasty little female dog and she just took your Milk Bones."

"Dad!" she wailed like a brat.

"He's right," Keith's father said. "You do resemble a member of the canine family when you scowl like that. An ill-tempered Chihuahua. I love you, kiddo, but if your mother and I can respect Keith's choice to show his genitals to the public for money, you can be nice to his girlfriend, who—" he turned to me "—does seem like a nice girl, despite her chosen profession of removing clothes. No offense."

"We're not strippers," Keith said, rolling his eyes.

"Modeling is hard work," I chimed in. "There are great opportunities, though. I'm actually the designer for the line with my name on it. That part is intense, because you have to consider the fabric weights and think about the colors two seasons ahead, because of manufacturing times." (Okay, I was pulling that last part completely out of my ass, thanks to a few things I'd overheard during the shoot, but who doesn't fudge their credentials when meeting a guy's parents?)

Katy stared at me, her pretty brown eyes almost dazed.

"What?" I said to her.

69

"That sounds so cool," she said, and with that one compliment, my desire to punch her in the throat greatly diminished.

Ken asked me, "Have you always been a fashion designer, or was there something else before all this?"

"I used to, and still do, manage a bookstore in my hometown."

"That sounds respectable," Ken said. "Will you look for another bookstore here in LA? We've lost some of the bigger ones, but there are places, if you know where to look."

I looked to Keith for assistance.

"One day at a time, Dad," Keith said, and then he gave me a look that scared me.

It was one of those looks that lasts forever and communicates so much.

With his big, brown eyes and that handsome boyish face, he looked at me like he *loved* me, and that everything was going to *work out*. I'd move to LA, and we'd be together, and tonight was just the first of many colorful dinners we'd have with his family.

Were we still pretending?

~

The rest of dinner was actually enjoyable. Keith's family had a different dynamic than the Monroes, but what they did have in common was that they seemed to like each other. You have to love your family, of course, but *liking* the family you were born or otherwise brought into is both rare and precious.

For dessert, we had fresh brownies with a raspberry compote plus ice cream. Any two of these items on their own would have been good, but the trio was perfection.

Keith's family howled with laughter as he picked up his plate and actually licked the pink raspberry and ice cream soup off his plate. Did I then follow suit and lick my plate? You bet I did, and I'd do it again, because I am classy like that.

After all the plates were cleared and after-dinner coffee was served, Katy asked if I wanted to "see her room."

I stared at her in disbelief. "Why? Do you have poisonous spiders?"

"I'm *trying* to be nice," she said.

Everyone else was quiet, and I felt the pressure to try to be nice as well. "Sure, I'd love to see your room. I guess you just moved back home after living with Keith?"

She got up and nodded for me to follow her.

CHAPTER 8

We went to the back of the house, then down a set of stairs, to a lower floor that was so cool, it was practically chilly. The decorating style was nice and modern, and the ceilings were a good nine feet high, but it still had the faintest musty basement smell.

Katy's room was an L-shape, with a gas fireplace, sofa, and TV at one end—more of a bachelor apartment than a bedroom.

"Swanky," I said as I admired the framed prints of flowers and hummingbirds on the wall. "You have your own apartment, practically."

She flopped back on her double-sized bed, sprawling on the white comforter. "What's the deal with you and my brother?"

I looked closer at the prints on the wall, all tastefully framed in white frames. "Did you take these photos yourself?"

"Yes. How did you meet my brother?"

Switching into Ursula mode, I quipped, "I clean house. He see me bent over toilet, scrubbing with brush. He like what he see, you know? Grab me by hips. Say be girlfriend with me!"

"What I really want to know is, do you love him?"

"That's between me and your brother."

I turned back to see a disgusted look on her face. "So, no, you don't. Great. Well, give me a call when you're done using him, so I can pick up the pieces."

So much for being nice.

I didn't have to take any more of her attitude, so I turned around and left. Katy didn't follow me upstairs, which was fine by me.

I joined Keith and his parents, and we went for a tour of the back garden, which was full of not just flowers, but more butterflies than I'd ever seen outside of a conservatory. One came and landed on the back of my hand. It was orange, black and cream. I nearly died when I realized how much its long freaky body resembled a dragonfly, but I managed to grimace through the horror.

Keith's father pulled his reading glasses from his shirt pocket and examined the butterfly. "You have a friend," he said.

My voice squeaky, I said, "Monarch?"

"Painted Lady. They're smaller than the Monarchs."

I thought the creepy butterfly would take to the air again, but it didn't. Finally, I yelped and shook my hand like a crazy person, which made them laugh.

Kendra squeezed my shoulder and said, "I hate it when they land on me, too."

After the garden tour, Keith took my hand and we said goodbye to his parents. They stood together as we walked away, like they were posing for a photo.

~

The sun was low on the horizon, the whole city of LA orange and glowing as we drove back to Keith's apartment. I was now so used to the dirt smell in the van, I wondered if any air freshener companies made a dirt option.

At the apartment building, we walked through the courtyard in comfortable silence. The apartment was still and quiet, as though not one dust mote could be bothered to float around if nobody was there to see it. My own house never had this time capsule feeling, because my roommate was usually coming or going during the time I was out. For a moment, I felt a pang of sadness for Keith, that he had no roommate, nobody to stir the air and toss all his shoes into the closet in annoyance.

He had me, but that was only temporary. Just a short-term arrangement between two wild animals with emotional wounds that needed licking.

I scarcely had my sandals off and he swept me off my feet, up into his arms.

"Careful," I said.

"Don't worry. I won't drop you."

"I meant your back."

He carried me through the apartment, toward the bedroom door. "Nonsense. You weigh less than a tree."

I laughed. "That's the nicest thing anyone's ever said about my weight!"

We got into the bedroom, and he didn't set me down right away. "You feel good in my arms."

"I sure do."

He gently set me down on the soft bed. "Let's light some candles and meditate."

I laughed, then abruptly stopped. He was serious.

"For how long?" I asked.

"Does it matter? Have you got somewhere to go?"

I started to get a twitchy feeling all over, especially in my fingers. "I really need to check my messages."

"Right now?"

"Sure. You get started meditating, and I'll just go check my messages in the other room."

He frowned, clearly disapproving, but still waved me away.

I retrieved my phone from my purse and went into the other bedroom and closed the door. A minute later, some new age music started to play. I tried not to think of Keith sulking because I didn't want to meditate with him.

He'll get over it. I fluffed up the pillows on the spare bed and got comfortable.

Soon enough, I was completely distracted by my messages.

My friend Golden had sent me a half-dozen texts asking questions about Adrian. She asked, what did I think it meant that he had asked her to hang out a few times, but nothing physical had happened? Was it the height difference? Was she just too short for him to kiss? Everyone's the same height lying in bed, she said.

Golden and Adrian? Blech.

Because I still had a lingering crush on him from high school, I didn't like the idea of Golden putting her tiny paws all over him, so I wrote back: *Is Adrian depressed about his recent life failure? Maybe he's on one of those anti-anxiety medications that makes your willy soft.*

Then I cackled to myself like an evil witch in a Disney movie. (Not Ursula.) I wasn't going to hit the send button, but then the witch in me made me do it, and my words flew off.

Next, I opened up the one and only text message from Dalton. I was expecting him to tell me again I was being ridiculous, blaming him for something in a script, or maybe even for him to beg me to come back to him. (It would feel amazing to say no.) What I didn't expect was a simple, two-word message: *I understand.*

What did *that* mean?

I understand.

WHAT?

I gave the phone some serious facial expressions and jabbed out a response: *GOOD.*

Then I sent the missive, and immediately wanted to take the message back. Saying nothing at all would have been the appropriate thing to do, but I can't shut myself up—not in person, and not on the phone.

My best friend and roommate, Shayla, had sent me two messages.

Shayla, 6:37pm: *I'm serving a table of adorable firemen and they won't even flirt with me. I'm going to change into Trisha's tiny shirt, and if I don't get at least one number, I'm going to quit this stupid job, because there are no perks.*

Shayla, 7:40pm: *Your roommate is unemployed! Hey, do they need any extra help at the bookstore?*

It was ten o'clock on the nose when I wrote her back: *Please tell me you didn't actually quit. How can we afford all our fancy brand name salad dressing if we're not a double income household?*

I tried to hide my concern with a joke, but I actually was worried. I'd be getting some money from the modeling and underwear line, but not pay-the-whole-rent money.

Shayla: *I got a raise! I quit, and then Cameron hired me back for another two hundred a month!*

Me: *At last, Cameron does something decent and useful for a change.*

She sent back a smilie face, then phoned me instead of messaging.

"Talk fast. I have ten minutes for my break," she said. "Did you find anything else exciting at Dalton's house?"

"I'm not exactly staying there anymore," I said, and then I explained everything from the last two days as best I could without triggering a pity party.

"I told you so," she said.

Wait, that isn't true.

She did NOT say *I told you so.* Not in so many words. But the consoling words she said next still carried that exact connotation.

"That sucks donkey balls," is what she actually said, which sounds empathetic, but she said it with no emotion at all.

"It does suck donkey balls."

"We'll get through this together," she said, even though it sounded a lot like, *Next time, you'd better listen to me, you astoundingly stupid book-smart girl.*

Attempting to lighten the mood, I said, "Keith is actually really fun. I hardly feel broken at all when I'm around him. Maybe there's something to this whole rebound arrangement."

"Hang on, I'm just Googling his name to find a picture of this Keith Raven dude, and… OH-MY-GOD."

"Not bad, right?"

"That boy is so hot, you could use him to heat a whole room."

I chuckled. "He's in his bedroom right now, meditating."

"Meditating? Oh, Peaches. The guys you pick. They just keep getting hotter and weirder."

"I guess that's my type."

"What if Dalton begs to get you back? Then you'll have two guys fighting over you."

"Not gonna happen. Dalton isn't the begging type."

"Still, he seemed really into you. And he's back in town Wednesday?"

"Yeah, but that doesn't matter, because I won't see him ever again."

"You can't stay away from that man and you know it."

"Whose side are you on?"

She grumbled something, then said, "Send me a selfie pic of you and Keith. I'll know when I see you together."

"No way. Our arrangement is just while I'm here. I don't want any photos of us together, for me to sob over in the future when I'm feeling lonely."

"No pictures together... except for the underwear campaign all over billboards and magazines."

A wave of nausea washed over me like a sewer backup over basement carpet.

"I've made a huge mistake," I whispered into the phone.

"At least your huge mistake has... hmm, I'm zooming in on a photo of Keith, and... holy breadsticks, that certainly is a huge mistake. I've seen huge mistakes before, but this one is making me re-think my life choices."

"Stop looking at Keith like that," I joked.

"Why don't you come here and make me?" In the background, dishes crashed to the ground, followed by sarcastic applause. "Great," she said, then, "I may need to quit again. That could be my new thing. I'll keep quitting every shift."

"I miss you, buddy."

"I miss you, too. Hey, before I go, what's wrong with Keith? Why aren't you open to a relationship with him beyond this trip?"

Without thinking, I said, "He's not Dalton." Hearing my own words gave me a strange feeling, like walking by an electronics store and seeing your own face on the large TV.

"Interesting," Shayla said smugly, then she was gone, and I was alone with the truth. I didn't want to be with Dalton, but I didn't want to be with anyone who wasn't Dalton, either.

I rolled across the bed and stood the framed photo on the nightstand back up again. Katy and Tabitha. The nasty, overprotective sister, and the mysterious ex-girlfriend. His parents had let it slip during dinner that Tabitha was a model, and her career was doing well, albeit mostly catalog work and nothing too glamorous.

What was the story of their breakup, and why wouldn't Keith tell me? Why did I care?

I came out of the room and gently tapped on Keith's door. The earth muffin music was still playing, and he didn't answer. I pushed open the door to find him sitting cross-legged on the bed, a relaxed expression on his face.

"How's it going?" I asked.

His eyes stayed closed.

"You seem busy," I said.

His mouth twitched up momentarily into a smile.

"Maybe I'll just watch some TV," I said, backing away.

He seemed to nod in agreement, so I closed the door again and went in search of the television.

After twenty minutes, I finally found the television, not in the most logical place—the large armoire in the living room—but inside a smaller armoire in the spare bedroom. Nestled in alongside the old tube-style set were multiple purple rocks—amethyst crystals—and a lamp made from a big yellowish rock that smelled like the ocean.

On a hunch, I leaned forward and licked the lamp. It was salt.

I settled in to watch some quality programming, but the salt taste in my mouth made me crave something to drink. Back out in the kitchen, I found some cranberry juice in the fridge. I should have known something was off when I poured the juice and saw that it was a little cloudy, and not as bright red as I was used to seeing it.

Have you ever taken a big glug of unsweetened cranberry juice? It's like drinking straight lemon juice, only not as pleasant. As my face tried to invert itself via my mouth, I poured the death-juice back into the bottle and returned it to the fridge. After that, I didn't trust anything in Keith's kitchen I didn't recognize the brand of, so I poured a glass of water and snagged some Premium Plus soup crackers (whole wheat, of course) to snack on.

Back in the bedroom, I wondered if I was going to get in trouble for eating crackers in the bed. I hoped I would, because then Keith would have to spank me.

Unfortunately for me and my spanking needs, Keith wasn't very social the rest of the evening.

At one point, he came to the door and asked if I needed anything before he went to bed.

"Should I just sleep in this room again?" I asked, not sure where I stood.

"That might be better, considering we have the photo shoot bright and early tomorrow morning."

"But this bed has cracker crumbs in it."

Ignoring my confession, he came into the room and gave me a quick kiss. "Goodnight, gorgeous lady."

"Goodnight, Mr. Raven. If I'm cramping your style, just let me know, and I'll find somewhere else to bunk."

"Nonsense." He kissed me again, taking more time. His face smelled like scented candles. "Give me tonight to catch up on my sleep, and I'll show you such a good time, you'll never want to leave. You think my face is cute now, wait 'til you see it between your legs." He licked his lips suggestively.

My eyes flew open and I was momentarily speechless, and then he was gone, off to the washroom to brush his teeth and torture me by leaving me hanging for the second time that day.

"Weirdo," I grumbled after him, then I pulled out my phone to give Shayla a full report.

She replied: *WHAT?! You need to show him who's in charge of the sex.*

Me: *Call me a Wearer of Reasonable Shoes, but isn't it supposed to be mutual?*

Shayla: *You're the one with the girl parts, so start acting like it. You're the tops! You're the boss, baby!*

Me: *Drunk?*

Shayla: *I think it's someone's birthday… somewhere! LOL!*

Me: *Have fun, and I'll see you next Wednesday, if I don't die of sexual frustration.*

Shayla: *Someone just called me a word I've never even heard of. I'll have to look it up on Urban Dictionary. Do you think that's a compliment?*

Me: *Definitely.*

Her next text was a photo of either her breasts or her butt, her flesh marked with a felt pen drawing of a penis. I'd like to say this was particularly shocking for a post-shift Monday night party at the restaurant she managed, but it was not atypical.

~

Tuesday morning, I insisted that I walk into the photographer's studio ahead of Keith, so people wouldn't know I'd been staying at his house. As far as they all knew, I was still dating Dalton Deangelo.

The same crew who'd been there Sunday were there again, plus about twice as many more people, though most of them were doing other shoots.

I said to the nice girl doing my makeup, "I guess I lucked out having my first shoot on the weekend, when it's not so crazy around here."

"It wasn't luck," she said, sounding like she had a truckload of gossip she was dying to unload, if only I'd say the magic words.

"What do you mean?" I asked.

She looked left and right. "I shouldn't say."

"I'm sure if it's important enough for me to know, Mitchell will tell me. He's really sweet. Come to think of it, everyone here has been so nice. I'm just a wide-eyed yokel from Washington, in way over my head."

She pursed her lips. Oh yeah, the pre-gossip lip purse.

MIMI STRONG

CHAPTER 9

I was just about to crack the makeup girl. Any second now.

"You didn't hear this from me," she said. "Everyone was worried the photos were going to be a disaster. You-know-who had you come in on Sunday so there'd be fewer witnesses putting you here. They all had the big review on Monday. After a heated debate, they decided to move ahead with today's shoot, but there's a change. One change."

I smiled sweetly and tried to make her feel good about giving me news that didn't sound so good. A disaster? Because of me, no doubt. Coked-up starlets who showed up hours late were probably just fine, as long as they were skinny. But curvy me was going to ruin everyone's reputation.

"I understand," I said.

I understand.

The same phrase Dalton had sent me was so simple, yet vague enough to fit any heartbreaking situation. *I understand*, you say, as your heart and happiness shatters under the brutal sledgehammer of reality.

I closed my eyes and focused on not flipping out as she continued to work on my makeup. Flipping out now would get mascara in my eye, and I didn't want that.

She wanted to tell me more details about Monday's meeting, but I changed the topic, saying, "Are you from here? And if not, how long did it take you to get used to LA's smell?"

"Oh, you have to get soy-based candles," she said.

"For eating?"

"For burning. Regular candles put more toxins in the air."

As she talked about the wonders of aromatherapy, I got more and more nervous about the one change she mentioned. What was the change?

Please, please let it be more airbrushing, I prayed.

~

My suspense over the big change didn't last long.

I walked onto the set in my snazzy purple underwear to find the tallest, blondest man I'd ever seen. He wore a pair of purple briefs that were the size of a bow-tie, and he seemed to be smuggling an entire daschund inside the briefs. His golden abs went on for miles, like a giant, Christmas-stocking-sized, white chocolate Toblerone bar.

Reaching out to shake his hand politely, I said, "I didn't know the human body had that many abs."

"These ones are implants," he said, pointing to the top row.

"No way! They look real."

"You can touch," he said, his accent sounding Swedish.*

*I watched all the *Girl with the Dragon Tattoo* movies in their original Swedish versions, plus that creepy-kid-vampire movie, so I'm practically an expert.

Just as I reached out to touch the round bumps, Mitchell grabbed my hand and said, "He's full of monkeyshines. Those are real muscles, but Sven here is quite the prankster."

I turned to Mitchell. "Thank you for saving me from the horror of touching this man's abs. Can I buy you dinner?"

We grinned at each other.

"Good to see you again," Mitchell said. "We ordered Pop Tarts, just for you. Shall I toast one for you now?"

I threw my arms around the short blond man and squeezed him. "Thank you so much. I had a parsley smoothie for breakfast."

I didn't tell him who made the parsley smoothie, because it wasn't his business. I looked around for Keith, who'd come into the building just behind me, but I didn't see him.

One change.

Catching the attention of a person with a headset, I asked if she'd seen Keith Raven around.

"He won't be in today," she said curtly, and then left.

The crew on set all started laughing behind me, amused by something Sven was doing. He strutted around with his bare chest stuck out, saying, "How about this? *It's not a tumor.* Arnold Schwarzeneggar, you know? *I'll be back.*"

Sven was a real jokester, all right.

I knew he wasn't to blame for Keith being let go, but I still wanted to karate chop him in his ridiculous abs. How dare he push out Keith?

He opened his mouth wide and stuck his whole fist in, to everyone's amusement.

Something told me it was going to be a very strange day.

~

Big-mouthed Sven was truly gorgeous, no doubt about it, but posing with him felt like a competition, not a collaboration. Any charm or charisma he had was funneled straight into the camera, bypassing me.

"You're in my light," I had to keep telling him.

He gave me a suspicious look. "I thought you were an amateur."

"Not after Sunday, when I worked with the immensely talented Keith Raven."

Sven responded by rubbing his trouser anaconda against my hip.

"Excuse me," I said as he prodded his wang into me like a bratty kid poking all the fresh loaves at the bakery.

"Am I in your light?" he asked innocently.

I started to wave my hand in the air, to call for Mitchell's help, but then I caught a look at all the bored and irritated faces around me. The horrible truth of the situation sunk in. If I complained, I'd be the girl who went to a sexy underwear shoot and couldn't take the heat. Was I overreacting? I mean, sure, if I was working at Pizza Hut and my coworker stuck his barely-covered wang into my back, I'd have him fired. But this? Gray zone.

Mitchell came running, having caught enough of my wave.

"Bottle of water?" I asked.

He ran off for water.

We took a short break, and I said to Sven discreetly, "I don't care where you put your hands, but my body is penis-free and I'd like it to stay that way."

"I do not control him," he said.

I turned away in disgust, only to feel a familiar body part grinding into my back once more.

Mitchell returned with a full water bottle. "Ooh, nice and cold," I said, turning to smile sweetly up at Sven.

"How cold?" he asked.

I held the bottle to the center of his smooth chest. He closed his eyes, grinning.

And then I let go. The large bottle sailed straight down the front of him and ricocheted off his overly-intrusive semi-chubby.

He howled a string of nonsensical swear words, clutching himself.

It was the first time I'd heard such a colorful expression, and—judging by the laughter—the first time for everyone in the studio as well.

I apologized profusely, of course, blaming my sweaty fingers. He kept whimpering, so I told him, "Maybe if you loosened the Velcro strap and let a little air out of the tires, there wouldn't be so much sticking out to get caught on things."

"Thanks for the tip," he said, giving me a wary look.

We got back to bright lights and photos, and Sven behaved himself. In fact, he seemed almost frightened of me, because when I suggested we take a few pictures of me slapping him—the classic rom-com slap—he cowered and pleaded for me not to.

"How about a nipple twist?" I asked. "Or love bites?"

Poor Sven looked like he was about to cry, which was an interesting look for a seven-foot-tall man.

We finished the shots with both of us, and then I did a few more solo pictures, thankfully some of them with a chair, because my feet were killing me in the high heels I'd been wearing to bring me closer to Sven's height.

I kept wondering where Keith was, and how he was feeling. I hoped he was still getting paid, and that he wouldn't be mad at me.

We worked straight through lunch, with me eating a spicy tuna salad sandwich between bra changes. As I munched away on the pickle that came with the takeout, I marveled at how quickly I'd gotten used to the whole modeling scene.

The scene. Granted, it was just letting two women stick their hands inside my bra cups to rearrange my peaches, not going off to fight a war, but I felt proud of how much I was able to endure.

The long day and all the scrutiny did eventually get to me, though.

We'd just wrapped up the shoot, and I was in the dressing room when Mitchell walked in and found me with my face in my hands, feeling vulnerable.

He sat his immaculately-styled skinny butt down next to mine on the bench and gave me a sideways hug. "Don't be sad! You were even better today. Are you sad because Keith's off the campaign?"

"Yes," I whimpered from within my hands, because that was a big part of it. How could we still be friends if he felt humiliated about getting fired?

"He just wasn't a big enough presence," Mitchell said with a sigh. "Keith is a good-looking man, but we needed someone more masculine, to accentuate your femininity."

I took a breath and tried to pull myself together. It had all happened so quickly, this mood slump. I'd gotten a text message from home, and then I felt like I'd fallen off a diving board, at the deep end of the pool. The message was still on the screen on the phone in my hand, and I couldn't deal with those emotions, plus talking about the model change.

"At least the photo shoot's over," I said. "Just the commercial, but that's days away."

"The change to use Sven was nothing personal."

"I understand. They wanted someone bigger to make me look less big."

"I respect you too much to lie to you. You're not wrong. But don't worry. These things happen all the time."

I looked down at my phone again, my breath catching in my throat.

"What's this?" He tilted his head down, and I showed him the phone.

He read the message out: "Kyle says he misses you and wants you to come home. Your father and I wish you would check in with us more. Why have that fancy phone if you're not going to use it? Love, Mom. P.S. What's the shower like at Dalton's house? Is it one of those deals with the seven sprayers?"

Hearing the message in Mitchell's voice gave me some perspective. It was just them checking in on me, not trying to break my heart.

"I guess I'm homesick," I said. "I haven't seen Kyle very much these past two weeks, and it just hit me. I'm a terrible person."

"I have a little black cat," Mitchell said. "His name is Pretzel, and he lives with my parents in a little town called Squirrel Mountain Valley. Don't laugh; it's a real place. Now, when I moved to LA, the apartment wouldn't allow pets, and I figured I'd eventually get settled and send for him, but I haven't. Every day, I miss his little whiskers and the shiny spot on his chin below his lips."

"Is this supposed to make me feel better? You're bringing me down, Mitchell. Way down, like a sad country ballad."

"The point of my story is that Pretzel is just fine, because he is a cat, and as long as there's food in his dish, he's good. Parents, however, will use any dirty trick in the book to make you feel guilty about running down your dreams."

"My parents are supportive."

"Sure, they want you to do as well as they did in life, but they don't want you to do *better* than them. They don't want you to *get above yer raisin.*"

I chuckled. "Do you want to go get that sushi now and tell me all about it?"

"Aren't you sick of me after working with me all day?"

"You're the nicest person I've met in LA, except for Keith."

Mitchell winced. "He really sucked you in, didn't he?"

I grinned. "Nobody sucked anything. We're just friends." (This was, at the time, somewhat true. We'd had sex once, and nobody had sucked anything, though I was looking forward to trying, if he didn't hate me for the photo shoot disaster.)

"Just friends?"

"Totally," I lied.

"Honestly, I don't know Keith at all. But I do know male models, and I can tell you that, without a shadow of a doubt, every single one of them is a narcissistic, lying, using, son-of-a-whore."

"And you know this because…?"

"Because I keep dating male models. It's terrible, I know. I can't stop, and there's no self-help group. It's like when you open a tube of Pringles to put out on set, and you think you'll just have one or two, but pretty soon you're cramming them into your mouth by the dozen, and you can't get enough, even though they're shallow and bad for you."

"By the dozen?"

He rolled his eyes. "Okay, just one at a time, but a guy can dream."

With that, we got to our feet, I grabbed my bag, and we went out to the parking lot, to Mitchell's little blue Miada.

Was going for sushi the right choice?

I took out my phone and mulled over my options. Keith had programmed his address into my phone that morning, because we figured I would have to stay longer at the shoot and take a taxi to his house. We'd been rushing around, arguing over how much parsley he was putting in the fruit shakes, and I'd neglected to get his phone number. The proper thing to do would have been head straight to his place and find out how he was doing, but I'd forgotten about him just long enough to get myself into dinner with Mitchell. That made me feel twice as bad, but I was already on an I'm-a-terrible-person kick anyway.

Mitchell kept driving, and I crossed my fingers that Keith wouldn't be too upset if I popped out for a quick dinner.

"Mitchell, do you think someone can tell if they're a narcissist?"

"Nope. But it's like alcoholism. If one person tells you, ignore them. If two people tell you, it's true."

"So, am I a narcissist? Do you have to be one to feel okay about taking your clothes off in front of the camera?"

"Oh, girl models are nice. It's just the guys."

"But you don't date the girls."

"They mostly have Daddy issues, and eating disorders."

"Shape aside, I don't fit the profile. My father's in my life, but I do have a problem with cupcakes."

He grinned, staring ahead at the traffic, then giving me a quick glance before looking the other way to change lanes. In the golden early-evening light, Mitchell looked cherubic with his blue eyes and curly hair.

He said, "You're going back to your real life right after this, aren't you?"

"That's the plan."

"What about Dalton Deangelo?"

"We're done. Broken up. Kaput. Over. Please don't tell anyone, though. I'd rather go quietly back to Washington without a lot of nosy questions."

He reached over and patted my knee, which was such a sweet and perfect gesture, I nearly told him I loved him.

We got to the sushi restaurant, parked, and went in quickly, only to have to stand in line to be seated. The place was packed, and unlike the few sushi places I'd been to, didn't smell of bleach, but of food. Waitresses sailed back and forth with plates of food—tempura vegetables, teriyaki beef, and rolls of spectacular size.

Mitchell turned to me. "There's nothing quite as life-affirming as a great live band, or a busy restaurant after a long day's work."

"Thanks for taking me here. Everything looks really good."

The hostess took our name and told us the wait wouldn't be long.

Mitchell, looking sly, turned to me and said, "Didn't you come here Sunday, with Keith?"

"No, we, um…" My cheeks were burning with embarrassment. "We went to a steak house. I forget the name. He's friends with the owners."

Mitchell's blue eyes got huge, his blond lashes blinking to accentuate his interest. "Tell me you didn't. No. Tell me you did, and then tell me everything."

"I thought you didn't approve."

He waved his hand. "Cat's out of the bag now. May as well have some fun while we're all on this planet." He leaned in closer and whispered, "Is Keith the reason you and Dalton broke up?"

"No, those were completely separate events." As I said the words, I detected a lie. It was a small lie, but the events weren't entirely unrelated. I'd already kissed Keith, and I was at his apartment when I broke up with Dalton. If I'd been at Dalton's house that night, or even at a hotel—one that didn't have the waiting arms of another man on the other side of my door—would I have done the same thing?

Did Keith break us up?

I felt dizzy. Everything in my life was happening so fast, out of my control.

Dalton would be back in LA the next day, and my stuff was still at his house. The clothes were expendable, but I had to get my laptop. What would seeing him do to me?

The hostess took us to a seat in the window and told us we were a beautiful couple. I wrinkled my nose, because Mitchell was shorter than me and probably weighed the same as my purse, but he gave her a heartfelt thank-you anyway, which I suppose is the proper response to a compliment.

The menu had twelve pages, with photographs of everything. I'd never seen anything like it, and admitted to Mitchell I was in way over my head, and that he should order for me.

He did, and we enjoyed a sumptuous feast with a bit of everything. Even the rice was delicious, and it was just plain rice, but cooked perfectly. The thing that surprised me was the spinach *gomaae*, which was lightly cooked spinach with a peanut sauce. It was delicious, and probably my second favorite thing of the night.

My *favorite* thing was Mitchell telling me all his hilarious stories about dating models. He dated one guy who was obsessed with crafting the perfect root beer, and succeeded mainly in spraying sticky soda all over the kitchen. Another one had a chew-and-spit eating disorder that was the cause of many fights—not so much about the disorder, but the wasting of pricey food, because he also liked fancy restaurants. A third male model was just exceptionally dumb and sent sexy text messages that were incomprehensible. Mitchell received one of his texts, then responded with a naked torso shot, which he thought was what the guy wanted. It turned out the man's brother had been shot in the chest and was at the hospital. Now, before you get all bummed out thinking that last story was just sad and not funny at all, I should mention the brother was just fine, as he'd actually been "shot" in the chest with a champagne cork, right before he fell over a railing and broke his leg.

I could have stayed all night, eating green tea ice cream and hearing Mitchell's stories, but I had to get back to Keith's place.

Mitchell drove me there, and made sure we had each other's phone numbers in case I needed anything else from him while I was in LA.

"Just gimme one of those awesome Mitchell hugs," I said, and he gave me one.

~

I knocked on Keith's door, which had regular music playing on the other side—top forty stuff.

He opened the door wide, wearing absolutely nothing but a big grin. "Hi, honey, you're home!"

I herded his naked body back into the apartment and pulled the door shut behind us. "Are you drinking?" I asked, though the empty bottles on the kitchen counter should have been my first clue.

"Let's go swimming," he answered, his goodies waggling back and forth.

"Only if you put some shorts on."

CHAPTER 10

Keith waved his hand clumsily. "They don't care around here. The neighbors are very lacka—" He hiccuped. "Lacka-da-da-daisies. That word."

"Lackadaisical."

"Yes. Let's go swimming. Just us. Nobody else."

I looked around the apartment for signs of drugs, but this seemed to be a garden-variety, one-person booze party, and I can't say I haven't done the same from time to time.

He walked into his bedroom, so I followed his cute buns and watched as he rooted around inside dresser drawers for a swimsuit.

"Keith, I'm so sorry they pulled you off the shoot. They're absolute idiots. That Sven guy is a big jerkwad, and I'm sure the photos won't be good. I'll probably have a look of disgust on my face in every shot."

He stopped rummaging and turned to me. "Disgust? Did he do something to you?"

"Nothing I couldn't handle. Don't worry about it."

"I'll kill him." He seemed to sober up instantly.

"Let's go for that swim," I said, reaching into the drawer around him and pulling out what looked and felt like swim trunks. "It's been a long day, and I'd love to go for a swim with you."

"Swim first, then we find and kill Sven."

"The hippie boy has a caveman side."

"Grrr."

I ran my fingertip down the center of his tanned chest. I would have much rather posed with him all day, but at least we were together now.

"I bet we can think of some other things to do after a swim," I said.

"Just like a woman. Always trying to prevent war and homicide."

"I do what I can."

As he pulled on his red swimming trunks, I stripped off my clothes down to my underwear. The bra and panties I had on were black, and as long as nobody looked too closely, they would pass for a swimsuit.

Keith pulled me in for a kiss, and his lips felt good, but he smelled of something I didn't like—maybe whiskey—and I held back.

"I'll go brush my teeth," he said, picking up on my reluctance right away. "I'll grab some towels for the pool, too."

I followed him out of the bedroom and waited on one of the chrome kitchen counter stools, checking my phone messages.

There was a reminder for my commercial shoot on Monday, along with directions to be wearing loose-fitting clothes when I arrived. Thinking about that little adventure in my future made me glance over at the booze available, but luckily the wooziness passed in a minute.

A message from Amy, my junior staff member at the bookstore, simply said: *I'm sorry. It was really fun working with you.*

The next message was from Gordon Oliver, my boss and the owner of Peachtree Books, telling me that those sheep-lovers from the other bookstore in town (hate them!) had poached our employee, and he was on the verge of shutting the whole thing down. I don't want to get Gordon in trouble, but he seemed awfully vengeful. He actually used the words "fire" and "collect the insurance."

With my hand on my forehead, I shook my head like a weary father in a TV sitcom. I leave Beaverdale for business, and before a week goes by, all hell breaks loose? Would there be any buildings left standing amidst the rubble when I returned next week?

As I was holding the phone, it tickled my hand with another message. The number wasn't in my address book, but the sender seemed to know me, because he or she said: *Hey, Peaches.*

I asked who it was, and the tickle spread all through my body when he said: Adrian Storm.

Hot buttered noodles with cheese.

Me: *What's going on?*

Adrian: *I'm your new coworker.*

Me: *You didn't.*

Adrian: *Oh, yes, I did. Gordon hired me just now. And I'm going to reorganize this whole bookstore before you get back. I think there should be more of an emphasis on Men's Adventure books.*

Me: *Don't touch anything! You are my subordinate!*

Adrian: *Yes, boss.*

Me: *Your secondary job is to sell books. Your main job is to speak to Gordon in a soothing voice and talk him out of expanding the wine store into our space.*

Adrian: OMG! *I think that wall just moved.*

Me: *Very funny.*

Keith came out of the bathroom, two bright orange towels in his arms. "What are you getting all giggly about?"

I felt my cheeks flush hot, like I'd been caught lying.

"Everything's falling apart at home without me."

"And that makes you giggle?"

I batted my eyelashes, and in a funny voice, said, "I'm not like other people."

"You can say that again." He went to the front door and pulled it open.

I followed him out to the courtyard in nothing but my black underwear, and the sun's evening rays glanced off my milk-hued, Washington-white-girl skin and blinded everyone in a thirteen-block radius. (Sorry, LA.)

I watched Keith lower himself into the pool, which was rectangular and tiled with mostly blue and green tiles, dotted with the occasional yellow tile, standing out like a dandelion in a lawn. Surrounding the pool were a few weathered teak loungers, some potted palm trees, and a trio of ceramic turtles that made me look twice—not because they were realistic, but because I am gullible.

"Hey!" Keith said. "Some kids left their pool noodles." He grabbed two of the long, foam pool toys and wrapped them under his armpits so he could float easily.

I came around to the side with the steps and stepped down cautiously, pleased to find the water was warm.

"You need those to float," I said. "You have no body fat."

We were alone in the courtyard, and if there were kids living there who owned the pool noodles, they were quiet ones.

I swam up to Keith and wrapped my legs around his waist playfully, pretending to pull him under like a shark.

Smiling, he said, "Be gentle. I've had a tough day."

I looked down at my body under the water, warped and rippling, a distorted version of myself.

"I feel awful about what happened today," I said.

"Don't. It wasn't your fault." He gave me a pretend-serious look. "Unless it was. Did you have me fired?"

I wrapped my arms around him, pulling him in for a hug, the two plastic pool noodles between our chests keeping us afloat without effort.

"Of course I didn't," I said.

He stared down at my lips for a moment, then kissed me. Despite the cool water surrounding us, I felt a heat rise from my core.

Pulling back, he said, "I'm going to be fine. Please don't let any of this stuff take away from what is actually a victory."

"A victory?"

His hands found my buttocks and massaged me there, and up and down my legs as I continued to hold on tight to him.

He kissed my eyelids, my cheeks, the tip of my nose, and then my mouth, before moving down my neck. The pool water splish-splashed with our movements. I ran my hands through his damp hair.

"Today is a victory for curvy women," he said.

I reached down into the water with both of my hands and grabbed his firm, muscular ass. "Today is a victory for my hands," I said.

"Be serious for a minute. You're part of something that's bigger than just you."

I reached around between us and grabbed something interesting through his shorts. "Speaking of bigger…"

He took in a quick gasp of air, raised his hands over his head, and quickly sank, slipping out of my grasp. He reappeared at the other end of the pool, slicking his inky hair back with both hands.

"You're not very patient, are you?" he asked, grinning at me.

"My roommate flips to the last page of every book to read the ending. I'm a lot more patient than she is."

He swam close enough to retrieve one of the pool noodles for himself, then swam away again.

"When you were ten, did you long to be twelve?" he asked.

"Doesn't everyone? I wanted to be sixteen, so I could drive a car."

"I wanted to stay ten forever." When he said that, his youthful face looked even more innocent, his brown eyes wide and honest. He continued, "When our eleventh birthday came, I told everyone that only Katy was turning eleven, and we weren't twins after all. I said I was younger than her, and the whole twin thing had been a prank."

I took the pool noodle he'd left behind and wrapped it under my legs, balancing on it like a chair.

"I didn't know you and Katy were twins. Did people believe you?"

"Yes. Even teachers believed me. I knew it wasn't true, of course, but the idea that people would just believe whatever an eleven-year-old told them—it shook me. That's my first memory of realizing how chaotic the world is."

"That's a tough age for a lot of people. I was about that old when I figured out that eventually everybody dies. Not just sheep dogs and goldfish, but everyone."

"It's tough to be a kid," he said solemnly.

"It's tough to be an adult."

The courtyard was so quiet, I could hear cars in the distance and people inside their apartments running water and washing dishes.

As the sun set and the light disappeared, Keith's muscle contours picked up shadows, and he looked less like a boy and more like a man—like a sinewy god of the sea, with a lavender pool noodle.

We both started paddling, moving in a clockwork direction. We moved slowly at first, then sped up, like each was trying to catch the other by the foot, but pretending that wasn't the real goal.

Finally, Keith snarled like a dragon and shot out of the water, seizing me around the waist. I let out a startled cry, then was pulled under.

Once underwater, he released me, and we opened our eyes and found each other under the surface. He opened his mouth like he was speaking, but only bubbles came out. I did the same, and he smiled. We repeated this until we were both out of air and had to surface, laughing and gasping to catch our breath.

He caught me in his arms, and as his skin connected with mine, I realized the water had cooled me, and I craved his heat. With one look into his brown eyes, I craved even more than his heat.

He asked, "What do you like to have after swimming?"

"Hot chocolate with mini marshmallows."

"You're in luck. I actually have the stuff to make that."

I leaned over and slurped the water beads off his beautiful shoulder. Once I started, I couldn't stop, and soon I was slurping my way up to his ear, sucking on his earlobe.

He growled with enjoyment as I gave him a nibble, then he steered me over to the side of the pool, so he could hang onto the tiled edge and grind against me.

We kissed, my legs wrapped around his waist again, then he said, "Would you like me to take you before, or after the hot chocolate?"

"How about after? I'm trying to practice my patience."

"As you wish," he said, in his best *Westley-from-Princess-Bride* voice.

For the second time, he jumped up and then slipped down and away from me, through the water. He surfaced, and started up the steps. Once out of the water, he picked up the two orange towels, holding one between his knees for himself, and holding the other one open for me to walk up to and get wrapped in.

I stepped up out of the pool and into his waiting arms.

"You make me feel pampered," I said as he rubbed me dry with a towel for the second time since we'd met.

"It's the least I can do for someone who makes me feel so happy."

He gave me a quick kiss, then switched to drying himself.

Oh, Keith, I thought. *You're too good to be true.*

Sure, the meditation stuff was kookier than a barn full of cuckoo clocks, but sweet mercy, the man was as thoughtful as he was gorgeous.

Following him back into the apartment, I tried not to think about how this short-term relationship of ours was doomed.

As we stepped inside and he pulled me into his arms and rained kisses all over my shoulders, I tried not to think about how a long-term relationship would be equally doomed—assuming he would even want one.

"I was promised hot cocoa," I said, pushing him away playfully.

After a sly wink, he moved into the kitchen and started preparations.

"How old are you?" I asked.

"Ten. I refused to blow out the candles at my birthday parties, so I'm only ten. Ask any grown-up. That's how it works."

"How old is your sister?"

"Old enough to manage the landscaping business on her own, just as soon as I catch my next big break."

I sat on a kitchen stool and looked down, feeling worse than ever about him losing his big break.

"Maybe I'll ask around on your behalf," I said.

"I didn't tell you about Milan, did I?"

I looked up, surprised by how upbeat he sounded, considering he'd been drinking when I got there.

"Flying scares me," he said. "I actually turned down another job to do Peaches Monroe." He laughed.

"Uh, to *do* me?"

Still laughing, he said, "Little did I know that doing Peaches would lead to doing Peaches."

"Keep saying my name like that, and you won't be doing anything tonight but listening to whale songs and playing a five-finger solo on the man-banjo."

He stirred some hot cocoa mix into boiled water, in two matching red mugs.*

*The only thing better than hot cocoa is hot cocoa in a red mug.

He said, "I need to call my agent and do a little B-B-B, but I think I can still book the job. They really liked me."

"What's B-B-B?"

"Beg, Bribe, Blow. A great business plan for anything you want to do in life."

"Gross." I accepted my mug of cocoa and took a sip, inhaling the tiny marshmallows into my mouth. "Perfect. Tell me more about this other modeling job."

He scrunched his face. "You'll just find the details boring."

"If it's important to you, it's important to me." (Wow, I totally just quoted my mother there.)

Keith got a happy look, and started telling me about the clothing line. As he talked, some of the details flew over my head, but I discovered something beautiful. When Keith talked about this job, his face lit up the same way it did when he named the different tree species at the big garden.

I was relieved to see he wasn't turning away from his life's passion of gardening to do something his heart wasn't into. He was really excited—about everything *but* the plane ride. He said the idea of facing his fear had scared him into drinking earlier that evening, but he assured me he was feeling better.

"Quite the day we've both had," I said.

He took the empty mug from my hand and kissed my palm.

The stool I was on rotated, and he used my arm as a handle to spin me around, so my back was to the countertop. He knelt down on the hardwood floor at my feet and rested his chin between my knees, then looked up at me, a glint of mischief in his dark eyes.

CHAPTER 11

I was still wearing nothing but the black underwear I'd worn in the pool, and my gleaming white thighs squished out on the stool, making me feel self-conscious, but I didn't move or draw attention to my nervousness.

He kissed my knee, then rubbed his chin along the edge of my thigh. He'd shaved that morning, but had just enough stubble to accentuate his touch and make me shiver.

Inch by inch, he made his way slowly inward, toward my underwear. He pushed my legs apart with his chin, and when I wouldn't budge, he grabbed my knees with both hands and helped me.

He was certainly right about one thing: his face did look even more gorgeous between my legs.

Once he reached my underwear, he extended his tongue and artfully licked all the way up, over the black fabric, still damp from the swimming pool.

"This is happening," I moaned, leaning back against the countertop for support.

He continued to tease me, through my underwear, for several more minutes. After a while, it didn't matter anymore that I had underwear on and his tongue wasn't against my skin. I still felt him, still saw his gorgeous model face between my thighs, and the idea alone sent multiple waves of pleasure through me.

When he finally reached up to the waistband of my panties and started to tug them down, well, I've never gotten a pair of underwear off so quickly.

With my bare bottom back down on the seat, Keith pushed my knees together and moved back. He kissed the same knee as he'd started on, then rubbed his chin along my thigh the same way as before. We were starting over and doing the same thing again. Knowing what was coming next made the waiting more painful and delicious.

When his hot tongue finally hit my pink inner ridges, I couldn't believe how good it felt. And how *right*, as if balance in the universe was being restored—like rain on Sunday night, after a blistering hot weekend.

He wrapped me up in his tongue and clutched me with his lips. I held my breath for an instant, when it was almost unbearable to not come yet, and when I started breathing again, I felt our energy entwine, like our bodies had in the pool.

He slowly pulled away again, kissing his way down my legs and to my knees, which were now sensitive to the point of being ticklish. I realized my arms were outstretched, my hands gripping the edge of the countertop like I was riding into battle. I shook out my hands and laughed nervously.

Keith bit my knee and gazed up at me with a playful expression.

"You bite me, I'll have to bite you back," I said.

"Promises, promises."

"Trade spots with me and find out."

"If your bite's as mean as your bark?" he asked, laughing.

"Just get your man-shorties off and take a seat."

I jumped off the bar stool and gasped in horror at the little puddle of saliva and whatnot sitting there. Keith pulled off his bathing suit shorts and gave the surface a quick swipe with the shorts. "No worries," he said casually, like it was no big deal.

"About that," I said, thinking about splashes.

He sat on the bar stool now, completely naked, and pulled me toward him using his foot as a hook. "C'mere. Kiss me some more. I really like it when you kiss me, and when you run your fingers through my hair."

He was lower than me, seated as he was, and I bent down to kiss him. Everything felt different this way, like I had more control as the taller party.

As we kissed, our lips and tongues tangling, I thought about the thing I'd been meaning to mention—the fact that if I had an orgasm after a long build-up, it might be more than intense. It had only happened once so far, but a torrent of fluid, healthy and natural though it was for some women, could be upsetting if it was unexpected.

My hands moved up Keith's thighs, my fingers moving through his leg hair to where his legs were nearly smooth, by his hips. I felt him shudder with anticipation as I traced back and forth along his hip creases with my fingertips. The heat let me know when my fingers got near it. We kept kissing, and I put the warning out of my mind. Strange and surprising things happen during sex all the time, and people keep banging away on each other.

I gripped him around the base with one hand, and he became very still, his mouth barely moving against mine. As I began to tug rhythmically, he breathed in deeply, his nostrils next to my skin cooling my upper lip with air flow.

"That feels so good," he murmured.

"Do you want me to lick it like a lollipop?"

He groaned. "I think I have some more of those mini marshmallows. You could lick it for a bit and stick those all over to decorate it."

I started laughing, and he held his arms tightly around me so I wouldn't pull away.

"You act like an earth muffin, but you're a sex freak," I said.

"So? You act like a kitten, but you're a tiger."

I made an admirable attempt at purring, but the sound came out as more of a gurgle.

"Now you're scaring me," he said, his voice high-pitched with mirth.

"That was supposed to be a purr."

He clutched me tighter and growled in my ear, "Get the marshmallows."

I reached over his shoulder and grabbed the bag. When a sexy, naked man with a giant erection tells you to grab the mini marshmallows, you grab the mini marshmallows.

I got down on my knees on the floor before him and began kissing his knees, the same way he had kissed mine. He trembled slightly as I pulled his legs apart and moved into the V-shape gap. I nuzzled my face against his inner thighs, which smelled faintly of chlorine from the pool, but just musky enough to be exciting. I rubbed my chin across his sack, while watching the one-eyed tower looming above me.

I got the giggles for an instant (one-eyed tower, tee-hee), but then I ran my tongue up half the length of his shaft and got more serious. Being on my knees, looking up, I felt younger, and less experienced than I was. Feeling reverent, I lavished him with attention, running my fingertips gently around the ridges, and then my tongue.

I didn't take him into my mouth, though, no matter how much he quivered with anticipation as I exhaled hot breath upon the head for a moment before returning to licking.

After a few minutes of this sweet torture, I nudged the bag of marshmallows at my knees and remembered them. I retrieved a handful, and then slowly started to work, like an artist making a sandcastle on the beach. The marshmallows ran up in a swirling line, starting from the base and ending at the tip.

"Wow," I said when my masterpiece was complete. "It looks like a unicorn's horn."

Keith opened his eyes, looked down, and gasped. "That's what you were doing?" He started to laugh. "I had my eyes shut the whole time. No wonder it smells like cotton candy down there." He stopped laughing and frowned. "I'll never be able to un-see this. I'll be shooting a magazine spread, imagine marshmallows on everyone's peckers, and lose it."

"Look on the bright side. I love eating marshmallows, and the bag's empty now."

Smiling, he closed his eyes and leaned back against the counter.

I started at the top, engulfing him in my mouth along with the sugary treats. Candy or not, he seemed to appreciate this very much.

To get the last ones around the base required deeper throating than I could manage, so I cheated them up with my fingertips.

Once the sweets were gone, I savored the salty taste of his skin, and the pulse of him in my mouth. He was so hard, so ready to burst, but he kept holding back. I wanted him to come, wanted to feel him splash in my mouth and moan as he lost control. With one hand on the base, I worked him strong and steady.

Gasping, he grabbed onto my shoulders with both hands and gently pushed me away.

I looked up at him through my eyelashes. "Come for me," I said.

"Not like this. I want to be inside you, and I want to feel you come first."

He slid off the bar stool, grabbed my hand to help me to my feet, and led me to the bedroom.

In there, where it was dark and intimate, with only the light coming through the doorway, he unfastened my pool-damp, black bra and held my breasts in both hands as he kissed my lips.

A moment later, we wordlessly moved to the bed. I got a condom and put it on for him as he lay on his side. Resting with his shoulders propped up on one elbow, he looked so relaxed and comfortable, so I got onto my back perpendicular to him and scooched down to lift my legs over his hips.

He nodded with approval and used his hand to guide himself into me. He used his free arm between my legs, finding the right spot and working me as he stroked his length in and out.

Wouldn't you know it, I barely had time to look up at the ceiling, close my eyes, and I was coming. I gasped and let out some noises to let him know, in case the shuddering deep inside me wasn't a big enough sign.

He let me finish coming, and then he changed positions, pushing my legs to fold them up against my torso as he climbed on top of me. With my knees folded over his upper arms near his elbows, I had nowhere to go, nothing to do but enjoy the sensation of him sliding in and out of me. He straightened his body like an arrow, his legs straight behind him, and all of his beautiful muscles did the thing they were supposed to do—allow him to do me like a superhero.

My eyes rolled up into my head, and either I started to come again, or I hadn't finished the first one.

His breathing got ragged. His body glistened with sweat. When he leaned down to kiss me, his chin was wet with perspiration.

I opened my eyes to find him staring down at me, a look of curiosity in his brown eyes. His eyelashes lowered, his face contorted, and he groaned as he thrust into me harder than ever. As he touched me deep inside, sending off more quivering waves, he pulsed once, twice, three times. And then he collapsed on top of me, his body weight folding my legs up so my knees were around my chin.

We were still for a moment, and then I wiggled, suddenly uncomfortable.

With a satisfied moan, he rolled off me and said, "That was worth the wait."

"What was your favorite part?" I cooed, rolling over to face him and trace a line down the center of his sweaty chest.

"Not the marshmallows," he said, wincing.

"Oh, please. You loved the marshmallows."

"Fine. I did. Don't tell anyone."

"We're all out of marshmallows."

"Maybe next time, we can try chocolate chips."

"Mmm, s'mores."

"Stop, you're making me hungry," I cried.

"It's not that late. We can watch a movie and eat some kale chips."

I laughed. "That's funny. I could have sworn you just said kale chips."

"Oh, I did." He nodded, looking very serious. "Stick with me, kid, and I'll show you plenty of new things."

I covered my face with my hands. "And to think, I have another week of this."

He rolled over to me and kissed my hands and the parts of my face sticking through them. "You can stay as long as you like. Stay forever."

I kept my hands over my face, so he wouldn't see my expression. I didn't know how I felt, but I didn't want him to see my face and get any ideas before I knew.

I coughed abruptly. "Water?"

"Give me a minute to deal with this bag of expired fun, and I'll be right back with some water, my sweet."

After he left the room, I stared up at Keith's bedroom ceiling, which was smooth and plain white, with a simple dome light fixture. The ceiling was dark and provided no answers.

Why couldn't Keith live in Beaverdale and be anything other than an underwear model? Fooling around with Dalton hadn't been nearly as dangerous, because he was larger than life, and I never thought we had a future. Keith, though, was so down to earth. Sure there was quite the difference between us as far as percentage of body fat, but his family seemed the equivalent level of crazy-normal as mine, and by the look of his things, he wasn't I'll-just-buy-away-my-problems rich.

Ah, but he was on the rebound.

No matter how great we were together, Tabitha had been there before me, and I got the feeling I was just keeping him warm until he found his way back into her arms. Why else would he have kept her photo?

Keith came back into the bedroom, lugging the TV set from the other room.

"Movie night!" he said.

He got the TV set up on his dresser, and we started arguing over the remote control and what movie to watch first, just like a completely regular couple.

We snuggled. When Keith relaxed, all his muscles became softer and more snuggly. We tried out a variety of cuddling positions, settling on spooning, and it was delicious.

~

Wednesday morning, I volunteered to run out for bagels while Keith made some important phone calls alone in his apartment.

"Get poppy seed bagels," he said.

"So, you do eat carbohydrates?"

He was walking around the apartment completely naked, a towel slung over his shoulder for the shower he was about to take. He slumped his posture and stuck out his stomach jokingly, then rubbed the tummy bulge. "What are you implying?" he asked. "Don't you like what you see? You liked it plenty this morning. I was dead asleep and you just had to wake me up and get some."

"Oh, please. You started it, pawing and drooling all over me like a dog with a new squeeze toy."

He grinned. "I sure made you squeak, though, didn't I? Come, get in the shower with me."

I'd already showered and was fully dressed, so I backed toward the door, pretending to be scared. I fumbled with the door handle, giggling, then ran out and across the courtyard.

A white-haired lady was reclining in the teak lounger next to the pool. She called out, "What are you running from?"

I stopped, not wanting to be rude, and said, "Emotional intimacy, I guess."

"You must be young," she said as she applied coconut-scented lotion to her gold-brown, wrinkled arms and upper chest. "Are you living with that nice gardener, Keith?"

"Just for another week. I'm not from here."

She grinned, her teeth big and bright white in her wrinkled face. She had sunglasses on, so I couldn't see her eyes, but could tell she was smiling with her whole face.

"No kidding," she said. "Now, what's so scary about emotional intimacy?"

"Oh, I was just joking about that. I say a lot of crap. If my life were close-captioned, half of it would just be blah-blah-blah, and the close-captioning person would probably quit and go back to school to train for a better job."

She shook her head. "The greatest lies are the ones we tell ourselves. God bless denial, and I don't mean the river in Egypt. Now, could you do me a favor and move that umbrella over so I can read my magazine without so much glare on the page? I have sciatica, plus I just got comfortable."

"Sure." I grabbed the base of the standing sunshade, which was filled with sand and quite heavy, and shifted it closer to the woman. She started flipping through the pages of *Small Town Life in America*, which made me feel homesick.

"I'm Petra," I said. (I use my actual name around some people, just when I sense they'd feel more comfortable with Petra than Peaches.)

"Nice to know you, dear." She didn't look up from the magazine, so I muttered that I'd see her around, and continued on my way.

After I left the courtyard, I noted that the woman might have been a ghost, and that was why she couldn't move the umbrella stand. Ghosts can't move things. Perhaps anyone watching would have seen me standing there, talking to myself. Maybe Keith was the only live human who lived in the complex, and all the other units were... like, a ghost hotel or something.

I got so engrossed in my own story, I nearly got lost on my way to the bakery Keith had given me directions for. I never had an imaginary friend as a child, but I read a lot, and if I went too long without reading a book, I'd start to make up stories. Some of my favorite tales, both the ones I read and the ones I imagined, were about ghosts acting like regular, everyday people. Ghosts in laundromats, doing laundry. Ghosts standing in line at the post office. Ghosts with their hands pressed up on the glass, watching puppies inside a pet store, not knowing they could just go in and cuddle all the puppies, ignoring the posted rules for the living.

~

The woman was still in the teak lounger when I returned, so there went my theory about her being a ghost. She was asleep, with the magazine on her chest. I adjusted the umbrella again, angling it so the shade would last longer as the sun moved across the sky.

Inside Keith's apartment, I found him pacing the living room, his phone to his ear.

I whispered, "Any news on Italy?"

He shrugged. "On hold."

I set his takeout coffee—black—on the coffee table, fixed myself up a bagel with cream cheese, and went into the second bedroom with my breakfast and mocha, closing the door to give him some privacy.

This would be our comfortable life together, I thought. *Bagels and coffee.*

Sure, after a few years of marriage, not to mention the stress of a kid or two, we'd have our differences, but being with Keith felt good. It didn't feel like a rebound, but like a relationship I'd been destined to have, no matter the length.

I pulled out my phone, annoyed to see a message from Dalton: *What am I supposed to do with this laptop?*

He was back in LA. Today would have been our joyful reunion, if not for that stupid script.

Me: *You could just shove it somewhere dark and out of the way.*

He texted me back immediately.

Dalton: *Like my butt? Let's not beat around the bush. We know each other too well to not be honest.*

Me: *Yeah, shove it up your butt. And the blow dryer, too.*

Dalton: *Should I unplug the blow dryer first? I'm no electrician, but something tells me that might be dangerous.*

I laughed quietly to myself, my hand over my mouth. Why was it so therapeutic to threaten bodily damage to people? And why did Dalton have to go along with it and ruin all my hard feelings for him by being funny? How angry can you be at someone who jokes about putting small appliances in their butt?

Me: *Stop being charming.*

Dalton: *Stop walking through my dreams and abandoning me when I awake.*

Me: *Stop quoting your dumb movie script. Now you're just insulting my intelligence.*

He didn't reply for at least five minutes, which gave me conflicting feelings. Had I gone too far in calling his movie dumb? He probably had high hopes for it, and his career. Don't we all, Dalton Deangelo, don't we all.

After a long wait, a next message came in.

Dalton: *You are one of the smartest girls I've ever known. I'm utterly intimidated by you.*

Me: *Puuuuuhhhhhhleeeeeeze.*

Dalton: *What was the real problem? Was it that I borrowed a few phrases, because that's ridiculous. Or did you just get scared and run away like you always do?*

Me: *I told you on the phone. The script is offensive, and you used me.*

Dalton: *Which of those two things was worse?*

Me: *Using me.*

Dalton: *And you didn't use me? You didn't leverage our relationship to get yourself an underwear line?*

Me: *That's not fair. I was humiliated when those photos were published. And let's not forget it was your weird step-daughter/step-sister who took the pictures. From your messy life.*

Dalton: *That's the real problem, isn't it? My life is too messy for you.*

I threw the phone down on the bed and shook my hands at it. Huffing angrily, I pulled my hair back, twisted it in a bun, then huffed even more because of course I didn't have any elastic bands. They were at Dalton's house, along with my laptop.

I grabbed the phone again and jabbed back a response: *We're done and I'm already seeing someone else, so forget about trying to mess with my head and make me mad enough to sleep with you.*

Dalton: *You're sleeping with someone else?*

Me: *I'm dating someone else.*

Dalton: *Wow.*

The last message made my stomach lurch. Why did I have such a big mouth, even when it came to my fingers on the touch-screen? Even though he didn't say the phrase, I felt it reverberate through my body. Fat whore. It's the kind of phrase that's tossed around thoughtlessly in even the nicer high schools. Not just whore, but *fat whore*. Every damn time, thanks to several old classics that combine size and sexual appetite.

Was it true?

Was I trying harder?

I'd slept with a handful of guys in my life, but thanks to the last few weeks, with the addition of two new guys, my score had gone up. My number was nowhere near all the fingers of both hands, but I could imagine getting there in a couple of years, unless I got married soon. Ha ha. Like that was going to happen.

I knew I wanted to have a few experiences before I settled down with just one guy, so I wouldn't always wonder about what it would be like with other people, but was I out of control? Is it okay in today's day and age for a twenty-two-year-old to sleep with two nice guys in the same summer? Not at the same time, of course.

I sent a new text message, this time to Shayla: *Shay, am I promiscuous? Be honest.*

Shayla: *You need to come home from LA immediately. Those pretty people are eating your soul. Also, I miss you.*

(Notice how she completely ignored my idiotic question. That's what the best of friends do.)

Me: *I miss you too.*

Shayla: *The house misses you. It makes weird noises when you're not here. The fridge is possessed. I miss your face. I looked at photos of you on my phone last night, and you're really beautiful. Even the photo of you eating onion ring crumbs out of your food-catchers.*

Me: *You always know how to cheer me up.*

Shayla: *Now I want onion rings so bad. Or pie. Hurry home. When I pick you up at the bus depot, we'll go straight to Chloe's for pie. Mile-high lemon meringue. My treat.*

Me: *Do you really think dating pretty boys is eating my soul?*

Shayla: *Yes. No. I don't know. They're not regular people.*

Me: *The sex is insane.*

Shayla: *Sex is always insane. That's the whole point of sex. Turn off your brain and check your sanity at the coat check.*

Me: *There's a coat check for sanity?*

Shayla: *Yes. Don't forget to tip the girl who works the counter. She's got a freezer full of vegan hot dogs and nobody to smother.*

We texted back and forth for the next hour, getting progressively weirder and more *in-joke-y*, like all the best conversations, until my phone beeped sadly, begging for a charge-up.

In the main area of the apartment, Keith was off his phone and bustling around tidying up, by the sound of it. I checked one last time for new messages and saw one.

Dalton: *Come get your laptop before five o'clock today, or I'm throwing it in the trash.*

I growled several nasty swear words at my phone.

I burst out of the bedroom and told Keith I had to run an errand, and also beat some sense into someone.

He said, "How did my sister get your phone number?"

"Not her. Dalton. I need to get my stuff from his house before he does something even stupider than all the stupid things he's done to date." I held my hand out, palm up. "Do you think I could borrow your van? Or should I call a taxi?"

"I'll drive." He grabbed a lightweight jacket and slipped on some leather sandals.

MIMI STRONG

CHAPTER 12

I crossed my arms and allowed a small amount of sanity to wash in around my crazy. "You could drive me to Dalton's, but you'd better not come inside the house."

Keith grinned, looking boyish and adorable, his black hair ruffled up from him messing with it while he talked on the phone. "Don't worry, Peaches. I'm a pretty zen dude, or hadn't you noticed?"

"Eep." I grimaced. "Pardon my selfishness, but I forgot to ask how things went on the phone. Are you going to Italy?"

He shrugged, then jingled his keys. "To the Batmobile."

"My dad used to say that."

We were almost out the door, when I caught sight of my reflection in a mirror and begged for some time to fix myself up.

"I'll eat my bagel," he said.

I ran into the bathroom and shut the door. Alone with a big mirror, I frowned at my face. Hot sex was supposed to make you glow, not give you bags under your eyes from the sleep you lost. I put on my concealer and foundation, then had to start all over again, because my regular makeup looked too pale thanks to the sun I'd gotten over the previous few days.

I was putting on dark brown mascara when Keith knocked on the door and said, "Please tell me you're not taking half an hour to pretty yourself up for your ex-boyfriend."

"No," I lied. "I'm totally… taking a big, smelly one in here. Don't get too close to the door crack."

I flipped on the switch for the fan, then quietly died of embarrassment. To his credit, Keith demonstrated what a gentleman he was by laughing on the other side of the door.

Being a classy lady, I can assure you that I've certainly never farted in my entire life, much less taken a "big one." Oh, I've *heard* about pooping, but it's just something other people do. When I was a baby, babysitters loved my never-soiled diapers. I bet if I had to make one, some day, it would smell like rose petals and look like potpourri.

~

In Keith's green van, we drove up to the Hollywood Hills. We fit right in, because the roads were populated with both fancy convertibles and gardening trucks.

"So, this is what smoldering vampire eyes gets you," Keith said as he parked in front of Dalton's gate.

"Apparently." I unfastened my seat belt and pointed at Keith. "Stay."

He looked hurt by my command, his brown eyes puppy-dog-like. I appreciated everything Keith had done for me, including the ride up there, but I had enough sense to know bringing him into Dalton's home would be a disaster.

Glowering just a little, Keith stayed in the van, with the engine off and the windows rolled down. I opened the heavy gate and started toward Dalton's front door.

The door itself was tall and plain, cold gray brushed metal. I pressed the doorbell three times before someone finally came to the door: Dalton's butler, Vern.

"Vern!" I was so happy to see him, that I just hugged him without waiting for an invitation.

"What's happening?" he asked softly. "Mr. Deangelo is all worked up."

He waved me into the space. I wiped off my shoes on the matt in the foyer, then followed Vern into the large entertaining space, with its polished concrete floor, fifteen-foot-high ceilings, and giant ceiling fans that looked like airplane propellers.

Dalton was reclining on one of the white leather sofas, watching something on his phone.

"Vern, her things are in the master bedroom. Please pack everything in her luggage."

"*Her* luggage?" I sputtered. "I'm right here. You're going to pretend I don't exist?"

He glanced up briefly from his phone, his dazzling green eyes looking wounded. "It's either that or offend you in some way," he muttered.

Vern glanced over at me. "I'll just go pack your things and give you a moment." He exited quietly, leaving us alone.

"I'm not falling for the old madder-than-you trick," I said. "You're not allowed to hate me, because I didn't do anything wrong."

"You got your fame ticket to LA, sweetheart, but guess what? It's a round-trip ticket this time."

Quietly, I assessed the situation. I knew someone else who acted offended when he was in trouble. Kyle. Who was only seven years old. And what was the best way to deal with him when he acted this way? Sympathy.

I crossed the room and took a seat in the chair adjacent to Dalton's sofa. He was still lying there, so the top of his head faced me.

"I can see that you're not happy," I said. "Do you want to talk about this?"

He sighed and rolled over, still not looking at me. "I knew it was over when I left you that morning at your house, but I hoped I was wrong."

"Dalton, I only took the modeling contract because it made me feel like I was somebody—like how you're somebody. If I had my own thing, and wasn't just some small-town girl who worked in a bookstore, then a person could sort of squint and see that maybe you and I could be a couple."

"But I liked you exactly how you were." He sat up slowly, and turned to face me. As he looked into my eyes, he said, "I like you exactly how you are."

I folded my hands together nervously on my lap. The room was cool, but suddenly felt hot and dangerous, like the ceiling could fall and crush us.

"When we first met, you said we were future old friends. Can't we just skip to that now? I can get over how hurt and betrayed I feel over you stringing me along with lines from a script, if it means we can be friends."

He looked down, and I searched his beautiful face for clues. He had a scar I hadn't noticed before—a tiny pock like a chicken pox scar—right between his eyebrows.

He turned his eyes back up slowly, a sly grin on his face. "Does being friends mean you'll come for a dip in my pool? It's not a natural hot spring, but it can be refreshing."

"Stop looking at me like you're thinking about eating me."

He didn't stop smirking. "Just one of the hazards of playing a vampire for so long."

"If you're always playing roles, how do you know which personality is you?"

"Does it matter? I'm whoever you want me to be. We all are."

I shook my head and thought about storming out in a huff, but I had one question I'd been dying to get an answer to.

"Why'd you do it?" I asked. "Did you seduce me for research, or because you needed entertainment?"

"Seduce you? Excuse me, but you were the one grinding against me at your cousin's wedding, running your hands up and down my body every chance you got. You were the one who said she wouldn't be shushed, but shoved her gorgeous lips or breasts in my mouth whenever I said something you didn't like. You were the one who took what she wanted and ran out like a thief in the night on more than one occasion."

"Stop changing the subject. I know what I did, because I was there. My eyes are wide open. Now answer my question."

He pursed his gorgeous lips once, twice. "Research."

The word hung in the air like noxious gas.

"Research in the beginning," he said.

"I knew it." I slammed my palms on the armrests of the chair, making a slapping noise.

He shifted along the sofa, moving closer to me. He put both of his hands on top of mine, and then held my hands in his.

"But it stopped being research when I made love to you."

I yanked my hands out of his, and started scrambling back to get out of the chair and away from him, but the doorbell rang, and I froze.

Vern came jogging through and went straight to the door.

Dalton grabbed my hand again, and stood up over me, learning forward so his face was inches above mine. "What's scaring you?" he asked. "Was it the idea of love? The idea of making love?"

I looked around his shoulder, at the foyer. Keith would be coming in any second, and I didn't want him to see me like this.

"I'm not scared," I said. "I'm not scared of the dark, or of things in the woods, and I'm not scared of love. I love my family and my friends. I just don't feel it for you."

"Do you love this new guy?"

Keith walked into the room, looking young in his leather sandals and camouflage-print shorts, yet walking with a deliberate swagger, his chest puffed out.

Dalton leaned in and whispered in my ear, "Tell me. Do you love him?"

The idea that he thought my private feelings were any of his business, coupled with the fact he was trapping me in that chair and making me claustrophobic, made me seethe with rage. I could have punched him in the solar plexus, and if the wind had been blowing another direction that morning I might have, but I had another way to hurt him.

"Yes," I whispered. "We just met, but yes."

He stood up slowly, his expression cold. "Nice." He flipped his chin at me in a gesture of detachment.

Turning, he reached his hand out. "Dalton Deangelo," he said to Keith, his voice way deeper than I'd ever heard it.

"Keith Raven," Keith said, his voice equally deep in pitch. "This is quite the home you have here. I was looking at a Spanish in Outpost

119

Estates, but the renovation wasn't as high quality." He looked up at the ceiling fans, his hands on his hips, and his chest broad enough to take up half the spacious room. "Are those functional?"

Dalton snorted, but not with derision. It was a good-natured snorted. He raised his arms over his head in a V-shape. "The central air keeps me chill, but I like to turn those bad boys on and feel the power." He glanced over at Vern, who nodded and went to some switches on the wall. A second later, the fans were moving the air, and the room took on a different dimension that included swirling motion.

Keith also raised his arms in a V. "Ah, that's good."

Dalton lowered his arms, but moved to the concrete coffee table and propped one foot on the surface, displaying the bulge in his trousers my way while also taking up more space in the room. "With fans that powerful, you need sturdy furniture that won't blow away."

Keith took a wider stance. Scoffing, he said, "That's good air flow, but my grandmother's wicker rocking chair wouldn't rock in that breeze."

Dalton nodded at Vern. "Turn it up to maximum."

Vern nodded and cranked the dial.

The huge ceiling fans whirred as they sped up, faster and more powerful than I'd expected, and then faster again. The indoor plants started swaying and rustling like a rainforest in a storm. The wind got stronger. The top sheet from a stack of papers on a side table lifted into the air and flew across the room.

Papers and plant leaves swirled through the air, and my hair whipped around, getting in my eyes and mouth.

Paper and debris swooshed by Keith, who took two steps back, looking confused and unsure.

Dalton began to laugh, and then he actually—and I swear, I fib about a few things here and there, but I'm not making this up—began to beat his chest like a gorilla in a nature documentary. He didn't yell out the Tarzan cry, but he did bounce his fists on his chest once, twice, before resting them back on his hips.

My voice full of sarcasm, I yelled over the sound of the industrial fans, "Thanks for the amazing demonstration. Really." I gave him two thumbs up. "Very impressive. You're obviously the big man here."

He grabbed a piece of paper from the air and crumpled it up. "Thanks for dropping by! I really should entertain more. This is fun."

Across the swirling room, Vern waved to catch my eye, and pointed down at my luggage.

That was my cue to leave, so I grabbed Keith in one hand, the handle of my luggage in the other, and ran for the door.

Dalton beat us to the door and offered Keith his hand to shake. We were in the foyer, which was windy, but more like an unenjoyable vacation than a full-fledged tropical storm.

With a sportsmanlike nod, Keith put his palm in Dalton's. Dalton grabbed him in a bear hug and murmured something in his ear.

Whatever.

I tucked my chin against my chest and let myself out the door. Keith appeared at my side a few seconds later, looking dazed.

We walked in silence to the van, and Keith helped me get my bag loaded into the back, on top of the bags of soil.

Inside the van, I held my hand over my face, not sure how I felt, exactly, but part of the emotional mix was definitely humiliation.

We started driving, putting space between us and the strangeness.

After a few minutes of driving, I said, "Tell me what he told you by the door."

Keith frowned and shook his head. He wasn't telling.

"Was it something depraved and sexual? Turn this van around. Turn it around right now and I'm going in there to punch him properly, like I should have the minute I got there."

"Let it go." He fiddled with the stereo and put on a station with easy listening music. "People are like living ghosts, haunting their lives with their issues. If you don't like the story, change yourself or change your location."

"Meaning?" I reached back and dragged my suitcase closer to my seat so I could check that my laptop was inside.

"He's got his life, and his house, and I wouldn't trade him, because he's lost you, and none of his rich-guy stuff matters compared to losing a woman as precious as you."

My heart did that thing where it squeezes up when someone says something kind and unexpected.

"You're just saying that because you want to bury your face right here between my peaches." I pushed my girls together with my upper arms and flaunted the food-catchers his way.

"Don't." He shook his finger at me. "Don't turn away from contact by making a joke. Don't distract from true, deep physical intimacy by bringing candy into the bedroom."

"Technically, it was marshmallows, not candy, and you asked for it. And if we're going to talk *depth* here, I took you pretty deep. Getting those last marshmallows from around the base made my eyes water."

He grinned. "Which I appreciated."

"I'll say you did."

We drove in silence for a minute, then I asked him again, "What did he say at the door?"

"He said it to me, not to you, for a reason."

"Fine. Don't tell me. I don't even care anymore." I retrieved my laptop from my bag and opened it to make sure everything was working. I tried really hard to act like I didn't care about what Dalton had said, even though it was killing me.

"Wanna get some lunch?" Keith asked.

"Definitely. Acting like a trash-monster from a reality TV show, picking up my things from one guy's house with another guy as my escort, has really worked up my appetite."

"You're not a trash-monster."

"I didn't slap anyone or throw a drink in their face."

"The day's not over yet."

"What was up with you two guys and the alpha-male behavior? I thought I'd seen your chest puff out when we were modeling, but that was intense. I thought you two were going to start chimpanzee-screaming and throwing rocks around."

"Now you're making fun of me. I was in control of myself the whole time. If you ask me, Dalton could use a little meditation."

I giggled at the idea of Dalton meditating. He'd get so bored after two seconds, just like me.

After a minute, I said, "Thank you."

Keith looked over at me, his brown eyes gold in the bright sunshine streaming in the van's windows.

"Thank you for everything," I said. "Including coming inside, even though I told you to wait in the van."

"I'm all for equality, but sometimes a man has to be a man, and stand behind his lady, so she can see how much he cares."

"Are you trying to get into my pants? Because you don't have to try so hard. You are really, really sexy."

He shot me another moody look. "Be serious."

I shook my head. "It is really hard to be serious when I'm thinking about getting icing and sprinkles and decorating your body like a cupcake."

"Are all the girls from Beaverdale like you?"

"No. Some of them are weird."

He started laughing, and soon I was, too.

I stopped laughing abruptly when he pulled into the parking lot for an all-salad restaurant.

~

I survived lunch at the salad place, but just barely. They had a few interesting salads that challenged my salad-as-a-meal prejudice, including one with grilled turkey and candied pecans. Paired with a fruit smoothie, it promised a delicious meal.

Keith and I both commented on the Niçoise salad, because it sounded good, but he ordered something with kale and goat cheese instead.

Our waiter was a rugged-looking older gentleman with silver hair at his temples, and whenever he came by our table, a wild animal thing happened. Keith stuck his chest out like a threatened primate, and his voice got so deep, I worried about vocal chord damage.

I decided that most guys have a little alpha male in them, even if they're not spanking you and bossing you around like Christian Grey.

After our lunch, we browsed on our phones for other things to do during the day in LA, and I admitted that going on a bus tour of star homes was something I "could probably be talked into," meaning I *really* wanted to go and was embarrassed by how cheesy that made me.

If I didn't already think Keith was a sweet guy, his reply that he *insisted* I accompany him on a bus tour of star homes would have won me over.

As we boarded the bus, elbow to belly with tourists, Keith suggested we introduce ourselves as newlyweds from Nebraska. I thought that was an excellent idea, and told everyone my name was Pam. Keith said his name was Jack, which gave me the giggles, because he was not a Jack at all.

The tourists were friendly enough, except for a few older guys who grumbled about the cost and inconvenience of everything while their wide-eyed wives made the I-can't-believe-I-put-up-with-this-for-thirty-years faces. We met a newlywed couple from Queensland, Australia, named Trevor and Heather, who suggested we join them the next day for a tour of Universal Studios.

Keith said we had to stay in the hotel room all day because I was ovulating and we were trying for a honeymoon baby. The couple got red-faced, and then Trevor leaned in and said they were doing the same. Heather rolled her eyes and said, "Yeah, but it doesn't take all day."

We laughed and laughed, because everything is a billion times funnier when an Australian says it.

For the rest of the bus tour, I wondered if I was ovulating, and Keith somehow knew, thanks to his earth muffin, meditating, salad-eating ways. I'd had my period right before the trip to LA, so probably not. We'd been using condoms, but staring at Keith's face and thinking about him fertilizing my lady garden got me flustered. Bare skin on skin. Juices commingling. Extremely raunchy metaphors and mental images. For example, him coming inside me and painting me with his ecstasy, slicking my walls with one coat after another.

I kept crossing my legs and trying to focus on what the tour guide was saying, but pretending to be a newlywed had gotten in my head and there was only one cure for the fever I had.

CHAPTER 13

"I feel dirty," I said that evening as we were driving back to his apartment. The sun hadn't set, but the sky was like milky tea on the horizon.

"I can draw you a nice bath. I've got some aromatic epsom salts."

I reached over and squeezed his bare knee, right at the hem of his camouflage cargo shorts.

"No. I mean I feel *dirty*. Like *Reverse Cowgirl dirty*."

"Is that a dance? You want me to take you out clubbing?"

Squeezing his leg again, I simply said, "Not a dance."

He nodded slowly. "Good thing we're going straight home, then. Wait, I know what Cowgirl is, so wouldn't Reverse Cowgirl just be… Missionary?"

Feeling both embarrassed and turned-on at the same time, I said, "It's still with the girl on top, but the girl faces your legs."

"Would this girl be you?"

"Unless you want me to phone our new Australian friends about a swap. That Trevor was one tall glass of water."

He laughed. "No swapping. You're all mine for one more week."

One more week.

I didn't like him saying that, even though it was the truth.

He grabbed my hand, pulled it up to his lips to kiss sweetly, then moved it down to his crotch. I stroked his hardness through his shorts.

He said, "All this Cowgirl talk is making me *Cowboy Up*, if you know what I mean."

125

I shifted to the edge of my bucket seat and unzipped Keith's zipper so I could slip my hand into his shorts. "Hello, Lone Ranger," I said, gripping his cowboy tightly. "Or should I say Woody?"

He smiled, his eyes steady on the road despite the distraction.

"Call me whatever you like."

"Definitely Woody," I said, caressing the ridges. "And this is Woody's cowboy hat."

"I'm going to pull over this van and wear *you* like a hat, missy."

"Ooh, you're so manly when your voice gets deep like that." I switched into my high-pitched girlie voice. "You've been such a big ape of a man all day today, sticking out your chest and talking deep. I'm getting so wet for you."

He turned and gave me a look of respect. "Don't stop. And keep doing the voice. It's weird, like you, but I dig it."

The granite-hard manhood in my hand didn't disagree. Keith liked me talking dirty and ditzy to him.

"You know I'm no virgin," I said softly, my voice still high. "But I do feel innocent and scared by the big world. Except for when I'm in your big, strong arms. You make me feel safe."

"Go on."

I felt the pressure of being put on the spot, and my throat closed up. I pulled my hand out of his shorts and got some bottled water from my bag.

Keith chuckled and zipped up his shorts. "To be continued as soon as we get back to our apartment."

"Yes." I handed him the water, not commenting on him calling it *our* apartment instead of *his* apartment.

But, after a minute of driving, I said, "*Your* apartment, not *our* apartment. I am going home in a week. This is fun, what we're doing, but I'm not under any illusions. I won't be waiting by the phone, waiting for you come visit, pretending we have a future."

"You could come to Italy."

"Hah!"

He frowned, glancing over at me with a glowering look. "Fine, there's no deal yet, but they haven't said no, either."

126

"Sorry. I didn't mean to doubt you'd get the job. That was just my honest reaction to the idea. I mean… Italy? What would a flight out of Washington even cost? Never mind. We've had a nice day, Keith. Let's keep having a nice day."

"Sure." He tapped his fingers on the steering wheel, eventually falling into rhythm with the song on the radio.

We got back to the apartment building, and I felt heavy on the walk to his door. My feet were swelling in my shoes, the way they do if I eat a ton of salt and get too much sun. I still felt dirty, but I did not feel sexy.

Inside the apartment, Keith grabbed two towels and said, "Swim time."

I just wanted to lounge around with my phone, texting Shayla, but I stripped down to my underwear and followed him to the pool.

Once in the cool water, weightless again, I started to smile.

"What are you grinning about?" Keith asked, paddling around me with a pool noodle wrapped under his armpits.

"Just happy." I stared up at the sky, which was turning navy blue as the sun disappeared. "Do you use this pool every night?"

"Used to. With Tabitha, or with my sister. The three of us typically had the place to ourselves. We used to play this game…" He paused, looking troubled. "Never mind."

I rolled onto my back in the water, the other pool noodle stretched across my upper back to make floating easy. Keith was paddling with his back to me, and I hooked my feet under his armpits to tag along like a caboose.

"What happened with you guys?" I asked.

He continued to paddle, towing me with him. "I don't get why people are always so curious about breakups. What happened doesn't matter. If I tell you Tabitha went with her cousins to a party in Las Vegas and slept with her ex-boyfriend, I don't know what good that accomplishes."

"I'm sorry to hear that."

He kept paddling, his back to me. "Sorry? Nobody does shit with sorry. Sorry and a dollar will buy you four quarters."

I wiggled my toes, which were still hooked under Keith's armpits. "Some people say talking about the bad stuff helps. Every time you visit a bad memory, you get to re-frame it in a new light."

He threw his arms up and submerged again, slipping away from me. A few seconds later, he came up near the edge of the pool.

Grinning, his dark brown eyes mischievous, he said, "That sounds like a lot of new age talk coming from the person who says she's not into meditation."

"I went to therapy. Therapy isn't new age talk." I splashed water his way.

"Why'd you go to therapy?" He swam toward me, looking shark-like.

I put my foot on his chest, keeping him away, but he leaned down to kiss the top of my foot and stroke my legs, massaging my calf.

"That feels so good," I said.

He quirked his eyebrow sexily, then grabbed my other leg and propped both feet on his broad, muscular chest.

"Why'd you go to therapy?" he asked more insistently.

I floated back on the water, closing my eyes. "Have you ever been in a sensory deprivation tank? They're full of saltwater, so you float more easily. Sounds kind of fun, but also terrifying."

He rubbed his hands slowly all the way up and down my legs, making them feel about a mile long, and really sexy.

"You're avoiding my question," he said, his voice low and husky.

"I kinda freaked out over some stuff at college and had to drop out. My parents thought I was fine, but my family doctor referred me to a therapist."

He squeezed my calves and then the backs of my thighs, making me shiver, even though I wasn't cold.

"I used to get really worked up," I said. "I'd get so worried about things that didn't matter, and I'd be paralyzed with fear. I'd miss exams and deadlines for papers. My marks were bad, and that only made it worse."

"Then you turned to drugs."

"No, I did not." I laughed at the idea. "Who knows. Maybe the right drugs would have helped, and I'd have a degree right about now."

"Trust me on this one, drugs would not have helped."

I opened my eyes and tilted my head to look at him. "Oh my god. I'm so sorry, Keith. I totally forgot, and I'm being so insensitive."

"Cocaine is great for dieting. But you didn't hear it from me. Expensive, though. I mean, you think Jenny Craig is pricey, with having to buy all the special meals from them. Coke is way more expensive."

"Jenny Craig destroys lives, though."

He laughed at my joke, then pulled my feet away from each other and pulled me against him. I wrapped my legs around his waist.

"Tell me more about your struggles with Jenny Craig addiction," he said. "Is there a support group? Do you meet in a church basement three nights a week to talk about your struggles with Jenny Craig and drink bad coffee?"

"Not anymore. I've been three years clean."

He grinned and ran his palms up and down my back as he stared into my eyes. The sky was darker than the pool now, which was lit by recessed lights a foot under the water line. The pool around our bodies was dark blue and green, with tiny highlights of yellow tiles glinting like precious metals.

Keith asked, "Do you believe in free will?"

"I dropped out of college before getting heavy into philosophy."

"You don't need a degree to have thoughts."

"I've read about these identical twin studies, and I think a lot of our fate is predetermined, just by how we are."

"Me, too."

"And here we are. So it must be fate."

"Everything in our lives has led us here," Keith said. "Bad habits, bad decisions, bad temper."

"I don't have a bad temper."

"Excuse me, Peaches Monroe, have you *met* yourself? Yesterday I flushed the toilet while you were in the shower, turning your water cold, and you whipped your face around the shower curtain like you were going to take my toothbrush, turn it into a prison shiv, and stab me repeatedly. And that was just for a small water temperature infraction."

"A small temperature infraction? Are you kidding me? Your shower barely spits out water, then suddenly there's a fire hose pinning me to the tiles. I only looked around the shower curtain to get some warning about what plague was coming next."

"I have a soup pot full of snakes, but I'm saving those for Sunday brunch."

"What makes you think I'll still be here Sunday? Maybe I'll—"

The water churned around us, and then he had his hands on my buttocks, squeezing my buns and pulling me close as he shushed me by kissing me.

I wrapped my arms around his neck and rocked my hips, eliciting a reaction within his swimming shorts. In seconds, he was hard and pressing back against me, grinding me in a way that was not unpleasant at all.

Around his lips, I said, "Maybe I'll stay."

He pulled back from the kiss and gazed into my eyes. The blue lights under the water line made his face look upside-down, all the shadows pointing in the opposite direction as normal. His eyebrows had triangular shadows above them, like the eyebrows of jack-o-lanterns.

"I had fun with you today," he whispered. "I'm glad I'm not some jerk with a nice house in the Hollywood Hills, but nobody to cuddle tonight."

I reached down between us and grabbed his hardness. "I'm going to cuddle you so hard."

"Reverse Cowgirl," he said. "You promised."

Before I could try to wiggle out of the promise, he grabbed my hand and hauled me out of the pool. We raced back to his place and barely toweled off before we were in bed.

My skin was cool from the swim, so I insisted we climb under the covers for a cuddle and warm-up before the main event. We kissed for an eternity, all warm and cozy together in the dark, our bodies entwining. Whenever his manhood nudged between my legs, I had to hold myself back from pushing down onto it, bare.

Finally, I grabbed a condom and rolled it on before it was too late.

"Cowgirl time," he said, pushing me into position.

"Close your eyes. Don't look at my butt!"

"That's the best part."

Since he wasn't going to close his eyes, I closed mine. With my weight on my lower legs, my back to Keith's upper body, I straddled him. He slipped in easily, but instead of taking him all the way in, I arched my back and slowly leaned back, until I was lying on his chest. I craned my neck to kiss him.

"This is amazing," he said, reaching both hands up to cup my breasts. "I can touch you everywhere." One hand moved down between my legs, making me gasp as he grazed my swollen bump.

He groaned as he rotated his hips and dipped further into me. I shifted down a few degrees, taking him deeper, then deeper still. He kept stroking my nub and thrusting in and out at the same time, while his other hand squeezed one breast, then the other. The stimulation was so intense—almost as if there were more than the two of us, yet we were aligned, with his arms moving in the same range as my arms would, so we also felt like one person. One very sexy person.

He got me close to coming a few times, and I was in no hurry at all, until I was. And then I desperately needed to come.

Ignoring all the worries about him seeing the view of my rump, I sat up, ready to ride like a cowgirl in reverse. His length was firm and full, limiting my angle at first, but after some assurances from him that his flagpole really did bend that way (and felt good), I leaned forward even more, grabbing onto his muscular upper thighs for purchase.

"Ride 'em cowgirl," he moaned.

I rocked back and forth, enjoying the angle of penetration. With my eyes clenched shut, I heard the sound of his breathing become more ragged as he got closer to coming. The sound of his raspy breaths were the sexiest things I'd ever heard. When he started to moan, I began to quiver, my inner walls clenching him tightly. He was hard like a fist, and as his breathing changed again, relaxing, I started to come.

And for a moment, I felt like I really was riding a bucking bull. I threw one hand up over my head. "Yeehaw!"

He grabbed me by the hips and thrust into me, raising his hips all the way off the bed and me along with them.

I grabbed onto his knees and held on for dear life as I shook with a rapid succession of orgasms that made me see flashing lights.

Everything was still again. I caught my breath, then sighed. I looked down to find my right leg was straight out in front, alongside Keith's legs, and my left leg was folded, my foot under my buttock.

Interesting. I could work with that. I rolled to my right, and soon I was lying on the bed, both of us in spooning position.

"Hmm," Keith said, tickling me as he reached between us to hold the condom tight as he withdrew. "Um."

"What?"

"Just a little wetter than I expected. Hang on." He rolled away from me and flicked on the side table lamp.

"Bright liiiight!" I whined.

"Phew," he said. "The rubber's not broken, so I guess it was just water from the pool."

"Oh, damn." I reached my hand down between my legs. Yup, there was a puddle.

"Are you okay?" he asked.

I didn't answer, but I heard him sniff as he leaned back toward me.

"Keith, I didn't pee the bed."

"I didn't say you did."

"Uh, you just smelled me. I heard you sniff."

"I'm just breathing normally, I swear."

We were quiet for a moment, Keith being careful to breath so quietly I couldn't hear him at all.

Finally, I said, "Fine. You got me. I'm a squirter. Not every time, but I guess certain angles trigger this totally natural function that's totally not pee. It's a real medical thing. You can Google it if you don't believe me."

He grabbed some tissues from the bedside table and handed them to me. "Two for you, and two for me. There's a little garbage bin right over there. You can go have a shower if you want, but I'd like to get tidied up and have that nice cuddle you promised."

I used the provided tissues, and then a few more. Even dried off, I still felt a negative emotion. Not shame, because I knew I hadn't done anything wrong, but I was embarrassed. I think any girl would be.

Keith was back under the covers. "C'mere," he said, patting the bed.

I thought through all the excuses I could give to run out of that room.

"C'mere," he said again, softer this time.

He patted the bed. Pat, pat.

Sometimes, after a long, weird day, all you really want is for a guy to pat the bed next to him. If he happens to be a good listener with a kind heart, take him up on the offer. You'll be glad you did.

~

We had a great cuddle that led to comfortable pillow talk. I told Keith about my birthday ritual of going to DeNirro's* with my family and taking pictures of us all around the red-checked tablecloths.

*No relation or connection to the actor Robert DeNiro, one R.

Keith told me there were plenty of red-checked tablecloths in Italy, and then I tickled him until I found his ticklish spots, under his armpits and along his sides.

I switched the birthday topic back to him, since his refusal to have birthdays was so fascinating. What is it about people who refuse to partake in things everyone else loves? Like people who've never watched *Titanic*, for example? My cousin Marita, who used to babysit me, has never seen the movie, and I swear it's become a part of her identity. When she met her much-younger husband James at a bar, they got into an argument over a trivia game—specifically, a *Titanic* question. He mocked her, asking if she could call herself a girl if she didn't know what Rose did with the diamond. Marita claimed she didn't even know who Rose was, much less anything about a diamond, and James bugged her about it all night, because it was a rather tall tale. (I mean, please. I love Marita, but the girl knows damn well who Rose is.) James ended up taking Marita back to his house that night to "watch the movie," and you can guess what happened next. To this day, Marita still hasn't seen *Titanic*.

I wondered if Keith had stopped celebrating birthdays to make himself seem more interesting as an adult.

We cuddled and I pressed him for more details.

He admitted the decision was partly because he liked the beefy look of the number ten much more than eleven, with its two boring, thin lines, but mainly he refused birthdays to aggravate his twin sister. Katy was competitive, always pointing out that her birthday present box was bigger, or heavier, or that she had more girls attending the party than he had boys. Katy was the queen bee at her school, both popular and controlling, so there was no way he could compete. He first mentioned the idea of abstaining from birthdays as a joke, and it infuriated her so much, that... well... how could a brother *not* commit to doing something that bugged her so much?

I rolled over in the dark to face Keith, my hand against his warm chest.

"You seem to put a lot of energy into annoying your sister," I said. "I have to admire your commitment and dedication."

He reached over and played with my hair, pulling it across my cheek, and then tucking it behind my ear.

"When I make up my mind, it stays made up," he said.

"I wish I was more like you. I'm a softie, in body and spirit. Remember how easy it was for you to talk me into spending the first night here?"

"You were so beautiful in the dark, like you were this divine statue carved from alabaster. I swear you were glowing from the inside, full of stars and lightning bugs, and all I could think about was kissing you. I'm glad you kissed me back, or I might have tossed myself down the canyon."

"I'm always shocked when guys try to kiss me. I think half the time they do it just to shut me up."

His eyes went wide, mocking me. "No!"

I nodded. "It's true. When I was a kid, my mother used to carry these ultra-sticky caramels in her purse. I thought they were her favorite candy, but it turned out she can't eat them because of her dental work. I had no idea. She brought them everywhere because they totally filled my mouth and shut me up. She didn't like me telling people at the post office that we had Pop Tarts for dinner when my father was out of town on business."

Keith laughed. "You're a tattle-tale."

"No. I just thought she was the greatest mom ever and wanted everyone to know." I stared into his eyes, trying to memorize his face in the dim light, painfully aware of how easy it is to forget. "Both of my parents are great, actually. They'd probably get along well with yours, except for the cayenne pepper thing. That's weird."

"I'm sure your family has some secrets."

I laughed, my voice high-pitched. "Well, there is this one thing."

"Mmm?" His eyebrows tented up with intrigue.

"My mother has banned my father's hideous recliner from the living room, so he lugged it all the way up to the attic, along with a beer fridge. There's no bathroom up there, and my mother suspects he's going in a bucket and throwing it out the window."

Keith started laughing, rolling on the bed and holding his sides.

"That's not all," I said. "Back before I came along, they paid the deposit for our house with money my mother got from getting rogered by a movie star."

Wheezing with laughter, Keith slapped the bed between us. "I guess the apple doesn't fall far from the tree!"

"Excuse me?"

He stopped laughing and wiped at his eye. "You and your mom both slept with movie stars."

"But I didn't get paid for it."

"You should have. That guy is a serious Grade A Douchebag. And his acting is terrible. He's always—" Keith turned his head sideways and gave me a super-intense brooding stare. With his dark hair and high cheekbones, he did an alarmingly accurate Drake Cheshire.

"This isn't funny," I said, now feeling sweaty and claustrophobic in the bed with Keith.

"Look at me, Peaches. It is funny. It's *damn* funny. And making fun of our exes is an important part of the rebound experience."

"The rebound experience? Please, Keith, in all your infinite wisdom, tell me more about what emotions I should be feeling."

He wiggled his way backward, to the edge of the bed, then lifted his arms and rested his hands behind his head in a relaxed pose. He looked quite pleased with himself, as though he'd helped me with some spiritual breakthrough. The nerve.

"He still has power over you," Keith said. "Making fun of him takes that power away."

I gave him stink-eye for a minute, trying to hear what he was saying without rushing to judgment, and without smothering him under my pillow.

"I'd make fun of your ex, Tabitha," I said. "Except I do a lousy impression of skinny-butt-having, ex-boyfriend-banging, Las-Vegas-slutting, bag-of-hair-best-friending, meek little shrew-faced witches. Mainly because of my cheekbones."

He nodded slowly, opening his mouth with a crisp smacking sound. "I deserved that."

I covered my mouth. "No, you didn't. I'm being a monster, and I don't know why."

He studied me for a moment. "You're good at protecting yourself, like a momma bear. It's an admirable quality."

"Hmm." That sounded like an insult wrapped in a compliment.

"You have many admirable qualities. You're confident, and brave, and lots of things."

"Keep going." My irritation was subsiding.

"You're the whole package," he said. "You're real, and you have more class than most girls, even if you do swear like a truck driver sometimes."

I adjusted my position in the bed, squeezing my breasts together to put them on display. "Plus don't forget my peaches."

"You're good at changing the subject, too."

"Kiss me," I said. "Kiss me like my lips are on fire and you need to smother the flames."

He grinned. "You look so cute right now, I want to get my phone and take a picture."

"No time! Kiss me like I'm the judge of a kissing contest."

He laughed, but still wouldn't go for the kiss.

I meant to say something original, something funny, but I found myself using the lines from Dalton's movie script—the lines I'd been so pissed that he'd used on me.

"Kiss me like I'm bad for you. Kiss me like I'm dangerous."

His expression serious, Keith whispered, "You are truly a dangerous woman." He leaned in and kissed me with an urgency that caused my pulse to race. As we kissed, our hands found new places to hold on, and we rolled back and forth, trading top and bottom with every breath. I knew using the movie lines was wrong, though I wasn't sure why. I couldn't shake the feeling Keith and I were in some sort of war, and by manipulating him with words that weren't my own, I had won this battle.

MIMI STRONG

CHAPTER 14

Thursday morning, a gorgeous, raven-haired man tucked the blankets around me.

Groggily, I said, "Why are you putting me in a cocoon?"

"Keep sleeping."

"What time is it?"

"Early. You sleep in and relax. I have to take care of some gardening business, but I'll be back by dinner."

"Take your pants off and come back to bed."

He climbed on top of me and ground his hips against mine through the blankets, growling sexily. "Don't tempt me, woman."

I broke my legs free of the blankets and wrapped them around him.

"Just a quickie," I panted.

He reached down under the covers with one hand and stroked between my legs.

I swore in frustration, or maybe it was more of a plea.

He nudged one finger, then two, inside me and stroked in and out. I closed my eyes, bit my lip, and whimpered for more.

"I really have to leave," he whispered.

"Never leave."

"I'll be back before you know it. All day, I want you to think about me touching you." He stroked in and out more firmly with his fingers, moving my whole body. "Just like this."

I sighed with pleasure.

Then he pulled away and left me aching for more.

I heard him leave, and I reached down between my legs to rub myself the way he had, but it wasn't the same, and I gave up in frustration.

After a few minutes of angrily devising ways to torture him, I realized I was sleepy, and had only slept for four hours. The ache in my pelvis was annoying, but sleep was a good consolation prize.

I rolled over and went back to my dream, where I was putting flower petals back onto flower stalks, because I was a mouse inside a video game. (It really made sense at the time, and I was so close to getting to the next level.)

When I did finally roll out of bed, it was nearly lunch time. Keith had left me a spare key for the apartment, a note saying he'd be back by four o'clock, plus a fifty-dollar bill for groceries.

I looked at the money and remembered the night I'd ordered pizza with grocery money my parents had left behind. That whole night was… a dark spot in my memory. How could I have been so stupid? I still felt like the same person, so I had to assume I was still capable of colossal idiocy.

I folded up his money and tucked the bill back under the corner of a coaster on the coffee table. I had to laugh that he thought I couldn't pay for groceries, but I truly appreciated the gesture.

Leaving money was just such a Keith thing to do. The guy was the nurturing type. He knew how to grow plants, and he'd generously coached me my first day of modeling. Even the smiley face on his note made me feel loved.

I snapped a photo with my phone, just because the still life was cute: the note, the spare apartment key, and the bright red apple he'd set where I couldn't miss the suggestion.

I looked out the window as I planned my day. The weather was exactly like the previous five days—perfectly nice.

I put on a casual sundress I'd brought with me. The dress had thicker straps that covered my bra straps, and my mother owned the same one, but hers was blue and mine was green. One time we went out in our matching dresses and a man asked if we were twins. My mother has told that story at least twenty times—that I know of.

I sent her a quick message to check in, then I left the apartment on my quest.

My main mission was to pick up ingredients for making dinner for me and Keith. I stopped by the coffee shop I'd been to before, and had my mocha and danish as I read the newspaper. As I sat there, a number of homeless guys came in and either used the washroom noisily, asked for a free coffee, stuffed their pockets with sugar packets from the mixing station, or all of the above.

I tried not to gawk at all of this like a small-town hick, but it was difficult not to.

We have a few people in Beaverdale who roam around with no fixed address, but it's not from simple poverty, as it seemed to be with some people in the big city. Back home, there's a woman everyone calls Sweet Caroline, and she uses felt pens to draw on her makeup, with big red circles on her cheeks. Some of the little kids think she's a clown and smile and wave at her, which I think is part of the reason why she does it, but I'll never know, because she doesn't talk to anyone. She hums, smiles, and shoplifts, and most people around town turn a blind eye and call it charity.

After my leisurely breakfast, I found the nearest grocery store and picked up everything for Salad Niçoise. I'd been craving one ever since seeing it on the restaurant menu the day before. It's similar to a Cobb Salad, but with tuna, green beans, and red-skinned baby potatoes, instead of chicken and whatnot.

I'd just gotten back to the apartment and set the groceries on the table when my phone started vibrating with messages. I kicked off my sandals and got ready for a conversation with Shayla, but it wasn't her.

Adrian Storm: *Why does Gordon keep rocks in the drawer?*

Ah, it was my new coworker. I'd hoped Amy would have come to her senses and left those sheep-lovers to come back to Peachtree Books, but apparently there'd been no such luck. Adrian was there, getting into all my business and messing it up by the sound of it.

Me: *Those rocks are to remind you to put the cash drawer by the door at night when you lock up.*

Adrian: *That makes exactly zero sense. Try again.*

141

Me: *We've had a couple break-ins over the years, but none since we started putting the cash drawer by the door.*

Adrian: *Should I take the money out of the tray before I put it by the door? Because if I don't, that seems like it's just encouraging the break-ins.*

Me: *You put the money in the safe.*

Adrian: *I know. I'm just pulling your leg. How's LA? I hear you're shacked up with some underwear model. Shayla told me.*

Me: *I'll be back there Wednesday. Don't mess with my organization there. I have everything exactly where it needs to be.*

Adrian: *This store is like Lady Town. I just hang out and talk to women all day. I think I might start menstruating.*

Me: *Don't. Menses is totally overrated.*

Adrian: *If I start a garage band, our name is going to be Menses Is Overrated.*

Me: *There probably is one already. That sounds familiar.*

Adrian: *I bet there is a band, and they have really awesome mustaches, too.*

Me: *I hate it when other people take your best ideas straight from your brain.*

Adrian: *That's why you need to wear a tin foil hat. I'll make you one. I like to use the tin foil to line a regular hat. Nobody needs to know you're blocking them.*

Me: *I never was a hat person. It would be a shame to cover up such nice hair.*

Adrian: *You do have great hair. You always did. And it smelled nice.*

Me: *I always wanted to get cornrows.*

Adrian: *I used to braid my Barbie's hair. That's right. I had a Barbie when I was a kid. She fought alongside G.I. Joe.*

Me: *I bet she kept his tent warm at night.*

Adrian: *Now that you mention it…*

Me: *Anything else work-related? I should probably let you go if you have customers.*

Adrian: *Nope, it's just me and the books. I did have someone come in earlier and ask if I'd read all of the books in the entire store.*

Me: *We should keep a baseball bat behind the counter for people like that. Not a real one, but one of those Nerf ones, made of foam.*

Adrian: *The boss man Gordon said violence isn't part of the Peachtree Books experience. Not even cartoon violence.*

Me: *What is cartoon violence, anyway? Is it dropping an anvil on a road runner?*

Adrian: *I should know this because I'm the guy?*

Me: *You are a guy.*

Adrian: *And you're a girl.*

Me: :-(

Adrian: *I remember now, how I used to say that to you all the time back in high school. I'm sorry I was such a tool.*

Me: *That's okay.*

Adrian: *And of course you were in love with me so bad, and then I kept asking you for advice with Chantalle Hart.*

Eep!

I dropped the phone on the table and pushed my chair back. Adrian just mentioned my being in love with him in high school, as casually as you'd mention someone's experimental phase with spiral perms.

The phone buzzed with another message, but rather than endure more horror, I switched it off.

Stupid Adrian and his big, stupid mouth.

I bustled around the kitchen, getting the water boiling for the red potatoes and green beans.

~

Keith walked in the door at half past four, and his jaw dropped open when he saw the surprise welcome I'd set up.

"I have a dining table?" he asked, circling the small table.

"It was underneath your plants by the window, and I got the chairs from your patio. I hope you don't mind."

He looked around the living space, which I'd taken the liberty of rearranging for better flow.

"This looks good," he said. "I like the couch on a jaunty angle like this."

"Shut up. You hate it. Just come eat your dinner and I'll put everything back."

He came around behind me and grabbed me in a hug, his arms tight just under my bosom. "This is the best I've seen my apartment, and this food looks great." He nuzzled my cheek and kissed my neck.

143

"Are you wearing an apron?" He reached down and rubbed his palms up and down my legs just above my thighs, pushing up the apron. "So sexy. Grrr. My sexy little homemaker."

"Do you want a drink? I got vodka and soda. That's your favorite, right?"

He kissed my neck some more, getting that area moist... as well as other areas, including my entertainment center.

I made a few happy noises as he groped me all over, and it wasn't long before he had me bent forward over the kitchen counter with my dress up, my panties down, and his fingers visiting my amusement park.

"What are you doing?" I squealed between giggles and very serious moans.

He slid one finger in and out, and then two fingers, picking up where we'd left off that morning.

"Making you come for me."

"Oh," I breathed, my cheek pressed against the cool countertop.

He filled me with fingers, the sensation powerful and pleasant. I relaxed in my bent-forward position and took him in, fitting his hand like a very happy glove.

Soon, I felt the tremor begin, pushing me up onto my tiptoes. I rocked my hips, pushing down harder against him, chasing the high and worried he was going to stop. He thrust his fingers into me harder, thumbing me with skill and pushing me to new heights as I came undone.

I moaned, repeatedly.

He waited until the spasms ceased before gently withdrawing his fingers, careful not to tickle too much.

"Huh," he said.

I turned around and retrieved my underwear from the floor.

"You were expecting the squirting?"

He shrugged. "Maybe. But I guess, like you said, it doesn't happen every time." He went to the sink and washed up as I pulled on my panties. I could see the outline of his rigidness inside his pants, and I got a few ideas, but he was looking over at the food now, so my plans could wait. Keith liked to wait, but as long as he took care of my needs, that was fine by me.

After he dried off his hands, he grabbed me in another hug, this time facing me.

"Don't you look proud of yourself," I said, grinning to match his expression.

He kissed me on the tip of my nose. "You have the nicest, sweetest, tastiest little cunt. I want to crawl up inside there like it's a boutique hotel room."

My jaw dropped open. How could he say *that word* and make it sound so endearing?

He laughed at me, and my rare speechlessness.

Finally, I said, "Dinner?"

"Famished."

"Go sit down. I'll bring everything over."

He gave me one more kiss, then let me go to take a seat on a teak chair. "I totally forgot I had these chairs," he said.

I got ice cubes, made us some vodka and soda refreshments, and brought the drinks and the Salad Niçoise over to the table. He kept grabbing my thighs as I served up the food.

"You can't get enough of me," I teased.

He pulled me down onto his lap and started pillaging me through my clothes. I squealed and got away.

"Come give me a lap dance," he said.

"These little folding chairs aren't rated for lap dancing. I've got a lot to shake, and I don't want you to break."

He grinned and pulled his chair in to the table as I took my seat across from him.

"I'm glad you have a lot to shake," he said.

I pursed my lips and poked at the green beans with my fork.

After a moment, he said, "What's going on?"

"Just thinking. Me and my body are cool with each other. I like it when men appreciate my curves, but I only want to hear about it so much. Don't tell me you like my booty, show me, you know what I mean? That's how it is with some guys, but with you, Mr. Sexy Model

Man, you've certainly *shown* me your appreciation, and I plan to return the favor right after dinner."

He waggled his eyebrows and sipped his drink. "I like the sound of that."

"I'm going to yank off your clothes, and I'm going to worship your manhood—worship it like some pre-historic cave girl who's never seen one before, because she's been raised in an all-female tribe. I'm going to sing a song to your manhood, and lavish it with all my attention. Then I'm going to suck it so hard the top will turn purple."

Keith let out a nervous laugh.

"Oh, you'd better be scared," I said. "This cave girl has been having dreams about your pointy thing. Witch-doctor-mushroom-juice-prophecy type dreams. And tonight is the night of legend."

"We're going all *Clan of the Cave Bear* tonight?"

"As soon as we're done eating our salad."

"I can work with that." He took a bite of the food I'd made. "Mmm. This is good. And I'm not just saying that because you terrify me."

I started eating my dinner, and for a minute, I worried that I'd oversold the evening's planned activities. I had some vague ideas about prostate massage, but that was about it—no cave-woman costume or bones to twist into my hair. Then I remembered that Keith was a man, and as long as I didn't bite it too much, he'd be happy.

"How was landscaping today?" I asked.

"Not bad. Remember that restaurant we went to on our first date?"

"That was a date?" I waved my hand. "Never mind. We don't need labels. Yes, I remember the place."

"Edgar and his family were one of my first clients. Really good customers, and nice people, if you remember. I just went to oversee some work my company is doing for them."

"But you're not sweaty or dirty."

He grinned. "My manager is, though. And the three guys we have working for us. Actually, the manager is set to take over the whole business, because I'm switching to modeling full-time now."

"What about your sister? Isn't she your partner?"

"She'll be partners with Mikey now. This is all for the best, because she and I were too entwined in each other's lives. Now I get to be on my own, make my own decisions."

"I feel scared for you, going off to Italy by yourself."

"We have to do things that scare us, or hurt us, or we don't grow."

I sighed. "I don't want to grow anymore. I'm feeling pretty good about where I'm at. I don't want to get hurt anymore. I'd sincerely prefer to never cry again."

He quirked one dark eyebrow up. "What about crying at weddings?"

"I'd rather just be happy and smile. My cousin Marita's wedding was nice. Everybody was too tense about the age gap to get all emotional, which was fine by me." I picked up my glass and chugged the remainder. "I don't like being overwhelmed, good or bad, where you feel like a glass that's being overfilled with water."

"Meditation really helps with that feeling."

I rolled my eyes. "How can thinking about all my problems do anything to solve them?"

"Let's say you need to do a math problem. Long division. You need to do it on paper. Are you better off using a fresh sheet of paper, or the back of an envelope that's all covered in scribbles?"

"What are you getting at?"

"Don't get ahead of me. Visualize your two options and tell me. Blank sheet, or scribbled-on envelope?"

"The blank sheet, obviously."

"Meditation isn't about thinking through all your problems at once. It's for thinking about nothing. So you become the blank sheet, and then later, you can take on your problems, one at a time."

Maybe it was the vodka, or his model-gorgeous face, but Keith's explanation made some sense.

"I'm really glad you met me," I said. Laughing, I corrected myself, "That I met you!"

He stuck his tongue out and wiggled it. "How strong were these drinks? I can't feel my tongue."

"The first time I got drunk, it was with my girlfriends, and we kept trying to measure how drunk we were by standing on one foot with our eyes closed. The funniest thing was my best friend, Shayla, had better balance drunk than she did sober. I guess she relaxed and stopped trying so hard."

"Sounds like a metaphor for life."

I chuckled and went back to my salad.

We talked for a bit more over dinner, about life and philosophy. Keith had a lot of good ideas. I didn't agree with all of them, but I could see how they might work for other people.

After we'd finished eating, Keith jumped up to do the dishes. I stood beside him and dried after he washed. At one point, I put my head on his shoulder, and for a minute, it didn't feel like we were playing house at all. Our relationship was real, and our connection to each other was real.

He kissed me on the cheek and said he wanted to take a shower, since he'd gotten sweaty in the sun that day.

I waited for him in the bedroom—completely naked, under the sheets. When I heard the water shut off, I started to get nervous. The room was still bright with the evening sun streaming through the blinds. I hadn't closed the blackout curtains, because I was feeling more confident about sex in the light.

Keith walked in, wearing nothing but a towel slung low across his hips. I squealed and clapped my hands at the sight of him. From the defined muscles to the perfectly-tanned skin, he truly was a fine specimen. But more than that, he had a personality that was just as beautiful.

"C'mere," I said, patting the bed next to me.

CHAPTER 15

He had some clothes in his hand, and he tossed them on a chair. Then he turned his back to me and opened up the towel covering his lower body. He kept the towel in place, hiding his buttocks, teasing me.

"Woo!" I cheered, clapping my hands.

He moved his body, shaking his hips from side to side, lowering the towel a few inches, then raising it up before I could see his butt. He turned around, still holding the towel up, hiding his goodies.

"Tease!"

"Show me your body," he said.

I propped myself up against the headboard and pulled the sheet down to show him my breasts.

"Touch yourself," he said.

Making continuous eye contact with him, I cupped one breast and then both with both hands. I moaned and massaged myself while staring at him with my sexy face. (At least I hoped it was a sexy face.)

He still had both hands on the edge of the towel, and he nodded down. I watched as a bump appeared, pushing against the white towel and inching its way up.

I shrieked with a combination of amusement and surprise.

"Don't scare it," he said, still laughing.

I patted the bed next to me. "C'mere. I don't bite… hard."

He tossed the towel onto the chair and followed his direction-pointer straight to me. Over on the dresser, his phone started to wiggle around, vibrating with an incoming phone call.

"One minute," he said, grabbing the phone. "Hello." He nodded and breathed audibly, then leaned back against the dresser. "Okay. Yup. Okay."

His arrow was still pointing right at me.

It sounded like he was having to endure a really dull phone call, so I rolled out of bed, got on my hands and knees, and crawled over to him.

He shrugged, and kept talking on the phone.

I nuzzled my way up his beautiful legs and kissed the base of his penis. He patted me on top of my head, which I took as a sign of encouragement. Gripping the base loosely with one hand, I ran my tongue up the length of him and then around the contours of the head.

That beautiful ridge of skin is one of my favorite parts of a man—the way it fits a tongue or mouth so perfectly is amazing, every time. I took him in through my lips, moaning softly with pleasure as his flesh filled my mouth. He sucked in air through his teeth, and I smiled around my mouthful.

He kept talking, giving only one-word answers. Something told me it was his ex-girlfriend on the line, and it didn't bother me he was talking to her, because he seemed annoyed by her, plus I had him in my mouth.

More sucking. I was enjoying myself, and getting into the task at hand.

Above me, he ended the call and tossed the phone onto the dresser. I startled at the noise and grazed him with my teeth.

He cried out in alarm.

I popped him out of my mouth and blinked up at him. "Sorry."

He blinked slowly. "Don't be sorry. That was terrifying, but I think I liked it."

"Oh, really? In that case…" I took him in my mouth, but I didn't get him with my teeth. Instead, I brought my hands up to the tops of his thighs and lightly scraped my fingernails down his thighs. Not enough to leave a mark, but definitely a sensation.

He tensed up, and got thicker and heavier in my mouth. I alternated with soft and then tight pressure, and then I very deliberately dragged the tip of my eyetooth along the length of him. He started to tremble. I ran my hands up and down his legs, then moved my hands to his buttocks, where I pinched him.

He groaned, his breath ragged. "You are one crazy cave girl."

He seemed really surprised by everything I was doing, but I was in a wicked, horny mood, and wanted to blow his mind. The next thing, I didn't even think about it. I stuck my finger in my mouth, alongside him, to get my finger wet and slippery. Then I put pressure on the male g-spot, aka the prostate, I gave a light massage while at the same time, I powered down by mouth.

Keith became my hand puppet and completely lost control. He made some garbled noises, wove his fingers into my hair at the back of my head, and trembled as he spurted. I swallowed him down happily, my whole body tingling with excitement. When it was over, I sat back on my heels, gazing up at him.

Whispering, he said, "That was intense."

I licked my lips. "That was fun."

His phone started buzzing around again.

"Damn. That's Tabitha again," he said. "My ex."

"Figured as much. Now what? Does she really, really have to make popcorn, and you still have her other favorite popcorn bowl?"

The phone kept buzzing, demanding to be answered.

"Close. She wants her folding patio chairs back." He tipped his head to the side, looking apologetic. "Her grandmother was a medium. I wouldn't be surprised if this is her psychic side coming through, and she only thought of the chairs because we were using them."

"Really, Keith? Psychic stuff? What next, voodoo?"

He pushed the buzzing phone away from him, as if some physical distance would help.

"The world is a strange place, full of possibilities," he said.

The phone kept buzzing.

"Oh, just answer it," I said, feeling annoyed.

As he did, I got up and went to the bathroom to freshen up.

When I came out of the bathroom, still naked, he was just finishing the call. After setting the phone down, he said gravely, "She's coming over to get the chairs."

I shook my fist. "And for me to punch her some new freckles."

Keith didn't laugh. He didn't appear to be in a very good mood at all, considering the Top Grade blow job I just gave him. That was some premium servicing, and for my efforts I was getting a long, miserable face?

I got on the bed and rolled to my side, striking a pose straight out of an old-timey painting. "Hey, would you say I look Rubenesque like this?" I squeezed my tatas together, crossed my eyes, and stuck out my tongue. "How about now?"

He started sorting through the clothes on the chair, oblivious to my cuteness.

I relaxed my pose, pulling the sheet across to cover my nakedness. "Do you want me to leave?" I asked. "I could be elsewhere. I don't need to be here."

"Where would you go?"

My inner bitch dialed up a notch or two, and my voice got angry and sarcastic. "I don't know, Keith. Is Disneyland still open?"

He slowly finished getting dressed, keeping his back to me the whole time.

A little softer, I said, "I'll go to that coffee place that's walking distance. Jitter bugs. Jitter beans. Jitterpalooza. Jumping Bed Bugs. What is that place called?"

"Jitters?"

"Yeah." I got up and tried to get dressed with as much dignity as I could while still giving off the vibe I was mad as hell, yet also couldn't care less.

"Great, now *you're* upset with me, too," Keith said. "What are you unhappy about? I've been playing by your rules, but it's not enough, apparently."

"Uh, my rules? Do you mean *coming*? As opposed to holding back your pleasure like some sexual anorexic?"

He raised his eyebrows. "Really, Dr. Phil. Tell me more."

"I didn't mean it like that!" I had my green sundress back on, and took a seat on the edge of the bed. "That was out of line, and I'm sorry." I looked up with puppy-dog eyes. By this point, I actually had forgotten what I was angry about, and hoped he wouldn't ask. I may have a big mouth and be prone to fits of hilarious pouting, but I'm not without self-awareness. Keith hadn't done anything wrong. I was nervous and jealous about his long-legged ex coming over, and trying to hide my insecurity. Poorly.

"I'm completely over Tabitha," he said. "I don't care what she thinks about how I live my life, and I don't care who she's sleeping with. She can do every one of our friends if she wants. I don't need them, and I don't need her."

Keith picked up his phone and scowled at the screen. "This is so like her to suddenly need her chairs back."

I sensed a big speech coming, and I wasn't wrong. After a rant about her chairs, he went blah-blah-blah about Tabitha and how she liked to have picnics, but she had to buy a whole set of matching plates and bowls for four people, and God forbid Keith use one of the plastic bowls for his granola, because then it would go through the dishwasher more times than the other ones and the red plastic would fade, and…

Keith went on and on about all the things Tabitha used to do to irritate him. Honestly, the complaints weren't that bad. I found myself siding with her, because everyone knows you don't leave wet towels on the bed. Come on, Keith. Do you want your whole apartment to smell like mildew?

I just nodded and tried to be a good Rebound. Listening to Keith's laundry list of gripes got boring pretty fast. I surreptitiously pulled out my phone and checked for new messages. There were some details about the commercial shoot on Monday. Four days away. Time was just flying by. I smiled, thinking that if I could keep Keith talking about all his complaints about Tabitha, it would slow time down, like a time dilation field in a sci-fi show.

He sat down beside me on the bed, all talked out. He put his arm around my shoulders. "You're a good listener."

I tucked my phone away quickly. "Just trying to be a good whatever-we-are."

He lay back on the bed, his hands over his eyes. "Peaches, sometimes I don't even know if I want to date someone. I question if people really want to have relationships. Maybe what we truly desire is half an hour a day to complain about everything, while someone else pretends to care."

He patted the bed next to him, so I rolled onto my back and cuddled up next to him. "I'd love to have half an hour a day to complain. But it wouldn't be about anything important, like human rights or politics or global climate change. Just personal things, like when you eat a whole bag of chips thinking it's only three hundred calories, then you realize that was the *suggested serving* size, and the whole bag was ten servings. Who eats one tenth of a bag of chips?"

Keith chuckled. "Keep going. You have another twenty-nine minutes."

"I feel better already." I nuzzled my face against his chest. "I heard this talk, once, by one of the happiness scientists. If you list off three things you feel grateful for, every day, the gratitude changes your mood."

"I'm grateful for the beautiful dinner you made me. That was a nice surprise to come home to."

"I'm grateful for the surprise you gave me, when you bent me over the kitchen counter and stuck your hand in me like you'd lost your keys in there."

He laughed. "Wait, are you being sarcastic?"

"No, it was really..." I rolled one leg over his leg and nudged my pelvis against his hip. "Good."

He said, "Number two, I'm grateful for good health."

"Same."

"No copying."

"Fine. I'm grateful that I got embarrassing photos taken of me in my bra, because it led to me coming here to LA and having this adventure."

He kissed my cheek. "I saw those photos the day they came out. You've got nothing to be embarrassed about. That was the first day of my crush on you."

I squirmed, giggling. "You're so full of crap."

He continued, "Number three, I'm grateful for how comfortable you are in your skin, because you're teaching me how to relax and be more playful. I think of my body as this tool, that either gets me modeling jobs or lets me down when I don't. When I'm with you, though, in bed, or floating around in the pool, I can see that arms aren't just for flexing biceps and selling shampoo. Our arms are made for wrapping around each other."

I stretched my top arm over him and squeezed. "You're absolutely right. They're the perfect size for hugging."

"What's your number three?"

"I miss my family. I'm grateful that I'll get to see them again in less than a week." I squeezed him tighter. "No offense. I really like being here with you, but I miss them. Kyle's going to be an inch taller. He's only seven, but you know how it is."

"That's your little brother?"

The air in the room held its breath in the golden light.

"He's my son." My voice was soft and distant, like it was coming from somewhere else. "I had him when I was very young, and as far as everyone knows, he's my little brother."

Keith was silent for a while.

I started crying.

He heard me sniff, and pulled me against his chest, tighter. "Don't be sad. Why are you crying?"

"I don't know. It's this secret I have, and sometimes it feels like a balloon inside my heart. Everything aches, and I don't know if it's because of the secret, or if that's how everyone feels about their child." I sniffed and wiped my eyes on the corner of the bed sheet. "Why were you so quiet? Were you worried that I was a single mom? That I had a whole bunch of baggage and baby daddy drama?"

"Peaches, I was quiet because I'm not very good at math. How old were you? Fifteen?"

"Barely."

155

"Well?"

"Well, what?"

Laughing, he said, "Are you going to get out your phone and show me some pictures of the little guy, or do I have to beg?"

I pulled out my phone, realizing my hands were shaking. I'd never told anyone except my closest family members, my therapist, and Shayla. Even when I told people about Kyle, I said his name, and didn't specify he was my brother, because I didn't like lying.

I pulled up a photo of Kyle, shirtless and grinning with no front teeth. "This is my son," I said.

A chill went up and down my spine. It was a truth I felt in every cell of my body, but rarely got to say.

"He has your eyes," Keith said.

We scrolled through a few pictures. Kyle eating pizza. Kyle having a bath while wearing a cowboy hat. Kyle hammering things with his play set, in my dad's workshop, next to my father working with real tools.

"He was a nightmare when he was two. Terrible Twos. Always getting into my makeup, the little brat."

"Typical brother behavior, I think. I'm the same age as Katy, and I used to do terrible things to her dolls and stuff. There's something about making a girl cry that's just so appealing."

I laughed, snuggling against Keith's warm body. "I hope you outgrew that, because crying sucks."

He reached over and touched my cheeks. "Crying happens. I learned that from having a sister. You should always date guys who have sisters. We're more sensitive." He rolled over, on top of me. "Why are we both wearing clothes?"

"I don't know. You started it."

He kissed me, rolling his weight up and pressing against my chest. I love that feeling, where you're already breathless with lust, and then the guy shifts his weight on top of you and you can hardly breathe at all. I sucked on his lips and tongue, hungry for him.

Soon the hem of my dress was riding up, and he was between my legs, grinding against me with his jeans still on. Panting, I wrapped my legs around his hips and kissed his lips, his chin, his neck.

He shifted to the side, reached his hand down between my legs, and stopped.

His head lifted up. "Did you hear that?"

"What?"

Footsteps.

Someone was in the apartment. *A burglar?*

Something moved near the bedroom's doorway. I shrieked.

"Hello," came a girl's voice, sounding forlorn.

Not a burglar.

Honestly, I would have preferred a burglar to Keith's ex-girlfriend, but it was her, Tabitha.

MIMI STRONG

CHAPTER 16

Tabitha stood in the doorway, interrupting our intimate moment. At least she didn't have Keith's nasty-mouthed sister Katy with her this time.

Keith rolled off me and started straightening his clothes.

I jumped up and went to the door. Pointing feebly past her, I said, "I clean bathroom now. I clean real good."

Tabitha staggered back, then forward, both of her slender hands landing on my shoulders. Her hands were cool on my skin, my shoulders bare except for the straps of my sundress. She smelled like a variety of boozes.

"I know you," she said, slurring her words. "You're-the-fat-sssssupermodel."

"Yes, I was on that show with Tyra Banks. I'm America's Next Top Fat Supermodel. Very good. Now, if you'll excuse me."

The girl had a strong grip for a big-lipped girl under one hundred pounds.

"You're all woman," she said.

I glanced over at Keith, who was not making this any easier by sitting on the edge of the bed looking mortified.

Tabitha stared down at my breasts like a hungry baby who smells milk.

"So pretty," she said, smiling a goofy smile.

I looked over at Keith again. "Dude, I am *so* not down with having a threesome. Please tell her that."

159

Tabitha started to laugh, one of those slow-motion, drunk-girl laughs, then did a full-stop into Serious Mode. "You are so funny and pretty. I see why Keith likes you, because I like you. I like you a lot!"

I squirmed away finally, because she looked like she was about to kiss me. I love my ladies, but not like that. Maybe a tiny crush back in high school, but that was on Chantalle Hart and you'd have to be a robot to not feel something for her.

"The chairs are right over there," I said, pointing to the romantic set-up. "You're not driving, are you?"

"Oh, Keith," she said, transitioning into sobbing mode.

Drunk. Crying. At her ex-boyfriend's place. Classic. I rolled my eyes pretty hard, but just to keep me from cringing up into a ball of cringe.

"I'll just leave you guys to talk," I said, walking over to the other room.

She staggered into Keith's bedroom, shutting the door behind her.

My eyebrows nearly hit the ceiling. Oh, no. She did NOT just go into the bedroom with Keith and shut the door. No, she did not, because that's how you get your hair extensions yanked out.

I paced back and forth, then a calm broke over me. Whatever happened, it was out of my hands. I stomped back to the kitchen, being really loud to remind them I was still there, got the strawberries and Cool Whip I'd picked up for dessert, and took them into the spare bedroom.

I shut the door most of the way and turned on the TV to mask the murmuring of their voices. Keith had returned the set to the spare room because he didn't like the negative ions electronics gave off in the bedroom.

The two of them were still murmuring. At least they were talking, which meant nobody had their burrito in anyone's drunk mouth. As I watched some trash on the little TV set, I hit the mute button periodically, just to be sure.

The third time I hit the mute button, the apartment was silent, and I had to ask myself a question: if they weren't still talking, was I prepared to go busting in there like some not-very-hip parent, flipping on lights and whipping back covers?

False alarm. They were talking... and... laughing? What was so funny? The fact that Keith's rebound girl was in the next room? Yeah, really funny, guys.

I pulled out my phone and sent a message to Mitchell, my only other friend in LA

Me: *I think maybe you were right to warn me off male models.*

I got a message back almost instantly.

Mitchell: *What did he do? I'm telling you, they're barely house-trained. If only they weren't so hot, my life would be simple.*

Me: *In a parallel universe somewhere, models aren't hot.*

Mitchell: *What's bugging you? Does he wear a sleep mask? Does he have a satin pillowcase so he doesn't get sleep wrinkles on his face?*

Me: *Neither of those things. He has an ex-girlfriend. And they're both in the bedroom talking right now. She showed up drunk. Stupid cow.*

Mitchell: *Forget about them. Come dancing with me.*

Me: *I can't leave the apartment! They'll have self-loathing sex for sure. I think she's in heat. She had that look of a horny alley cat.*

Mitchell: *How would you know that look?*

Me: *Takes one to know one! I'll let you get back to your life. I just have to wait this one out. I can always pull the fire alarm, right?*

Mitchell: *LOL! Let me know if you change your mind about going out. I could use some adventure for a change.*

I put the phone away and tried to focus on the TV show. Competitors were making puff pastries and acting like they were getting their big break. I snickered at them, with their silly dreams, then realized I was no different from them, and probably looked just as foolish.

~

I'd nodded off, face down on a pillow with the remote control still in my hand. I was woken up by someone gently shaking me.

"I'm going to drive Tabitha home," Keith said.

"That's where she should be."

"Do you want to come along for the ride?"

"You only have two seats in that van. Is she going to sit on my lap?"

161

"Oh, right. Never mind." He stared down at me, his face in shadows. He looked like he wanted to say something.

Go ahead and say it, I thought. *Tell me you're getting back together with Tabitha, and you feel just awful about the whole thing. Say it.*

"I should pick up some ice cream on the way back," he said.

I smiled up at him. Keith was a good one.

"Anything but chocolate," I said. "Chocolate ice cream always tastes burnt to me."

Nodding, he said, "I'll get a variety."

He went back out, and they whispered to each other as they went out the door. The whispering made the hair on the back of my neck stand up. I told myself not to overreact, and I sat up to await his return, clicking around looking for a better channel.

I flicked past a familiar face, and stopped. It was Dalton Deangelo. I turned up the volume and shifted down the bed, so my face was practically against the set.

I'd been carefully avoiding news about him, or gossip about me, mainly by staying off the internet. But now, here it was—the exact thing I'd been avoiding.

I froze, too curious to change the channel.

A voice-over ran as commentary, while a series of photos of Dalton ran like a slideshow.

An excited-sounding woman said, *"Dalton Deangelo, best known for his role as Drake Cheshire on his hit TV soap, One Vamp to Love, was spotted this morning in a Marina Del Ray Pilates studio, working on that body millions of women love."*

The TV showed a grainy clip of Dalton inside the Pilates studio, talking to another man with a blurred-out face, and then a clip of him standing outside, drinking bottled water.

The woman continued, breathlessly: *"While his lips might be smiling that trademark Drake Cheshire smile, the sunglasses conceal the true windows to his soul, and the secret he carries. Millions of women love Drake, but Dalton is unlucky in love, heartbroken after his recent fling with up-and-coming sassy underwear designer, Peaches Monroe."*

A photo of me with my shirt off at the bookstore flashed onto the screen. The picture that put me in the spotlight. My eyes closed reflexively, and the static in my head overpowered all my sensory inputs for a moment. The woman was still talking, but it could have been in a foreign language.

I fell back on the bed and rocked in a fetal position for a moment, chanting a stream of nonsensical swear words, the way any grown woman in this type of situation would.

The woman kept talking, but now the topic had already shifted, to something about Lindsay Lohan. I have never been so happy to hear someone talk about Lindsay Lohan. My stomach lurched when the woman made a quip about poor ol' misunderstood Lindsay hooking up with Dalton, but everyone in the gossip headquarters office laughed, so I knew it was a joke.

The next segment was all about celebrity baby bumps.

"Get a life," I said to the TV, but I didn't change the channel.

~

Two hours later, Keith hadn't returned from driving Tabitha home. Even if she lived on the other side of the city, it was past eleven on a Thursday night, so surely he could have gotten back, unless...

Unless he was making her a trouser-meat sandwich with extra mayo.

GROSS!

I ransacked Keith's kitchen, then got started with a vodka and soda, easy on the soda.

~

Midnight.

Four drinks drinked. *Drinked?* Drank? *Downed.*

No sign of Keith. Obviously he was expending his coveted man-mayonnaise on Tabitha's bologne flaps.

WHAT?!

I called his cell, but he didn't pick up. I called it eleventy-seven times and still NO PICKY UPPIE.

Which was probably for the best, considering how juiced up I was.

I put in a call to the Last Good Man in Los Angeles. "Mitchell come get meeeeeeeeeee!"

163

He had me go outside and get the address for him off the side of the building, since he couldn't remember where it was, then he swore he'd come for me, with reinforcements.

~

One more drink later.

Mitchell showed up at the door, with two tall men towering behind him.

"Hello, boys!" I said.

"We're playing a game," Mitchell said. "One of these sexy boys is straight, and it's up to you to figure it out."

I pointed at the teutonic blond. "I hope it's that one."

"Gunnar," the blond man said, reaching out to shake my hand, then going in for the hand kiss.

Hand kiss? Oh, Gunnar was the gay one, *for realsies-for suresies.*

The other tall man, with sandy brown hair, said, "I'm Daniel. I've heard a lot about you, Peaches. Now I'm extra-sorry I didn't get a call-back for the shoot with you."

"Me, too." I grinned up at his bright, white teeth. Wow, they were really white. He looked like he just stepped off the hot-male-model factory line.

"May I?" Daniel leaned in and kissed me, right on the lips. He lingered, the scent of his skin and after shave getting into my head.

A mouth kiss? Daniel was over-compensating, which meant he was the gay one, not Gunnar.

I frowned at Mitchell, who merely shrugged and looked angelic. Classic Mitchell.*

*After six drinks, I could have sworn Mitchell and I went way back to high school. Did I say I'd had five drinks earlier? I meant six.

Gunnar looked past me, sneaking a peek at the apartment. The table was pushed back over to the window, and the folding chairs were gone.

He said, "Any girlfriends you want to invite along?"

I laughed, then veered dangerously close to sobbing like a drunk, hysterical girl. Shayla should have come with me to LA. I was not equipped to handle any of this stuff alone.

"Just me," I said, forcing a grin. "Mitchell, how will we all fit in your Miada?"

Daniel offered me his elbow like a gentleman. "We have a limo and driver. Come on, let's have some fun and get our pictures taken."

I gasped, my hands on either side of my face like some cartoon drunk version of myself. "Photos! The paparazzi! I look like crap!"

Mitchell helped himself to the contents of my purse. I didn't even know how he found my purse, considering I'd been searching for it the last half hour.

The boys deemed my green sundress to be party-appropriate. Mitchell quickly powdered my face and applied a pink lipstick to my lips. "Never go dark for a night out," he said. "The flash makes your skin look pale and even the smallest smear of lipstick will give you a fallen-star look."

"Perfect," Gunnar said. "That's a good pink, and you can leave some on my neck later."

"You're bad." I swatted at him.

Then we were on our way.

I walked out Keith's door and shut it behind me. Who would be returning there first? Not me.

The tall escorts each took one side of me, linking my arms with theirs, and we walked through the quiet courtyard and out the gate to a waiting vehicle—a stretch limousine.

"Now we're talking!" I said. "Let's find some trouble."

Mitchell smirked as he held open the door.

I climbed into the limo, and no sooner had I gotten settled than I had a champagne flute in my hand.

"Here's to new friends," Mitchell said.

"And future old friends," I added.

We clinked glasses and the air tinkled with magic. *Magic*, I tell you! Exclamation point necessary!

~

Going out in LA bears absolutely no resemblance to going out partying in Beaverdale.

First of all, nobody in LA wears polar fleece shirts or those fleece-lined jackets Shayla refers to as Canadian Tuxedos.

People have to dress *up* to get into the good clubs, and they line up out front behind velvet ropes. Yes, velvet ropes. That stuff you see on TV is real!

In our first line of the night, my three men posed for the lady with the clipboard. I didn't know what to do, so I smiled really big, like a pageant contestant.

She looked me up and down. "Team Peaches," she said, nodding. The woman had a little junk in her black-jeans-wearing trunk, so call it my lucky night that I encountered the only plus-sized club promoter in the city. She sent us in to the club, only to get smacked in the face by loud music and a cloud of cologne.

I coughed a few times and gradually acclimatized, like an alien visitor on Planet Swanky. We wandered through the club, which could also be called Planet Hoochie, and I spotted some upper levels separated by staircases and guarded by security staff with headsets. I craned my neck to see who was up there. In amongst some fine-looking ladies were a few men as tall as Washington fir trees. Basketball players. Famous ones.

I got the fame-proximity giggles. The next platform we walked past had a skinny white guy in a ton of jewelry, with two ladies on either side of him. This made me giggle so hard.

Mitchell looped his arm around my waist and asked, "What's so funny?"

I wiped a tear from the corner of my eye. "I don't know. It's like a petting zoo in here, but with famous people instead of zebras."

The four of us squeezed our way around an empty table and leaned in, elbows on the table.

The blond hottie, Gunnar, asked if I was having fun, and the other guy, Daniel, ordered a bottle of champagne for the table. Mitchell just gave me that look, like, *Do I know how to show you a good time, or what?*

I nodded back at him. *Yes, you do, Mitchell. Yes, you do.*

~

Three hours later.

I'd just tinkled on someone's front lawn, and my whole body was sticky from letting the guys drink champagne from my chest in the limo. Or did that start at the club? I couldn't remember, and it didn't matter.

My feet didn't hurt at all, which concerned me, because they'd been hurting an hour earlier, after all the dancing. I checked that they were still attached to my body.

I climbed back into the limo, saying, "Achievement unlocked! I just tinkled on someone's lawn. I've never done that before. It's quite liberating. Now I understand why you men are always widdling everywhere."

Daniel slid closer to me on the bench seat of the limo and kissed my shoulder. "Let's go skinny dipping."

I slid away, keeping a little distance between us. Flirting and dancing was fine, but I wasn't about to play hide-the-swizzle-stick with my second model of the trip. Besides, after all that booze, I couldn't even feel my woowoo.

The other guys didn't say much, because they were making out.

"They're so cute," I said, smiling at the two guys, one tall and one short, both blond, kissing in a tender way. "You don't see that much where I'm from."

Daniel wiped my hair behind my ear and gazed down at me. "Small town?"

"Not too small. Just the right size. Oh, we do have gay people. We have a big pride weekend in August, but it's not like in the bigger cities."

"I grew up in LA. Everything I know about small town life comes from movies or books."

Interesting. We were the exact opposite of each other. "There are magazines, if you're interested."

He touched my cheek, pulling away when he sensed my discomfort. Folding his hands in his lap, he said, "So, what's your story? Is it true what they're saying about you and Dalton Deangelo? Did you break his heart?"

"Hah! More like the other way around."

"I'm sorry to hear that." He got a sly grin, his ultra-white teeth flashing brightly inside the limo's interior. We were moving, driving

167

somewhere, but I'd forgotten where we were headed. He said, "So, are you looking for a rebound?"

"Hah! Already taken care of. Long story. Doesn't matter. But you should know, I won't be doing anything with you tonight. I need to give my lips and heart a break."

He shrugged. "Can't blame a guy for holding out hope, though."

"Why bother? I mean, why me? You could have picked up a dozen girls at the club. You could have taken two, on account of how small and flimsy they are."

"Like those skinny sticks of gum."

"Exactly. So, why are you attracted to me? Is it because you thought I was a sure thing? That you wouldn't have to try as hard, like with a pretty girl?"

"You *are* a pretty girl."

"You know what I mean. I'm not exactly Los Angeles material."

He used his finger to tap me on the tip of my nose, once, like pressing a reset button. "Exactly."

With that, I felt my whole brain shift. *I'm not exactly Los Angeles material.* Ah, it all made sense. I was the alternative option. The flip-side. The special kosher meal on the long flight. The road not taken.

Everything about my life made sense, the way it only can after a night of drinking, dancing with hot guys, and illegal lawn watering.

The car came to a stop, and Mitchell and Gunnar stopped kissing long enough to open the door and get out.

"I should go back to the apartment," I said. "My friend's place, not yours, Daniel. No offense. I'm sure you're as tender and sensitive a lover as you are a good dancer, and you are a very good dancer."

"This isn't my place," Daniel said. "It's a friend's and there's the most amazing pool. We can watch the sun rise. Look how the horizon is pink. Won't be long."

"Come on," Mitchell said, holding out his hand.

I grabbed the unopened champagne bottle from the ice bucket as I climbed out of the car. "I guess we'll need refreshments."

Daniel followed me out of the car, and we made our way along a path, past a gardening shed, to the back of a mansion. We passed a half-dozen security signs that everyone ignored. We were in another ritzy neighborhood—Malibu, Daniel told me as we walked through an unlocked garden gate. The houses here were quite far apart, but the two or three I could make out the shapes of in the dark looked impressive.

I got the hiccups, plus the giggles, which made for loud hiccups.

We located the pool, which was set on the edge of a hill, and had an infinity edge—the wall was glass, and the water line met the top of the glass. The guys all stripped down to their underwear and splashed into the pool.

My head was woozy. Time had been passing in jumps, but I felt good.

I popped open the champagne bottle and took a seat on a lounge chair next to the pool. A spot on the inside of my hip bone felt sore, like I'd bruised myself. I wanted to rinse off my sticky body, but I also wanted to put my feet up and rest. Just for a minute. Just to catch my breath.

I took a long, refreshing drink from the champagne bottle, and lay back with my head on the padded headrest. The horizon glowed a vibrant shade of orange-pink, and soon the sun would be coming up.

The guys splashed each other in the pool, laughing and horsing around. I didn't know who lived in the main house, but it was so far away from the pool, they'd never hear us, nor would the distant neighbors.

"Not bad, Malibu," I said to myself.

I thought about how a pair of sunglasses would make everything perfect, then I glanced over to my left and saw a pair of sunglasses on the table next to me. I hiccuped again as I donned the sunglasses.

The boys kept splashing in the pool, having a great time.

"This is more like it," I said as I settled back into the chair to watch the sun come up.

CHAPTER 17

I woke up to a woman in mirrored, aviator-style sunglasses gently shaking me.

"Tell me right now, ma'am, do you have any needles or sharps on your person?"

"What?" I tried to sit up, but she pressed me down with one hand. The woman was strong, and she was wearing a shiny badge on her shirt. My grogginess evaporated instantly.

"Do you have any drug paraphernalia on you?" she asked.

"No, ma'am." I took a closer look at her badge, noting the name of a security company. She wasn't a cop, but that still didn't mean I wasn't going to get arrested and be made someone's jail wife. I wanted to have some fun in LA, but not as a jail wife.

"If you're not on drugs, why are you here?"

"We came here with Daniel," I said.

"Daniel who?"

"Daniel... um. Big teeth. Really nice. Tall. I think he's a model."

"Are you sure you aren't on drugs? Because your friend over there is not very tall."

She nodded toward Mitchell, who was sitting on a lounger across the pool from me. He was doing nothing but looking helpless, with a plastic strap around his wrists.

This time, I sat up, shoving her hand away. "Oh, no. You need to untie him immediately. This is kidnapping. You can't tie him up."

The woman put one hand on her hip, delivering me a whole lot of attitude with a side dish of oh-no-you-didn't.

"We'll see about that," she said.

As far as I could tell, she was the only person there besides me and Mitchell. I looked closely at her, but the dark sunglasses weren't giving away much. She wore a necklace with a locket that had popped open, showing a photo of two little kids.

"Are you arresting us?" I asked.

"You will be charged with trespassing," she said. "As well as theft."

"Theft!"

"Those sunglasses are worth over three hundred dollars. I know that because my no-good sister spent the money I gave her for food, buying a pair of those same ones."

I looked over at Mitchell for some sign. He sat frozen. My purse was at his feet, but looked unopened.

Trespassing and theft.

Before I tell you what I did next, please bear in mind I was desperate, and I was scared.

Sure, we were still in America, and I was pretty sure we had rights, but I wasn't totally sure what they were. The phrase *jail wife* kept flashing through my head.

I gasped. "Where's Ricky?"

The mean security woman put both hands on her hips. "Ricky who?"

I started crying. It wasn't difficult to pull off, because I actually was scared. Also, the hangover was making itself known by now, with its blistering brain-pain, made worse by the hot sun overhead.

"Ricky is my son. He's five. He went over by those bushes over there to pee, and I just laid down for a minute to rest my eyes."

"Ma'am, you brought your son with you to trespass on a Malibu property?"

I sniffed. "We're supposed to go to Disneyland today." I looked over her shoulder. "Ricky! Get over here!"

"You just stay right here for a minute." She lowered her sunglasses just enough to give me the Mother of the Year Award, then she ambled off toward the bushes.

I was pretty sure she didn't believe me, but then again, as a security guard, she'd probably seen a lot of bad life choices in action.

I didn't take long to consider my options. I tore off the stolen sunglasses and tossed them on the lounge chair. I hustled over to Mitchell, only to find his ankles were also bound with another thick, plastic strap.

"This is insane," he whispered. "How did we even get here?"

I unzipped my purse, grabbed my trusty nail clippers, and tried to clip through the plastic band. I growled in a threatening manner.

"Use the nail file," he whispered.

"There is no file. I took this on the airplane." I stared up at his angelic face. "I'll have to carry you," I said.

His eyes widened. "No."

I shouldered in and grabbed him before he could protest too loudly. I stood up with him on my shoulder, glad for all the practice I'd had hauling Kyle around this way.

"I can't believe I'm doing this," I groaned as I hauled Mitchell along the pathway, toward the side of the mansion.

He wheezed, "You're so strong. Don't take this the wrong way, but I'm a little turned on right now."

I slapped his butt.

We reached the side of the mansion, and Mitchell was slipping around due to all the sweat coming off of me.

"Gardening shed," he said.

I groaned, still moving forward with him on my shoulder, albeit slower.

"Gardening tools," he said.

"Right." I set him down and ran over to the shed, feeling feather-light without Mitchell on my shoulder. I quickly located a pair of pruning sheers, ran back, and used them to cut Mitchell's restraints.

The security lady had figured out my little ruse and was now yelling for us to return immediately. Yeah, right.

We hit the end of the driveway and kept running, down the adjoining road.

A vehicle pulled up behind us and followed us slowly. I peeked back to make sure it wasn't a security vehicle, ready to dive off into some bushes if necessary. The car was black, with tinted windows.

The passenger-side window rolled down, and a male voice called out. "You folks need a ride somewhere?"

Mitchell stopped, his hands on his hips as he bent forward gasping. "Yes, please. You're a lifesaver."

I caught my reflection in the window before it finished rolling down. I looked like someone covered in sticky champagne and dust, who'd just spent the night partying and had makeup smeared down her face.

"Sure, we'd love a ride," I said.

The window finished lowering, and I gazed into the devilishly handsome green eyes of Dalton Deangelo.

"On second thought, I'll walk," I said.

Mitchell was already climbing into the back, though, and I could hear the security guard woman yelling as she got closer.

"Fuck my life," I said, and I reluctantly climbed into the front seat.

~

Dalton's car was comfortable and cool—a black BMW that looked expensive, but not as flashy as I'd expected.

"Fancy meeting you here," Dalton said, looking like a vampire who just ate a nice family.

From the back seat, Mitchell said, "Hey! You're Dalton Deangelo. I'm a huge fan. I just want to say that Connor is the worst, and I'm Team Drake all the way. I don't like how Connor drags all his lines out. Just. Too. Dramatic. Oh, listen to me. I'm a total rabid fanboy. Please someone, just knock me out right now or I won't stop talking." He paused all of two seconds. "Is it true that Drake's backstory is based on your life? I mean, aside from the whole serial killer thing. Did you grow up in an orphanage and have to fight other boys in an underground fight club? Wait, I'm being stupid. We don't have orphanages these days, and you're mortal, so that can't be true." I heard the sound of his palm hitting his forehead. "Why do I always embarrass myself like this? Seriously, though, if I was a girl, I'd have your babies." He let out a shocked gasp, as though he couldn't believe the words coming out of his own mouth. "I'm so hungover! I'm not even thinking straight. Not that I ever think straight, ha ha.

Hey, what were those pills we were taking last night? Oh, Peaches, I don't feel very—"

Dalton interrupted, "Dude, are you going to throw up? Don't chuck in my car."

I turned back to see Mitchell's face turn a sickly shade of pale. He had his lips pressed together so hard, they were white, and sweat was streaming down his face.

"You should probably pull over," I said to Dalton.

Frowning, he pulled the car into what looked like a park, with one of those playground sets. It seemed ridiculously out of place, in the Malibu neighborhood full of giant mansions, and I wasn't surprised to see that the only people using the park were a teen couple making out on a bench under a tree.

Mitchell opened the back door, stepped out, and commenced with the water-splashdown sound. This triggered my gag reflex, but I fought it, hard.

Mitchell sobbed, "I'll never drink again," in between splashes. Then, after a minute, "Huh. That's interesting."

Curiosity got the better of me, and I stepped out of the car. There on the grass was a bright green plastic ring with a pretend diamond.

A memory danced through my brain. Mitchell, holding the ring up and pretending to propose to me. I said yes, then he swallowed the ring and chased it down with Jack Daniels, straight from the bottle.

We'd bought the rings and some other kids' toys from vending machines, right outside the...

My body turned icy cold, like a cloud just passed over my whole life.

"Mitchell, where did we go last night after they kicked us out of the club?"

"I don't know. I shouldn't have taken those pharmaceuticals."

I wiped my mouth, because the inside of it tasted like how I imagine an organic fertilizer factory smells. Something sat in the corner of my memory, but when I tried to reach for it, instead of the detail from last night, I got perfect recall of a news story about a woman who heard a scratching noise inside her ear that turned out to be maggots tunneling toward her brain.

I bent over and blasted the grass with bile, champagne, and what tasted not unlike pool water. Wait. It was pool water. "Gotta hydrate yourself," was one of the things I'd said the night before as I stuck my face in the pool water and took a good drink.

Okay, that was gross, but why hadn't I gone into the pool and washed my sticky body off? I love being in the water.

And why did I have something crinkly inside the waistband of my panties, just above where my pubic hair started?

I pulled up the hem of my dress at the front.

"Whoa, not here!" Dalton said. He'd gotten out of the car to either help or laugh, and he hadn't held my hair back when I chucked, so clearly he was there to laugh at me.

Ignoring him, I pulled out the waistband of my underwear. I had what looked like a paper towel, folded in a square, taped to me.

Right. The vending machines were right outside a tattooist's shop. And the boys had gotten temporary tattoos in their prize packs, but my plastic bubble had a bracelet that broke when I tried to put it on. Then I'd started crying about having big wrists. (Why couldn't I have forgotten that embarrassing detail?) Daniel cheered me up by offering to buy me a tattoo.

I dropped my green sundress back down. The sun was high overhead, and the smell of someone's stomach contents was getting to me. The square of paper taped to me was only two inches wide, so how bad could it be? Knowing me, the tattoo was probably a cartoon peach. I could work with that.

Dalton was hovering and had already come to the same conclusion as I had. "You got a tattoo?" he asked.

"Yup. Team Connor. I'm switching sides now for when *One Vamp to Love* comes back in the fall."

"No, you didn't." He looked amused.

"It's totally Team Connor, dummy."

He frowned. "Dummy? That's not nice. I picked you two up, and I could have kept driving."

I remembered his sensitivity about being called a meat puppet, and the reputation of good-looking actors being dumb.

Mitchell asked Dalton, "How did you happen to be exactly where you were? Peaches told us last night you don't live in Malibu." He was still hunched over, but appeared to be finished being sick, by the way the pink had returned to his cheeks.

Dalton gave me a devious smile, his green eyes as mischievous as ever, and that million-dollar dimple in his chin mocking me. "My little secret."

I tossed my purse down on the ground. "You had a tracking device implanted in my bag! You weirdo rich freak!"

He started laughing, then doubled over, and finally fell back on the grass, rolling with laughter.

Mitchell looked over at me. "That's a little paranoid."

Dalton sat up, still grinning. "Show me your tattoo, and I'll tell you how I knew you were in trouble."

"No way."

Mitchell got my attention and pointed to the nearby water fountain. We both dragged our bodies to the water like zombies, and drank deeply.

Normally, public fountains gross me out, but I would have wrapped my lips around this one happily. Sweet, sweet water.

I was still enjoying the water when Dalton grabbed my arm. "Come on, we gotta go."

Pulling my arm away, I snarled, "Don't touch me."

He held up his hands. "I'm done." He backed away slowly, hands still up. "You'll look awesome in the paparazzi photos. Really. Good luck with that, and have a nice life."

Photos? I spotted a car rolling into the near-deserted park, a long camera lens visible behind the front windshield. Paparazzi.

Mitchell and I ran toward the car, Mitchell muttering about Team Drake all the way, and me apologizing in between curse words.

Dalton let us into the vehicle, and we took off, kicking up gravel with the tires. Mitchell clapped his hands. The windows were tinted, and nobody could see in, but I still slouched down low in the front seat, covering my face with my hand.

"Let's get brunch," Dalton said.

Mitchell squealed and started back into fanboy mode again.

When Mitchell finally stopped to breathe for a minute, I said to Dalton, "Are you seriously inviting us for brunch?"

"I have the time off. You and I were supposed to be spending this whole week together."

"Right." I felt about three inches tall. Meekly, I said, "Sorry I snapped at you. I'm a little hung over."

"No, really?!"

"Can you lower the volume of your sarcasm before you make my ears bleed?"

"Someone had a fun night."

"And can we pull over at a gas station so I can take a whore's bath at the very least?"

He turned to me, one dark eyebrow raised magnificently.

I explained, "That's where you get a wet paper towel and just... do your armpits... and... oh, never mind." I covered my face again. "Stop looking at me. I can feel your eyes groping me, Dalton Deangelo."

Mitchell piped up from the back set. "We could swing by my apartment and freshen up. My roommate has some dresses that would look great on Peaches."

I turned back to face Mitchell, who was looking peppier by the minute. "I thought your roommate's name was Steve?"

"His drag name is Luscious Hilda Mae Sparkles. She's inspired by this plus-size vintage pin-up girl from the fifties, plus Mariah Carey. Of course."

"Of course," I said, trying to wrap my dehydrated brain around the concept.

Mitchell gave Dalton his address, and we were at the door in twenty-five minutes.

I took the first shower, while Mitchell very awkwardly entertained Dalton by showing him his collection of vintage LA postcards from the sixties.

Alone in the bathroom, I pulled off my sticky, sweaty dress, and stared at myself in the mirror. I still had a square patch of paper towel stuck to myself, a few inches inside my front hip bone, and I didn't have the nerve to see what lay beneath the bandage. The skin stung, like a scrape or a burn.

There was cellophane over the paper, so I made sure the tape was water resistant and got into the shower. The bathroom was really old, everything pink and blue from the fifties, but it was clean and welcoming, and I was grateful. The shower head was better than average for an old apartment.

Steve/Luscious Hilda Mae Sparkles was at her day job at the coffee shop he/she managed, but had given approval by text message for me to wear anything from the costume closet. After my shower, I zipped into a retro floral dress with a pink sash for a belt. I'd hand-washed my champagne-sticky underwear in the shower and dried them somewhat with the hair dryer before putting them back on.

I let Mitchell take over the bathroom, and I came out to find Dalton sitting at an easel with a paintbrush in his hand.

"That's random," I said.

"I like to paint."

CHAPTER 18

I took a seat on the orange-vinyl vintage sofa across from him. "You like to paint? Yup, that explains everything." The sofa cushion compressed slowly under me, letting out an embarrassingly audible wheezing of air.

Dalton continued to dab at a canvas with his paintbrush, loaded up with tangerine-orange paint.

He said, "Mitchell likes for guests to contribute to the decoration of the apartment, by putting a cheerful saying on a canvas."

I looked around the room, noticing that some of the paintings I thought were abstract color washes actually had words on them.

The biggest painting, on the long wall, read: *After a storm comes a calm, Matthew Henry.*

I said, "It's like we're sitting inside a Pinterest board."

Dalton laughed. "Is that an internet thing? I don't go online. Too toxic."

"It's a page where you share over-engineered craft projects you'll never actually do. But look at my man, Mitchell. He's really doing the whole make-your-own-art thing." I crossed my legs, feeling it was the only appropriate pose for such a low-rider sofa. People must have been way shorter a couple generations back, because the furniture legs are tiny.

Dalton got up and fetched us both bottles of water from the kitchen.

This is weird, I thought, and then I couldn't un-think it. Here I was, hanging out with Dalton Deangelo, in LA, only we weren't dating. I wouldn't be licking the side of his gorgeous neck or riding him like a pony back in his palatial master bedroom. We were going to have brunch. With our chaperone/fanboy.

And then, after a few minutes, it didn't feel so weird anymore. We could just be in a room, and not put each other's body parts in our mouths. That's how friends are.

I raised my water bottle. "To future old friends, which is what we are."

He cracked the lid off his bottle, but didn't move in for the toast. "Are we friends now? Have you forgiven me for words written on a piece of paper by someone who isn't me?"

"I wasn't mad about the words on the paper. It was you saying them."

"I thought you were mostly irate about the tasteless threesome joke in the manuscript. By the way, we cut that out in the final draft. I thought the joke made my character unlikeable."

"I hate your character. He sucks."

Dalton stared steadily at me, his green eyes giving away nothing but inner stillness and control. "Why were you out partying last night with your new buddy? What happened to underpants boy? Michael Crow or whatever?"

"Keith Raven. Don't act like you can't remember his name."

Dalton's sultry lips quirked up in a smirk. "You didn't answer my question. Why didn't you spend the night in your new man's arms?"

I looked down at the piping on the orange vinyl sofa and flicked at the worn-thin spots with my fingernail. Fine filaments like fur were sticking out along the cracks.

After a moment, I said, "I think he spent the night in the bony arms of his model skank ex-girlfriend. I'm not sure. I kinda just left and haven't checked in yet."

"So you ran out on him, lathered up in an emotional tizzy, yet he's the one in the doghouse?"

"Maybe." I chugged my water, still avoiding eye contact.

"I'm starting to see a pattern," he said.

The tissh-tissh sound of the paintbrush on the canvas started again, so it was safe for me to look up.

"What are you painting? Turn it and show me. My bare legs are stuck to this ridiculous couch and I can't get up."

"Peaches Monroe, guys always let you down, don't they?"

"No comment."

"They say every story has a happy ending, if you stop in the right place. I'd say you make sure your relationships have a bad ending, because you run out before a minor misunderstanding can run its course."

I swallowed hard. "If you're trying to make me feel like crap on toast, it's working. I'm dressed in a drag queen's clothes, I got a tattoo I'm too scared to look at, I narrowly escaped getting arrested, and now the world's most beloved TV vampire is telling me I suck at life."

Dalton slowly turned the wood-framed easel to face my way. The image was mostly blue, like sky above ocean, with an orange circle like the sun, and in white letters: *Trust the process.*

"I don't get it."

Dalton stroked his chin thoughtfully. "*Trust the process* is one of the things my best acting teacher used to say. Basically, it means... well, it means whatever you want it to mean. My process is not your process."

"Maybe you should be dating Keith. He's into all sorts of spiritual stuff. Do you like parsley shakes?"

"You don't suck at life. And Keith seems like a good guy. I feel protective of you. I'm your friend, remember? I knew it from the day we met." His expression got serious. "I feel rotten about the NDA I had you sign. I've never told anyone about my past before, and I was caught off guard by how exposed I felt. I'm sorry I put you in that position."

"I'm sorry... I'm sorry I freaked out and ran off all those times. Especially the last time." I drank the last bit of water from the bottle. "But here we are. No hard feelings. I'm ready to be your friend."

Mitchell came out of the bathroom in a cloud of steam just as I was finishing. "And I'm ready for bru-uuuu-uuunch!" he sang.

My stomach growled, because apparently my stomach recognizes the word *brunch*, even when flamboyantly sung.

~

We were going to try the Hollywood hot spot, Mr. Chow, but the swarm of photographers made Dalton keep driving. Instead, the three of us went to brunch at a bistro with white tablecloths and paintings of fruit on the walls—real paintings, not those cheap mass market prints you get at chain stores.

My breakfast was a spinach and olive omelet, and it came with gorgeous fresh fruit, including ripe pineapple and papaya. Oh, plus there were tiny slivers of various cheeses. So good. *Myam myam*, as they say in some circles.

Mitchell had finally toned down his fanboy-ness and was asking Dalton questions about the show—questions Dalton seemed quite pleased to answer, such as what did the fake blood taste like? (Corn syrup.) Was the director a nightmare to work with? (No, but the director's assistant was a control freak.)

They talked about photography, and then got onto Quentin Tarantino films, both of them becoming gushing fanboys about how much they'd love to work with him, or with Nicolas Refn, whose film violence was "stylish, but more chilling than Tarantino's."

The waitress was attentive, never letting my ice water get more than one third empty.

The conversation veered into the territory of some of my favorite movies, and it turned out Mitchell was a great conversational link, because he liked dude movies and chick movies. The three of us had a great talk, and two hours passed easily.

I'd had a number of mochas, and excused myself to the washroom, which had really great lighting and fresh flowers.

In there, I pulled out my cell phone and checked for messages from Keith. He'd only sent one, and it wasn't what I expected.

Keith: *Sounds like you're having fun! Thanks for checking in!*

I shook my fist at Last Night Peaches, who had apparently sent him a dozen messages babbling about hanging out with Mitchell (whom Keith had met at the photo shoot), talking about the club we were at, and even saying I was dancing with all the LA Lakers guys.*

*That was actually a teensy lie, because I remembered most of being at the club. I actually danced with a couple tall guys who were

184

LA Lakers *fans*, but when you're drunk and name-dropping by text, you get a little fast and loose with the facts.

There was no panic in Keith's single reply, because I'd apparently assured him I'd be crashing at Mitchell's place. Neither was there any explanation from him about what he was doing for three hours with his drunk and vulnerable ex-girlfriend, with her tears and her ratty fake hair and her quivering lower lip.

Just thinking about her nearly made me rage-flush my phone. I sent him back a message designed to get him squirming.

Me: *So, should I come back there to get my stuff, or what do you want?*

Perfect. Just vague enough I could play it either way depending on how he responded. If he was guilty, he'd assume I knew everything, and 'fess up. If he hadn't played Enjoy My Tasty Burrito with his ex, he'd tell me to get back over there and play a round with him.

I tucked my phone away and fixed my makeup. I'd spotted a couple photographers outside the restaurant, so I figured it best to be prepared.

When I came back to the table, the two guys were strangely quiet and grinning.

"What's going on?"

"We were just discussing your commercial shoot on Monday," Mitchell said.

I took my seat, careful to smooth out the floral skirt of the drag queen's dress.

"I wish I was done with all my obligations," I said.

"You miss your little town?" Dalton asked.

"No." Yes, I did, but I didn't want him to know, to think I was too weak to spend a week away from home—to think I was like those wimpy kids at summer camp who sob inconsolably on the first night.

"She's adapting just fine to LA," Mitchell said.

"Thank you." I gave him my sweetest smile.

Dalton put his elbow on the table, rested his chin on his hand, and stared at me as if Mitchell wasn't even there. "What are your plans for the rest of the day?"

I squirmed in my chair. "Keith is busy with other stuff, so I'm just going to hang out."

"Wanna come hang out at my house?" The light in the restaurant practically danced in his sexy green eyes.

"Stop looking at me like you're the fox and you just got the keys to my hen house."

"I'm not. You're projecting your ravenous sexual desires onto me."

"Oh my," I coughed, pretty sure the tables around us quieted down to listen.

"This is the downside to being a sex symbol," Dalton said to Mitchell, all the while keeping his gaze on me. "These women, and their craven fantasies. They have all these wicked ideas about what they want to do to you, but they're like domesticated cats who finally catch a rabbit. Once they have you, they get all kittenish and embarrassed. The truth is, despite all their one-sided fantasies, once they have you, they don't know *what* to do with you."

"Hah!"

He continued, "The thing about a fantasy is you can have magical spells and goblins in a fantasy. Or relationships with no rocky patches, ever. In real life? Not so much."

I put my chin on my hand, mirroring Dalton's pose. "In my fantasies, the guy doesn't lie to get into the girl's pants, passing off movie lines as his own feelings."

"But the guy touches the girl just right, doesn't he? And he keeps things interesting on their dates, takes her places she's never been. He lavishes the girl with affection, and he's true to her."

"He shouldn't be too intense, though. He should back off sometimes and give her space."

"Or what? She'll wail about needing to be alone, then immediately rush into the bed of another guy?"

Mitchell waved his hand between us to interrupt. "Guys, chill. You're causing a scene."

I shook my head. "We can't be friends. Maybe in the distant future, but not yet."

Dalton sighed, then gave me a contrite look. "We tried. I guess it just wasn't in the stars."

People around us were staring, so we quickly got up and made our way to the exit. Dalton had picked up the bill while I was in the washroom, and we both thanked him for lunch.

He put on some sunglasses before reaching for the door handle. He turned to me, his eyes hidden behind the mirrored lenses. "Hey, if you want to get some publicity for your underwear line, look cozy next to me when we step out of here."

"Right. Of course." He'd extended his hand toward me, and I took it. We walked out of the restaurant, hand-in-hand, for the benefit of the awaiting paparazzi.

Mitchell trailed along a few feet behind, largely ignored.

Dalton dropped my hand and wrapped his arm around my shoulders—for publicity, of course. And then he held my door open at the car. He twirled me, pressing me against the car frame, and he kissed me. Just one very deliberate kiss, right on the lips. For publicity, of course.

I got in the car, my head spinning from the kiss. It was as though he'd had a venom on his lips, and it was numbing my whole body.

Dalton and Mitchell talked some more about movies on the way back to Mitchell's place, but I didn't say a word. I just sat there. Numb. I got out at Mitchell's and thanked Dalton again for lunch.

As he drove away in his not-too-flashy BMW, Mitchell said, "I have to write about this on my blog. Please don't judge me, but I stole the napkin he used to wipe his mouth."

"Too late. I'm judging you."

"Can I smell your lips? Do they smell like Dalton Deangelo?" He laughed. "Wait, no. You kiss me and transfer some of his kiss to my lips."

"You are so weird. Maybe that's why I love you."

He linked his arm with mine. "Come on in. We only have about eight hours to figure out what we're wearing to go clubbing tonight."

"Clubbing again?"

"It's Friday. Duh."

He did have a point.

~

Some time later.

I woke up.

It was dark.

Oh, because my eyes were shut.

OW! Opening my eyes was a bad idea.

Something brushed up against me, beside me. I was on my back, somewhere soft.

Something—an arm—flopped over my chest. A human arm. Not my own.

I cracked open my eyelids. The arm was covered in dark hair, so it wasn't Mitchell's blond arm, and it wasn't the drag queen Luscious Hilda Mae Sparkles' arm, because he/she used Veet to remove everything, and I do mean *everything*. (We had kind of a nice girl moment getting ready to go out clubbing Friday night, and Luscious showed me this great after-care product for preventing in-growns.)

"Good morning, sunshine," said the man I was apparently in bed with.

I silently vowed to never drink again, and rolled over to face the end result of a series of questionable decisions, including taking whatever Luscious handed me the night before at the first club. She said it was like a No-Doz, but it was more like a Red Bull crossed with a hand grenade.

At least I still had my clothes on, which meant I probably hadn't done anything regrettable with...

Keith Raven.

"You look surprised," he whispered.

"This is just how my face looks in the morning."

CHAPTER 19

Keith chuckled. "I bet you don't remember anything you said to me last night."

"When I drink, I lie. Did I tell you I speak three languages? That's a lie. You can't believe anything I say when I'm drinking."

"What is the Closet of Regret?"

"Um... it's this second closet I have in my room back home. Someone who lived there before me carved out some walled-off space and put a door on it." I licked my lips. "Talking is hard work. Anyway, I put some of my regrettable purchases in there."

"Like your cuckoo clock."

"Um, yes. Keith, I'm sorry I bored you last night with stories about my online shopping problems."

"You weren't boring at all. We had a good talk. Really good. You said that you regret all the things you never did, and you regret not being more fun, and you'd like to stick your old self in the Closet of Regret and come out as someone new."

"Oh. Well, it's really more of a cupboard. I'm not sure if I'd fit."

"I think it was more of a metaphor, and you agreed that you dismissed the idea of going to Italy with me too easily."

I sat up quickly, then I lost about five seconds to time travel before the blood got up to my brain.

"Hey, I'm mad at you," I said.

"Because I came and picked you up last night when you'd had too much excitement, but your friends wanted to keep partying? Are you mad that I hauled myself out of bed, didn't even get dressed, and drove straight to you in the dead of night, even though you called me bad names on the phone?"

I swallowed hard. "What did I call you?"

He grinned. "You called me girlfriend-banger, and you called me cheese-banger. The second one made me laugh so hard, I had to come get you." He stopped grinning and got a serious look. "Mostly I came because you sounded scared."

I gasped as I remembered being scared and disoriented. "I got lost and I couldn't find Mitchell and his roommate. Oh no, they're probably worried about me."

"Don't worry. I found them before we found you, standing in the shadows behind the DJ booth, your eyes bugging out."

A cry caught in my throat as I remembered how relieved I'd been to see Keith's friendly face. I was so grateful, I didn't even make fun of his flannel pajama pants.

Memories flitted back.

We came back to his apartment, I tried to get into those pajama pants, but he insisted we talk for a bit instead.

And now here we were, both in the same clothes as the night before. I stayed sitting up, staring down at him.

"Thank you for being my hero last night," I said. "Sorry I act like such a jackass sometimes. I tend to shoot first and ask questions later." I traced the wrinkles on the duvet cover with my finger, unable to meet his eyes for the next question. "So, are you back together with your ex? Is she going with you to Italy?"

He snorted. "We're not back together. Oh, she'd like that. You know, the reason I was gone so late Thursday night was she took my van keys, and my phone, and threw them down the hill in her backyard. I had to beg her for a flashlight, and then it took forever to find everything."

"Hmm. I may be hungover, but I'm not an idiot. It's fine if you slept with her, just have the decency to tell me."

He sat up and retrieved his phone from the top of the dresser, where it was charging. The screen was cracked, dark bits of dirt within the crack lines.

"Landed on a rock," he said.

"Your screen looks like how I feel."

The corner of his mouth quirked up. "Cracked and dirty?"

"Used and abused." I swung my legs off the edge of the bed and prepared myself to stand.

"I'll take good care of you. I have an excellent hangover cure."

I rubbed the bandaged spot inside my hip. "Sounds awesome. Do you also have a tattoo remover? Apparently I got a tattoo two nights ago, and get this: I'm too pathetic to pull off the wrap and see what it is."

"Probably an *I Love Keith Raven* tattoo. Very popular with LA girls."

"I hope so, because I can think of worse things."

"Me, too."

I twisted my arm behind my back and pulled down the zipper of the dress, which was another borrowed one, and pretty cute: green with white dots, with shoulder panels of black lace. After wriggling out of the dress, I flopped back on the bed and pointed to the edge of the tape, sticking out of the waistband of my underwear.

"You look first," I said. "Break it to me gently."

He hovered over me, rubbing his hands gleefully, like a mad scientist, then peeled down the tape.

"Oh, that's sweet," he said, followed by, "Hmm. Weird. I don't get it."

I curled up to sitting, sucking my stomach in with the aid of both hands so I could see the little tattoo. It was dark blue, with a tiny squiggle shape—a bird—and then the words *Doves Cry*.

"Huh," I said.

"Okay, you have to tell me what it means."

"I dunno. Maybe I was playing a game of Tattooist's Choice." I twisted my spine so I could look at the tattoo from another angle. "Actually, I really like this. *Doves Cry*. It's like… everybody cries. And that's okay."

"Doves don't really cry, though, do they? Don't they coo? Coo, coo."

"Coo, coo to you, too." I pondered the puzzle of my new tat for a few seconds. Was it a reference to the cuckoo clock in my Closet of Regret? No, that was reaching too far.

Keith jumped off the bed and returned with a whole First Aid kit. "You need to better care of your tattoo," he said.

"I need to take better care of my entire person."

He squeezed out some clear gel and tenderly applied it to my skin. Mmm, that felt nice. He pulled out a giant bandage, like the kind you might use on a skinned knee, and applied it over my new ink. Then he kissed the top of my leg. "All better." He kissed my leg again, then sat up and moved toward my lips.

I stopped him by putting my hand up between us. "Sorry, I need to either brush my teeth or throw them away. I care about you too much to let you kiss me right now."

He tried to convince me that it didn't matter, but I squirmed away from him and ran to the bathroom, where I locked myself in, along with my purse.

I started tidying up, but got distracted. I was eager to show Keith how grateful I was for his heroic rescue the previous night, but I couldn't pass up the chance to check my messages.

According to my outbox, I'd sent him my location the night before using the GPS function. That made sense, as I was in no state to remember the name of the club, which had something to do with either seafood, or astronomy, or possibly both. Saturn Prawn? Dolphin Galaxy? Planet Oyster? Ew, no.

I snorted as I found some photos I'd also sent Keith's way—all pictures of either my cleavage on its own, or my cleavage along with a top-down view of my face in a goofy expression.

But I hadn't just sent those pictures to Keith. I'd also forwarded them to Shayla, and to Adrian.

Oh, and there was a picture response from Adrian.

The picture from him was a little blurry, and looked like a distant image of... some people? Some guy with a shaved head?

Eep!

I dropped the phone on the bath mat.

That was definitely... something.

Adrian had sent me a dick pic?

Oh, no, that was NOT the appropriate response to a little bit of cleavage. Unless…

The next picture sort of excused Adrian's, because it was my own nipple, being squeezed between my fingers. Now, most nipples are not that easily identifiable, and my own are certainly no exception, but Luscious Hilda Mae Sparkles did my nails for our night out, and those were my rainbow-painted nails.

What I did next was exactly what any modern girl in this situation would do. I forwarded the pic to my best friend, Shayla. Oh, I hesitated for half a second, wondering if there was any sort of dick-pic-sender-recipient privilege, but neither of us were lawyers, so I went ahead and sent that bald-man-from-a-distance straight to Shayla's magical wiener-viewing screen. I figured any dude sending a photo of his man-privates to a girl has to know that girl's one to six best friends will also get a gander.

After my phone-business was done, I got showered and scrubbed up.

I took another peek at the tattoo after I got dressed in some stretch jeans and one of my favorite T-shirts, navy blue with silver rivets and sparkles.

Doves Cry.

The letter O had a squiggle on it, so the tattoo could be read as *Daves Cry*. Daves Cry? I didn't know anyone named Dave, and even if I did, the bird over top would make no sense.

Regardless of what it meant, it was a pretty sweet tattoo. I took a picture of it, still red and puffy under the ink, but didn't send it to anyone.

"Don't you look adorable," Keith said as I came out to the living room.

"You, too." I gave him a hug and kissed his stubbly cheek. "You look super-fine in those flannel pajama bottoms. Has anyone ever told you that you could be a model?"

He struck a pose, stretching his shirtless torso to make his ab muscles ripple. "*Scusi, che ore sono?*"

"What?"

"That was my bad Italian. I think I asked you for the time."

I batted my eyelashes. "I always have the time for you, baby." Three more blinks. "Wait. Does this mean you're going to Italy?"

He grinned.

"No way!" I went in for the high five, and he grabbed me in a bear hug, picked me up, and swung me around. I squealed like a little girl.

He put me down, then he picked me up and swung me around again. And then a third time, and he would have kept going for a fourth if I hadn't been wailing, "Put me down before you stretch out my new tattooooooo!"

Keith looked down at me, his lovely brown eyes wide open. "Stretch out your tattoo?"

I rubbed the spot while giving him a serious face. "Yeah, you'll crack it or something."

"You could just say you don't like being swung around." He hooked his finger in one of the belt loops of my jeans and tugged me toward him. "You could also say you're terrified I might ask you to come to Italy with me."

I rubbed his biceps, which seemed bigger now. "Look at you, all pumped up."

"Grrrr." He posed, flexing everything, including the sinewy muscles on the sides of his neck. "I haven't worked out in over a week." His face grew red as he kept flexing and posing. "Hey, let's go to the gym after we have some lunch."

I laughed and pushed past him into the kitchen, where coffee awaited, next to powdered chocolate for my mocha.

"I'm serious," he said. "Come and work out with me. You'll burn off that hangover and feel awesome in no time."

"Not gonna happen. I like to walk, because it gets me where I'm going. I like to carry around boxes of books, because it's my job. I don't do Stairmaster, and I don't do torture devices."

"My gym is great, though."

I finished preparing my mocha and took it over to the sofa, since somebody's skanky ex-girlfriend took the chairs, and I felt a little too woozy for the kitchen stools. I could feel Keith's gaze on me as I took a seat, so I sat carefully without any groans, though the tops of my thighs were sore from booty-shaking the night before.

Keith continued, "They've got complimentary towels."

I reached for a magazine from the lower level of the coffee table, finding only *Men's Fitness* and one lone copy of *Vogue*, with Keith's ex-girlfriend's name on it.

"Tabitha's last name is Fartz?"

"Oh, that was kind of an inside joke. That's not really her last name."

I sipped my mocha, flipping through the magazine. "I have a difficult time hating someone with such an awesome fake last name."

Keith walked into the bedroom and called out from inside the room, "Your loss if you won't go to the gym with me. I have to go, though. After a week, it's not even optional. I've worked too hard to get this body how I like it, to let it all slip away."

With a grin, I called back, "I feel exactly the same way!"

He poked his head out of the bedroom. "Do you? Really?"

I kept flipping through the magazine full of skinny models until finally I tossed it away in disgust. "This is why I could never be in a real relationship with you."

He hung his head in a show of contrition. "Honestly, the gym is boring. I thought having you come along would be fun."

"You were trying to cajole me into going with you? You weren't fat-shaming me?"

"I want to spend every minute with you before you leave town." He held his hands up. "Busted! I'm clingy. Just call me Mr. Clingy or one of those other colorful names you enjoy so much."

I snatched up a copy of *Men's Fitness* and started flipping through. "Cheese-banger."

"You can read a magazine at the juice bar. They make the most unbelievable smoothies."

I let out an exasperated sigh. "I can't work out in jeans!"

"You do have shorts and runners, though. You shouldn't have unpacked your bag and spread everything out on one side of the room if you didn't want me to know you packed workout clothes."

I got up and stomped into the bedroom. "Keith Raven, you are the absolute worst, but I did make a New Year's resolution to go to the gym at least once this year, so I guess today's your lucky day."

"How do you feel about a session with a personal trainer?"

"How do you feel about a flying double-punch to the asshole?"

"So, just a standard workout, then."

~

We arrived at the gym (despite my suggestions we find a drive-through donut place instead), and Keith was an absolute sweetheart. First, he introduced me to the girl at the front counter as his "peachy love interest," which made me smile. Then, he took me to the stretching mats, where we took off our shoes and did some stretches. We did that one where you sit facing each other with your legs stretched out, then hold arms and help the other person lean forward. He kept making really sexy eye contact with me the whole time.

"People are staring at us," I whispered. "They all think you're my personal trainer and I'm some pervy rich girl who's paying to grope your hot body."

His eyebrows bounced suggestively. "For an extra fifty, you can touch my inner thighs."

I laughed. And then I looked down and thought about how much I wanted to touch his inner thighs, now that we were in public and I couldn't. I wore a pair of black shorts—black because I don't like showing off my crack-sweat on my annual gym workout, and clothing companies have yet to invent a color other than black that doesn't show crack-sweat.

The three absolute worst colors of gym shorts to wear, in reverse order from bad to worst, are:

#3. Salmon pink, or whatever shade matches your particular skin tone. Paired with a longer T-shirt, people do double-takes, thinking you forgot to put on shorts and are parading around your bare butt.

#2. Gray. Why the default color of athletic wear is gray astounds me. That flecked pattern does nothing to disguise damp regions.

#1. White. Perfectly fine for shirts, but a recipe for horror when worn on the lower half of the body—not just because of the magnifying effect of a light color, but because moisture increases transparency, and everyone's going to see your underwear, or, if you chose not to wear underwear, your lady shrubbery. I owe my least favorite day of tenth grade to a pair of white gym shorts, not to mention the three weeks of Oscar Dwyer calling me Triangle Bush.

"You're doing great," Keith said. "I'm already having more fun at a workout than ever before."

I winked at him. "Save a little energy for later."

His cheeks reddened. Noticing this caused my entire body to flush pink to match.

The gym was clean, but the air was moist from the adjoining steam room, and had the tangy scent of sweat. Spreading my legs even wider for the next stretch, I pondered how sexy a workout could be, given the right partner.

I felt the tingle at the back of my skull that someone was looking my way. I turned around, and a guy doing bicep curls quickly looked away, a smile on his face. He was cute. Actually, there were a few cute guys around. And no women, except for the girl we'd seen at the check-in desk.

"Where are all the girls?" I hissed at Keith. "Is this a gay gym?"

Keith stretched his neck and shoulders. "There's a ladies-only floor above here, if you wanna go up there."

"And miss all the eye candy? I think not."

He gave me a sidelong look. "Just remember who you came with."

I reached out and rubbed my index finger across his chest in a pretend-creepy way. "My personal trainer. Who I pay very handsomely. He knows how to work all my muscle groups."

"That's right." He clapped his hands. "Chop, chop. Ten minute warm-up on the stationery bike. Move it, move it."

"Yes, sir!"

We got on the bikes, side by side, and pretended to race.

Next, we did some work with free weights, and he showed me how to do these different reps with five-pound weights in my hands, all while lying on a bench.

"Exercising while lying down isn't so bad," I said. "And who knew there were so many positions."

"Five more, and keep your form. They're worthless if you don't have proper form."

"Yes, sir."

Oh, how I craved his approval. And for something as ridiculous as lifting a five-pound weight up and down, over and over. Every time he said, "Very nice," it felt as good as one of his kisses.

Once I was set up with a simple rotation, he picked up the heavier weights and got to work himself. All around us, men were panting on treadmills and grunting as they lifted weights. They were being respectful toward me, but there was something about the amount of testosterone in the air that made me feel funny. Alert. Alive.

Keith was right about the workout snapping me out of the hangover. A little sweating, mopped up quickly with the much-appreciated complimentary towels, plus many refills of my water bottle, and I was feeling downright heroic. I even did some reps with the ten-pound weights.

To my chagrin, I tried to do a bench press, but Keith had to remove all the weights and have me lift the bar only. I was embarrassed at first, but then I realized that if anyone was looking my way, it was at my peaches, and not my puny muscles.

We switched, and I spotted Keith while he lifted an impressive amount of weight. I worried that I was the wrong choice for a spotting partner, but he assured me that even if he came close to failure, he could still lift a portion of the weight, and just two fingers' worth of help from me was the right amount of help.

He was right, and when he finished the reps, with a little help from me at the end, I felt so proud of him. He'd been born blessed with great genes, but he'd taken his gifts and worked really hard to turn himself into the gorgeous, sweaty beast I was going to take home and shower with.

He stood up and leaned over to whisper in my ear, "Amazing what two fingers can do."

I giggled, remembering his homecoming surprise from Thursday.

Just then, a guy doing squats near us let out an audible fart. The smell drifted over. I'm just telling you this detail to be completely honest. I don't want you to think gyms are Paradise on Earth, with nothing but hot guys and sexy, sweaty muscles. There's a dark side to gyms. A tarty dark side. Also, I did accidentally see a few cracks I would rather not have seen. But, overall, the gym wasn't the worst thing, and I contemplated making my next New Year's resolution about going twice annually.

MIMI STRONG

CHAPTER 20

We got our juice smoothies to go, and went straight back to Keith's place. After a quick shower, we returned to the bedroom for a little Afternoon Delight.

Keith dropped his towel on the bed as he did a standing stretch.

"Towel on the bed." I shook my head and made a tsk-tsk noise.

With a groan, he tossed his towel toward the hook on the back of his bedroom door. The towel missed and fell on the floor. He let himself drop backward onto his bed with another groan.

"You didn't save any energy for me," I said. "Naughty gym rat."

"You go on top. Do all the stuff. It'll be hot."

"Roll over on your stomach," I said.

"Kinky." He rolled over, revealing that cute little bum of his that looked like two perfect dinner rolls.

I hung up my towel as well as his, then crawled onto the bed alongside him.

I started kneading his muscles, gingerly at first. Working the thick ropes on the tops of the shoulders, I asked, "What muscles are these?"

"Mine." He chuckled. "Trapezius," he added. "They go all the way from the base of my skull to my shoulders, and then quite a ways down my back."

I kneaded my fingertips into his muscles, fascinated by the change in firmness that happened just with a bit of work. He seemed to be melting, softening under my hands.

"They're beautiful muscles. I normally objectify men by staring at their abs, but these are nice. Also, I totally know they're called trapezius muscles. I was just checking to see that you knew."

He moaned in response.

I moved over to his upper arms on the outside. "Deltoids? Or are they Altoids? No, Altoids are the curiously strong mints."

Keith's body shook as he laughed.

"Don't laugh at your masseuse. She's doing the best she can."

"You have good hands," he said.

"Thank you for taking me to the gym today." I paused. *Wow, that was a string of words I never expected to hear come out of my mouth.* "And thank you for not weighing me or talking about calories or trying to make me sweat on the treadmill for an hour." I kept kneading his muscles. "Thank you for being patient."

"I just try to put myself in your shoes," he said.

I paused.

I just try to put myself in your shoes.

He'd said it as if this was the simplest concept in the world, and everybody did it.

My eyes welled up with tears. He was facing mostly down, his eyes closed as he enjoyed the massage.

I fought to keep going at the same pace, even as my vision blurred and I surreptitiously wiped my tears on my shoulder.

"This really is a good massage," he said.

I kept working, kneading his back muscles. My own body was already feeling slightly tender in some areas, so I could only imagine how Keith was feeling, considering all the much-heavier weights he'd been lifting.

I zoned out during the massage, and Keith drifted off. He started talking in his sleep, and I thought for a minute he was talking to me.

"My order."

"What?" I asked, surprised.

"Dijon mustard. And ham."

I prompted him for more. "What's that? Is that your pizza order, Mr. Raven?"

Sounding indignant, he said, "We weren't cutting across your lawn."

I crawled off the bed and stood for a minute watching him sleep. I've seen my mother do this with Kyle, and when I still lived at home, she'd sometimes call me over to join in watching him sleep. How did Keith's mother feel about him leaving for Italy, and being so far away from her?

I'd been away from home for a week, and whenever I thought of my son, I'd feel like I was being pitched from side to side on a boat in a storm.

It was strange to think of him as my son. In my thoughts, he was simply Kyle, or my mother's youngest.

I'd wanted nothing to do with him after he was born, and I will probably see my dying day before I forgive myself for refusing to hold him, let alone breastfeed him. The nurses at the hospital tried to sell me on the health benefits, one of them even telling me breastfeeding did wonders for losing the baby weight.

The baby weight.

I'd gained no more than twelve pounds during the pregnancy, and the baby weighed seven.

The doctor thought I was lying. He treated me like a criminal, like one of those girls who throws her baby in the garbage with the umbilical cord still attached.

I can't read those kinds of news articles. Literally. I don't mean I avoid them, or don't enjoy them, I mean I *can not read them*. My breathing gets shallow, my body starts to shake, and the words swim around on the page.

Life changes you, makes you into a lightning rod for certain emotions.

You know that show about the women who didn't know they were pregnant until they went into labor? Do you ever sit and watch in disbelief, thinking they must be lying?

I can't speak for all of them, but I can tell you at least some of them are telling the truth. Especially the smart ones, because smart people have a way of being incredibly stupid when it comes to things like an unexpected baby growing inside of them.

I avoid talking about what happened.

Maybe it wouldn't always be awful, though.

Keith had been understanding, listening without pushing for more.

Before me in the quiet bedroom, the curtains drawn against the afternoon sun, the tuckered-out underwear model muttered about oatmeal and stirred in his sleep.

I leaned down and kissed him on the shoulder blade before leaving him to his nap.

I closed the door so he didn't get woken up by me making lunch.

Ten minutes later, just as I was sitting down to enjoy my grilled cheese sandwich, someone knocked on the door.

Keith's ex-girlfriend Tabitha stood on the other side of the door, looking as surprised to see me as I was to see her.

"You look sober," I said.

"Unlike last time." She ducked her head, looking vulnerable as she tucked some long, wavy brown hair behind her ear. "Oh, I'm sorry, am I interrupting your dinner? That smells really good."

What was she up to?

"Yeah, I'm just making dinner."

"It smells incredible."

What's that expression? Keep your friends close and invite your enemies in for a grilled cheese sandwich?

I said, "Keith's having a nap. Do you want to come in and have something to eat? You can have the sandwich I already made, and I'll just—"

She bolted in the door and toward the grilled cheese sandwich on the coffee table so quickly, I swear there were cartoon motion lines behind her.

She moaned with pleasure as she ate the four-cheese grilled sourdough, and I tried to block the idea those hamster grunts coming out of her big mattress lips were also her sex noises.

I grilled up a second sandwich for myself.

We talked for a few minutes about how I was enjoying LA, how I liked the neighborhood, and blah-blah-blah.

I sat down next to her and went for the jugular: "All right, Tabitha, enough foreplay. Let's hear your side of the Las Vegas story."

She turned three shades of pink. "Keith told you?"

"I know everything. We did one of those meditation mind meld things, because those are totally real. Obviously you regret what you did and you want him back, right?"

She nodded.

"Do you want him more because I have him?"

Her mouth dropped open.

"So that's a yes," I said. "You don't know what you've got until it's gone. I'm familiar with the concept. I had this dress with dolman sleeves—that's where it's really big under the armpits, like bat wings, but narrow on the cuff. I thought it wasn't flattering, so I gave it to the charity shop. Two weeks later, I saw a woman in town wearing it —and I knew it was the same one, because that thing was vintage from the eighties—and I wanted it back so bad, I actually considered offering to buy it from her." I took a big bite of my grilled cheese sandwich. "But I didn't, because I'm classy. So I followed her into the community center gym and stole it while she was working out."

Tabitha moved further away from me on the three-seater couch.

"That's a joke," I said, spitting a few chunks of food out accidentally. "I actually beat her up and took it off her body."

Tabitha's eyes grew wider and wider.

"C'mon, Tabs. Can I call you Tabs? I'm just messing with you. I don't believe in violence. I'm more of a poisoner, you know? That's how most female serial killers take care of their victims."

Tabitha set down the remaining quarter of her sandwich, her eyes darting between me and the front door.

"So, tell me about Las Vegas," I said, acting as chipper as the head cheerleader at an all-cheerleader sleepover.

"I don't know if I should."

"Someone might be convinced to put in a good word for you with Mr. Underwear Model."

She bit her lip, not saying anything, but not leaving, either. I sniffed the air. Perfume? She looked more dressed up, her fake-looking hair more carefully teased to be full, than the previous two times I'd seen her. Oh, she had not been expecting to see me here at all. In fact, I was pretty sure if I pulled up that little skirt she was wearing, I'd find some slutty underwear.

I should have turfed her out before Keith even knew she was there, but my curiosity got the better of me.

"You were in Las Vegas," I began for her. "There was a hot tub at the hotel pool, and you were drinking Jagermeister shots, and then you wandered into the wrong hotel room. You took off all your clothes and got into a soft, comfortable bed, only to discover your ex-lover next to you. He'd just eaten room service food with cracked pepper, and you both started sneezing violently, and before you knew it, you both were sneezing and sneezing, with no clothes on, and his penis just slipped right in."

Tabitha snorted, hesitant to laugh at first, but then I started laughing and soon we were both going.

"Hey, accidents happen," I said with a shrug. "That happened to a friend of a girl I know, I swear. True story."

"It all started when we couldn't get tickets to see the Blue Man Group."

"Why couldn't you get tickets?"

"Are you going to let me tell you, or do you have to control absolutely everything?"

"Ouch." I relaxed back into the corner of the sofa, eating the rest of my sandwich and nodding for her to continue.

She said, "What they don't tell you with these coupons is that there are blackout dates, and some of these shows are really expensive, even with the coupon. My friend Twyla knew a girl at the Rio, though, so we took three different buses and got lost a bunch of times, and we ended up going to see the Chippendales."

"Oh! Those are the male strippers who wear the bow ties? I think I see where this is going. All that dancing around while the ladies screamed for more made you go crazy. You called up your ex in a moment of weakness."

"Close." She nodded her head toward me and raised her eyebrows suggestively.

"What? Your ex is a Chippendale?"

"Ten points for Peaches."

"Did you know he was a dancer? Or was it... like, he comes out from behind the curtains, all oiled up, wearing his little cowboy boots, and he looks familiar, but you don't realize until he's giving you a lap dance?"

"He was dressed as a construction worker, and I was so embarrassed about being dragged up on stage that I couldn't even look the guy in the eyes. I didn't know it was him until I had my hands on his butt. I thought I was having *déjà vu*, because his butt felt so familiar, but then I looked up, and we were looking into each other's eyes."

"That is insane!"

"He said fate must have brought us together so we could say a proper goodbye. We dated back in high school, then tried to make it work long distance when he went off to work on the oil rigs, but we broke up over the phone."

She stared off at nothing, at the spot on the wall where someone who was a better decorator than Keith would have hung up some art.

"And that's why you cheated on Keith," I said.

"I'm not saying I shouldn't have done what I did, but Keith and I were taking some time apart. We'd been fighting constantly, and his sister Katy was living here, and the three of us kept getting into these strange power struggles."

"Because Katy is a Level Ten Bitch-monster."

Tabitha laughed guiltily. "She's my best friend, but I know what she's like."

"Wait. You and Keith were broken up when you went to Las Vegas?"

"We weren't exactly together. I'd moved back home with my parents. Katy wanted me to move back in to the apartment with her and Keith, but I still had some hard feelings about things he'd said to me."

"I see." I nodded. "Let me see your underwear."

"What?"

207

"I just want to know if you were coming over here to talk to him, or seduce him."

"Just to talk, I swear."

I reached over and flipped up the hem of her skirt. She pushed it back down and slapped my hand.

What happened next was kind of a blur. Let's just say I did some things I'm not very proud of, but things that needed to be done. I don't appreciate being lied to, and it was in Keith's best interests that I found out if Tabitha was planning to seduce him, which meant determining whether or not she was wearing slutty, ridiculous underwear, with matching bra and panties.

What Keith saw when he came out of his bedroom to investigate the ruckus wasn't pretty. I was pinning down Tabitha on the couch, my head up under her top, yelling, "I knew it! I knew it!"

He tapped me on the shoulder and said, "Tag."

I pulled my head out from under Tabitha's shirt and whipped around to face him. "What? Tag?"

He was grinning, looking his usual sexy self in just a pair of shorts. "Yeah. Tag. I guess we're doing this threesome thing here?" He laughed, very clearly making a joke and not at all serious. "Kind of rude of you two to start without me."

"Hilarious." I crossed my arms.

Tabitha had already jumped up and was heading for the door. "You two are both nuts," she said. "I came over to apologize to you, Keith, but I can see you're having way more fun without me these days." She opened the door. "Have a nice life." She left and slammed the door behind her.

Keith turned to me. "I can't believe I was going to ask her to marry me."

I steadied myself, not reacting to this revelation. "You could do better," I said.

He frowned my way. "What *were* you doing to her, exactly?"

"Market research for my brand. Just wanted to see what kind of underwear she likes."

"Worn-out gray sports bras and granny panties."

Ah. Theory confirmed.

"Grilled cheese?" I jumped up and went to the kitchen.

"I really should eat something with more protein, since I just worked out. I've got some turkey breast in the freezer."

He joined me in the small kitchen area and bumped me out of the way with his hip. He got a foil package from the freezer, opened it up, and pulled out thick slices of roasted turkey breast.

I moved aside and watched as he grilled the turkey to thaw it, then put the turkey inside the cheese sandwich I'd started.

"Not bad," he said after the first bite.

"Smells like Hot Pockets."

"I've never had one of those."

"They aren't bad, but stay away from the one with the broccoli because it tastes like Satan's bunghole."

"Good to know." He took a seat at the kitchen counter on one of the stools, eating and watching me clean up.

"I prefer the Philly Cheese Steak flavor. All of them are improved by a sour cream dip, of course."

He grinned. "Of course."

I ran some hot water into the sink. "Tabitha's really skinny." He didn't respond to this statement of fact. "I suppose dating her is less of a hazard to your career than dating me."

"I can eat a little cheese now and then, Peaches. I am an adult."

"You never told me that you and she were on a break when she allegedly ripped your heart out and ran it over."

"There are plenty of things I didn't tell you, like how we had an accidental pregnancy and miscarriage in January, and she shut me out. She spent all her time with Katy, and I was the awkward third wheel roommate."

"Hmm."

"The situation wasn't healthy."

"When did everyone move out?"

"A few weeks ago."

"Not that long ago."

I looked up, meeting his gaze. The look in his brown eyes confirmed what I thought: the void in Keith's life had literally sucked me in to cork up the energy draining away. Yes, I was a girl-shaped cork. A rebound. And he was mine. And that was okay.

Keith pulled out his phone. "Too late to go to Anaheim today. I guess we'll have to go tomorrow."

I clapped my hands together, visions of princesses dancing through my head. "Disneyland? Are you for real? You would take me there?"

"You've never been, so I'm practically obligated to take you. I'd be a terrible host if I didn't."

I hugged him so hard, I nearly knocked him off the stool.

The funny thing is, I'd joked about going to Disneyland on my trip, but I hadn't seriously considered going. I didn't know I wanted to go so badly, until that moment. Like how I hadn't wanted to be an underwear model until the opportunity came up. How many other things did I secretly desire and not even know?

CHAPTER 21

On Sunday morning, while regular tourists were still in their hotel rooms, adding non-dairy creamer to mugs of coffee made on dressers in those mini-carafes, Keith and I lined up outside Disneyland Park half an hour before the rope dropped.

As soon as we were admitted, Keith grabbed my hand and hauled me through the empty park toward Adventureland and the Indiana Jones Adventure.

The ride was thrilling and every bit as corny and fun as it looks in the ads. As I screamed at the mummies and the insects in the creepy Bug Room, I mulled over the question posed at the beginning of the ride. The temple deity had offered us one of three gifts: earthly riches, eternal youth, or seeing into the future.

When we disembarked at the end of the Indiana Jones Adventure ride, I asked Keith which of those things he'd choose.

"Eternal youth, of course," he said. "The opportunities for models get slimmer with age."

"Then you'd be a model forever."

"I guess I would. A model with a big mansion and an amazing garden. I'd spend my downtime splitting plants and getting dirty." We both laughed. "What about you?"

I had to think. *Earthly riches, eternal youth, or seeing into the future.*

"Not riches, because I'd rather earn them. Eternal youth… sounds good, but I wouldn't want to have all my friends aging while I didn't. I guess I'd pick the visions, because who wouldn't want to see the future?"

"What if you could see the future, but it worked like TV, and you could only see one channel?" He pointed in one direction and started hauling me that way. "New Orleans Square. We're going to hit the Pirates next."

"Pirates are fun." I skipped to catch up, glad I was wearing tennis shoes with a favorite outfit I'd brought from home: olive green cargo shorts and a ruffled pink blouse, which I think of as my Barbie-meets-G.I.Joe outfit.

Keith continued, "What if you can see the future, but just the weather? And only right where you are. Not even globally, so you can't prevent human deaths from natural disasters."

"Did anyone ever tell you you're very unusual, Mr. Raven, guy-who-doesn't-have-birthdays?"

He blushed. I'd seen him blush once or twice before, but not like this. He looked like he was trying to act natural, but failing.

Something was off. Something I'd said had triggered a reaction.

"Keith, is today your birthday?"

We kept walking, him looking around and waving at Disney characters.

If I remembered correctly, he prevented birthdays from happening by insisting on doing only regular-day things. Going to Disneyland didn't fit the profile of regular-day things, not even for someone who lived nearby.

"Keith, squeeze my hand once if today is your twin sister's birthday."

He squeezed my hand.

We walked on in silence, until I said, "I'm honored that you'd choose to celebrate your birthday with me. And if anyone asks, I'll lie and tell them we did boring everyday things."

He stopped walking, stepping in front of me so we were face to face, him looking down into my eyes. The morning sun was behind his head, giving his dark hair a glow, like a halo.

Without a word, he leaned down and kissed me. The park had started filling up and people flowed all around us, and he kept kissing me. When he finally pulled away from me, he said, "You inspire me with your enthusiasm for life, and your honesty, and your passion.

Peaches, you make me want to grow up. So, Happy Birthday to me. I couldn't have picked a better way to spend today, and before you say it, oh, yes, there will be cake."

"With ice cream," I added, nodding. "Because someone was a bad boy on Thursday night and promised he'd pick up ice cream, but then he did not. Unforgivable."

"I told you, the stores were all closed! Stupid Tabitha throwing my phone down a mountain. Tonight there will be both cake and ice cream."

"Birthday candles? How many? Eleven?"

He grimaced.

"Okay, no candles," I said, laughing. "Enough personal growth for today, right?"

He grabbed my hand and got us walking again. "Pirates! And then the Haunted Mansion. Oh, and Space Mountain."

"It's your birthday," I said, smiling. "You get to pick everything, because it's your day."

"I like the sound of that."

He got a big grin on his face that didn't quit the whole day, and it was a long day. A very long day. We crossed over to Disney California Adventure at mid-day and crammed in as much as we could there.

As we toured the attractions and went on rides, I discovered that I did have the magical gift of being able to see the future, and it wasn't limited to the weather. I could see returning there in a couple of years with my whole family, or maybe just me and Kyle.

Kyle, my baby.

Kyle came home a few days ahead of me, because the doctors weren't sure about my mental state. I insisted I was completely fine for someone who'd eaten a whole pizza and gotten indigestion.

They told me I'd had a baby, and I rolled over and stopped talking. I couldn't tell you what I was thinking, because those thoughts are scribbled out in my head to this day, probably to protect myself.

Finally, I told the doctors I'd known I was pregnant, and I'd kept meaning to come into the hospital for pre-natal care, but I'd been scared and pushed it off one day at a time. They bought the story. I told it so many times, I started to believe it myself, these new lies overwriting my actual memories with every re-playing.

At home, my parents barely let me in the house before they sat me down to talk about adoption papers. My father had gone into problem-solving mode the minute they'd returned early from their trip, and once he starts, he's like an unstoppable cargo train.

The funniest thing about that night was that the two of them couldn't stop smiling. I honestly thought they were going to be furious with me as soon as we all left the safety of the hospital, but they weren't.

It's hard to be anything but calm when a newborn is sleeping in a laundry basket next to you, his tiny hands curled up like rosebuds.

All babies should be so lucky, to be as wanted as Kyle. I hadn't known this at the time, but my mother had tried for years after my birth—tried to have a younger brother or sister for me. She says she would have had four kids, if it had been possible. She had an abnormality in her uterus that they didn't discover until she was in the hospital having me, by emergency caesarian. The abnormality didn't show up on the ultrasound, but the doctors said she would have difficulty bringing another baby to term.

She chose not to believe them. But medical problems don't care what you believe.

They tried and tried in secret, and it wasn't until after Kyle came along, and we sat together at the table with him slumbering in the laundry basket, that she told me all the details about the miscarriage heartbreaks she'd suffered.

At last, I finally understood why she'd cried for two weeks, all during Christmas break, when I was twelve. I'd gone onto the internet that holiday and thanks to Dr. Google, diagnosed her with Seasonal Affective Disorder. I printed out some information about special lights you can get to combat the dark, rainy Washington winters.

She'd lost a baby on Christmas Eve. A boy. They named him Kyler and held a small memorial in January. I thought they were going to the funeral of a distant uncle.

And then, three years later, there was a healthy little blue-eyed surprise who needed a lot of care, and a name. Their hearts were so full. Their prayers had been answered, and, unlike the doctors, they believed me that I hadn't known. My parents were concerned, but they weren't angry. They were overjoyed.

"I love the name Kyler," I told them, glancing over at his little red face. He just looked like a baby, not a person, so what did I know? "I would name the baby that, but isn't that a girl's name?"

My mother started crying, the tears falling into her smile. "Sweetie, it's a boy's name."

We talked some more that night, and over the next few days, about responsibilities and care of the baby, now named Kyler—Kyle for short.

I'm not going to lie and say my parents were saints about the whole thing. We had *moments*. When my father was bleary-eyed from baby duty all night, he said a few cross things to me about certain clothes I was wearing and accused me of being "prone to whimsy."

I took his comments in the worst possible way; I heard him say I was a fat slut. Those weren't the words, but guilt has a way of twisting and balling things up to torture you.

My parents are smart people, but it didn't take a rocket scientist to figure out my friend Toby, who lived down the block, was the other half of the surprise baby equation. Toby was uninvited from "homework sessions" behind closed doors, and after a few tense meetings with Toby's family, he agreed to the terms of the adoption.

Toby's family claimed that there had been a job offer across the country in the works before all of this "baby daddy drama" had started, but none of us believed it. They moved away before Kyle's first birthday. Toby came over once (supervised) and held Kyle. The whole time, he looked like he was about to vomit.*

*Coincidentally, that's not dissimilar to how he looked the first time we had sex.

And now I will answer the questions I'm sure you have:

1. Yes, I knew how babies were made. I was fourteen and went to public school, people. But I looked up a monthly ovulation chart, and it made perfect sense to me, so naturally I felt I could outsmart the

main force that has altered women's destinies since the beginning of time.

2. I continued to get what I thought was an irregular period. I don't have the same abnormality my mother did, but there's a little uterine weirdness going on, for sure.

3. There's no such thing as a food craving that I would find unusual in any way.

4. Any body changes, I attributed to puberty, given I was going through puberty at the time.

5. My parents absolutely didn't know or suspect, not consciously. They wouldn't have gone on a three-day trip to Arizona and left me to go into labor at home alone if they had.

6. Except for the part where I nearly died, the delivery wasn't too bad.

~

"Thank you for an amazing birthday," Keith said as we ate our cake and ice cream at a neighborhood cafe near his apartment.

It was nearly midnight, and I felt twitchy with nerves, as if I had bug bites all over me instead of just one on my shoulder. Being outdoors in the sun all day makes my skin sensitive, even if I don't get sunburned.

My commercial shoot started the next day, Monday, and finished on Tuesday. I'd gotten myself through the print photos the week before, barely, but now I had movement and my voice to mess things up.

I'd been assured that the horrible, rude model, Sven, wasn't a part of the commercial, but I couldn't shake the idea he'd be there anyway, and they'd say "suck it up, princess" if I didn't like it. They had a lot of money riding on the new product line, and they had to pay me my modeling fee no matter what. Deep down, I worried the whole thing would be a colossal failure, and everyone would think I jinxed it with my jiggly buns.

"Stop it," Keith said.

I looked up from my cake and ice cream, confused by his words. Stop eating cake? But there was still cake on my plate. What kind of cruelty was this?

"Stop worrying about the shoot," he said. "Everyone on set tomorrow is there to make you look good. Think of them as *your* people, *your* team. If you're not sure about something, ask. And take your time. They've scheduled two days to shoot a thirty-second commercial."

"It's actually splitting into a couple different commercials."

He used his fork to separate his chocolate cake from the ganache. "A couple? In that case, you should definitely freak out. You're toast."

"You're not helping."

"Wait 'til we get home. I'll undress you and take your mind off your worries."

I smiled and took another bite of my treat, which was a lemon cake with white buttercream frosting and raspberry sauce. I'd opted to not get the ice cream, but only because I wanted to enjoy the flavors on their own, and not because I thought skipping ice cream would magically make me shed ten pounds before an underwear shoot the next day. I may be "prone to whimsy," but not straight-up insanity.

~

Back at Keith's place, we did something I'd never done with a guy before. Something intimate.

We sorted out our clothes into lights and darks and did laundry together. Hot!

My jeans mixed around in the washing machine with his jeans, inside the stacking washer and dryer units that had been retro-fitted into a storage closet.

When the clothes were dry, we took them out of the dryer, dumped them all on the bed, and folded them. I've never lived with a guy, so this was all incredibly novel to me, and made me feel like a sexy housewife—the way cooking for Keith made me feel.

He slayed me when he experimented with folding my panties, forming them into tidy squares or triangles. He was so serious about folding, and I couldn't stop laughing at him.

We got everything put away, and then it was just us and a freshly-made bed.

I said, "If only I had something to *give* you for your birthday present, this would be the perfect time for me to *give* it to you."

He grinned and started unbuttoning my frilly pink blouse, both of us standing at the foot of the bed.

"I could order you something online," I said. "It would take a few days to arrive, but you could print out the picture in the meantime."

He pulled the blouse away and let it fall, tickling my arms on the way to the floor. He leaned down and kissed the tops of my breasts, held up high and proud in the pretty pink bra. Nodding down, I smelled the top of his head, taking in the scent of his scalp, which always smelled so good. His hands moved up and down my back, and then he was kissing my neck, his hands in my hair.

I reached down for his T-shirt and tugged it up and off so I could put my hands all over his hot skin. He kissed my shoulder as we closed the distance between us and rocked from side to side to...

"We should have music," I murmured.

"Really?" He pulled away and turned the stereo on.

"Isn't this your meditation music?"

"You don't like it."

"No, no. This music is nice. Is that a sitar? I feel like a snake charmer." I moved my neck from side to side in a bad parody of a white girl doing a scene from Disney's *Aladdin*.

"You've already charmed my snake, so whatever you're doing, it's working."

I laughed and grabbed him so I could unfasten his pants and get him ready for the *real* snake charming event.

I pushed him, naked, onto the bed, and slipped out of my cargo shorts before climbing on alongside him, still wearing my nice underwear.

"You're not naked," he said.

"Think of me as a birthday present you unwrap a little at a time."

He lay back and closed his eyes.

Instead of starting at the top, kissing his lips, I began at the bottom of his body, giving both of his feet a light, invigorating rub. He had nice toes. Men always have good feet, without bunions, because they don't wear ridiculous shoes like we do. I rubbed his arches, then pulled his legs apart from each other so I could kneel in between them as I squeezed his calves.

I moved my hands up along the inside edges of his legs, making him laugh and squirm. He peered down at me. "I feel so vulnerable with my legs apart like this."

"Now you know how girls feel."

"Honestly, I don't know what you girls see in big, hairy men."

He was naked, so I leaned forward and kissed him somewhere personal. "You're big, but you're not that hairy."

I moved back down a few inches with my body, and went back to rubbing his legs again. Keith grew very quiet and still, his eyes closed.

As I rubbed his legs and then moved my fingers up gradually to gently rub his sack and shaft, I watched him, thinking about how many girls would be looking at photos of him and imagining themselves doing what I was doing.

I glanced down at my body, and at all the natural creases forming from the position I was in, and for the first time since I'd gotten the underwear modeling offer, I imagined men looking at photos of me while they jerked off.

I may not be everyone's cup of tea, but for a certain segment of men, I'm the bee's knees.

As I took Keith into my mouth, I thought about all those sexually frustrated men who couldn't have me, and I got even more turned on. I threw one leg over his leg and rubbed up against his shin as I sucked his beautiful hardness.

He was big and hard, like a tower that couldn't be knocked down. I got excited, moaning and breathing hard—so much so, that he tapped me on the shoulder to check I was okay.

Embarrassed, I wiped my mouth and took a break, saying, "Just wanted you to have a good birthday."

He sat up and put his arms around me. "I do have a request. Remember the first time? With our legs wrapped around each other?"

"That was fun."

"Lay back and let me kiss you before we get started."

I rolled onto my back and held my arms out for him, but instead of joining me for kissing on the mouth, he moved down and pulled my panties off. Oh. That kind of kissing. Well. Happy birthday to me, too!

He put a pillow under my hips, and then another pillow under his chest as he wriggled into place. "Perfect," he said, bending my knees up and making his way down between my thighs. "Now just relax your legs open a little more."

I giggled, because these sorts of instructions are funny at the doctor's office and even funnier in bed.

He dove in, his tongue pushing down, and I sucked in a deep breath, no longer feeling the giggles. I grasped handfuls of the bedcovers as he bore down on my sweet spot as eagerly as I'd enjoyed him a moment earlier.

Taking his time, he brought me up, up, to the point of the waves crashing, but eased off instead, allowing the waves of pleasure to recede.

I begged. I pushed my pride aside and I truly begged for release. "Harder? Harder? Don't stop. Don't... noooo. You bastard. You tease. I'm leaving this room as soon as feeling returns to my body."

Then he went in again, and I moaned and begged, and still he wouldn't let me come.

I even tried to be sneaky about it, but he had fingers inside me, and could tell by my tension or my breathing, or possibly the sheen of sweat that appeared on my stomach whenever I got close to detonation.

Finally, I just gave in. *You win, Keith, you sex-a-thon-having meditation-nut. Do to me what you want, because it's your birthday, and when we're done I'm going to acquaint myself with the massaging shower head in your bathroom.*

Once I was as compliant as Silly Putty, he climbed on top of me, his penis against my stomach, and kissed me until he was as hard as ever. We sat up together, wrapping our arms around each other and kissing. He put a condom in place, then sat up with his legs loosely bent, forming a circle with his knees under mine.

We were both still sitting, facing each other, legs interwoven. My butt was still raised on the pillows. I leaned back on my palms and raised my hips as he slid forward to merge with me, moving easily into me as a thrill raced up my spine. I wrapped my legs around him, sitting upright and feeling him completely within me, from his root and all the way up, his upper body wrapped in my arms.

We rocked back and forth like this, and when my legs started to shake from the position, he gathered up the pillows that had escaped and propped me up under my butt.

Now we were really in our groove, barely moving, but fully in contact. We stared into each other's eyes, and I wondered what he saw that made his expression so raw and serene at the same time. He kissed me, and we both kept our eyes open, as if we were afraid the other might disappear, like a dream in the morning.

MIMI STRONG

CHAPTER 22

Monday morning, Keith drove me to the studio for the commercial shoot, and I wouldn't get out of the van. It wasn't nerves that got the best of me, but I was addicted to that man! I couldn't stop kissing him and grabbing onto his sweet, sweet butt, and other parts.

"What have you done to me?" I said.

He growled and kissed my neck while fondling my chest through my zip-up hoodie jacket. "Me like pretty girl."

Finally, I pulled myself away and reluctantly opened the van door. "Wish me luck," I said.

"Break a leg."

"Anyone's leg but mine." I leaned back over to his side for one more kiss.

What *had* he done to me? Quite simply, he'd subjected me to a marathon tantric sex session the night before, thus ruining me for all other regular sexual encounters, for the rest of my life. Keith's super-slow lovin' fried out some of my dopamine circuits, and now I craved him like a chocolate addict craves the good stuff from Belgium.

I dragged myself away from the old green van and in through the austere door of the photographer's studio. The same guy who did the photos was directing the commercials, so at least I got to work with the same crew again, including...

"Mitchell!"

He stopped where he was, at the opposite end of a long corridor just inside the lobby. He started running toward me in slow motion.

Laughing, I did the same, lifting my knees high and pretending I was racing frantically toward him, but in slow motion.

We collided together in the middle, hugging and pretending to sob.

He pulled away and went back to regular Mitchell mode. "You, Miss Thaing, were a *handful* Friday night," he said, his blond eyebrows raised high.

"I sure was. Then Keith picked me up from the bar and I went home and got myself a handful."

"You did better than me! I went home and microwaved two Jenny Craigs and ate them both. For dessert, I ate jam straight from the jar with a spoon."

"That's quite the sad tale."

"I've had worse nights." He shook his head. "Come Christmas, everyone thinks it's *so* funny to dress me up like one of Santa's elves."

"You would make a cute elf."

"I know." He wrinkled his nose. "True confession? I like being an elf. I own three different costumes, but if anyone asks, they're rentals."

We started walking toward the hair and makeup room, where the illusion I was a professional model would begin.

"Hey, speaking of quirks," I said. "Do you happen to remember why I got a tattoo that reads *Doves Cry*?"

He gasped. "That happened? I thought I was dreaming."

"Any clue what it means?"

"Give me a minute," he said.

I got into the makeup chair, introduced myself to the sleepy-looking makeup girl with a pixie haircut, and got comfortable as Mitchell ran off to make me a mocha.

He came back with the drink and told me the story.

Apparently, we were listening to Prince songs in the limousine that first night we went our partying, with Gunner and Daniel, the models. I had really enjoyed Prince's *When Doves Cry*, and how the opening ba-wang sounds moved around the car's surround sound speakers. At my request, they replayed the song a couple of times, until finally I told the guys I was confused, because I still didn't understand what it sounded like when doves cry.

Daniel, the straight guy with the shaggy brown hair, said, "What it sounds like? You mean when the doves cry? It's a seven-note melody. Doot-da-doot. Doot-doot-do-doot."

As Mitchell relayed the story, making the pixie-haired makeup artist snicker, I dimly remembered all of that happening. I'd had one of those moments you only get when you're drunk or over-tired, and not yourself. That night, I realized I over-think everything. The key to life seemed so simple in that moment, as we were all laughing and playing music in the limousine. I just had to let go. If I had to cry, I'd cry.

Then I did start to cry, right there in the limousine. Messy tears. Snotty nose. The whole drunk-girl-crying experience. But they were happy tears. My only fear was I worried I'd forget my revelation when I sobered up.

We then did the only logical thing. We drove straight to an all-night tattoo parlor—not the nice kind with attractive people who won't tattoo you if you're drunk, but the seedy kind with scary dudes who can't spell, where you watch closely to make sure the supplies are sterile—and I got my tattoo.

Mitchell finished the anecdote, assuring me I didn't complain at all about the pain.

The makeup artist applying my extra eyelashes begged to see the tattoo, so I pulled my loose-fitting shorts down and showed her. The ink was looking less black and more blue every day as it healed.

"That is so cute," she said. "I'm, like, totally jealous. You have a great tattoo and an amazing story. All I have is a stupid tramp stamp."

She turned around and bent forward to show us a thorny mass of roses on her lower back.

"Um, the flowers are pretty," Mitchell said.

"It's nice," I lied.

She turned around, her lip curled up in a sneer. "You know what my guy does? He pulls out at the last second and says, 'Water the roses. Pew, pew.'"

I gasped. "No."

"Yes. He comes on my tramp stamp. He's mentally ill or something."

"I'm sure he loves you, though, right?"

She continued, "Of course he does. He rubs my feet when I come home after a long day, and he made me a bacon omelet this morning, and I love the big, stupid idiot, so what-cha-gonna do?"

With a straight face, Mitchell said, "He sounds like a keeper."

I pointed to the girl's wedding band. "How long have you been married?"

"A year. It's good, except for the tattoo thing."

I nodded, because that was perfectly understandable.

~

An hour later, I looked like a Vegas showgirl crossed with a lion. My hair was bigger than a drag queen's wig, having been teased mercilessly and augmented by another pound of blond, wavy hair.

They hadn't gone so crazy on the hair for the still photos, and I was surprised by how powerful a lion's mane made me feel.

The photographer, who had someone else on the camera as he was directing today, came by and frowned, then walked away.

I blinked up at Mitchell's reflection in the makeup mirror, both of us lit up brightly by the flattering light bulbs. "He hates me," I said.

"That was his good frown," Mitchell said, patting my shoulder. "Trust me, I know. That frown was him acknowledging that you look fierce, and now the pressure is on him to not blow it."

"I can't believe you said I look *fierce*. People actually say that word around here, don't they?"

A skinny guy came into the room with two dresses. "Hey, girl. You look fierce. So, we're all loving both of these dresses, but I'll let you pick which one you like."

"I won't be in my underwear?"

Mitchell took the dresses and shooed the guy away.

He explained, "The concept is... you're riding a bicycle in the park and as you ride by a cute guy, he sees you in your underwear. We shoot you in the dress, and then in the underwear, and do a little computer magic to mirror his eyes undressing you."

"Really?" My stomach flip-flopped. "Isn't that creepy? How does this sell the underwear? It doesn't seem very sexy or empowering to me."

Mitchell laughed, then stopped. "Oh, you're serious. You said *empowering* and I thought you were pulling my leg."

I squirmed in my chair and reached for my bottle of water. "You're right. I'm over-thinking again."

"You'll be smiling through the whole commercial, so it won't feel like you're being victimized."

I spat out my water, dribbling down my chin. "Mitchell, you don't know what it's like to be a woman."

"Sometimes I feel like I have a sassy big girl inside of me. Her name is LaShonda, and she makes me buy cupcakes." He blinked, looking as innocent as a curly-haired little cherub.

"Okay, I'll wear the ivory dress. Let's do this."

He made an unattractive expression. "There's one more thing. Promise you won't be mad."

"I'm not eating in the commercial. I already put that in the contract, and it's not negotiable."

"The cute guy is Dalton Deangelo."

"You mean someone who looks like him."

"No, it's really him. When you were in the washroom at the restaurant, he said he wished he could make it up to you, how he hurt your feelings, and I had a few ideas."

I sighed. "I guess that's fine. He's the reason I got myself into this mess, so he may as well be part of it."

"You still like him."

I rolled my eyes. "Not as much as you, fanboy."

Someone tapped on the door. My heart raced, anticipating Dalton, but the person who entered looked like a cross between a Vegas showgirl and a lion. WHAT? How could that be me? How could I be sitting in the makeup chair and also walking into the room?

"Can I get your autograph?" my look-alike asked, handing me a cotton T-shirt and a felt pen.

"This nice young lady here is your lighting stand-in," Mitchell said.

"Wow, for a minute I thought you had me cloned."

The girl's face squished up. "That's so nice of you to say. I love you SO MUCH. Like, I know this is weird because you don't know me, but I love you and I think we could totally be best friends."

Standing behind her, Mitchell grimaced and mouthed the words *I'm sorry.*

"Thanks," I said, and I signed her Team Peaches T-shirt, because that seemed like the thing to do.

She immediately began crying, and ran from the room.

"Did I do that wrong?" I asked Mitchell. "She seemed decent, but honestly, that was more terrifying than the paparazzi."

"Don't post any exterior pics of your home online," he said.

"I'm not Lady Gaga."

"No, but some of your Team Peaches people are quite organized. Yesterday, they staged a rally at a dog rescue in San Diego, because the place wouldn't let a woman adopt a Jack Russell terrier. The woman was... big enough to have some mobility issues, and she wanted a dog to help get her out of the house. They told her she was going to return the dog six months later, overfed and blown up like a sausage."

"Tell me you're joking, because I have to shoot a commercial right now, and I do not have time to fly to San Diego and slap the sense into those people."

"Everything worked out. She adopted the dog, and the shelter issued an apology and has promised to change their screening process. The dog's name is Barkles."

He held up his phone and showed me a picture of the little guy, being cuddled by his new person, all thanks to this group of people on the internet whom I had nothing to do with, but were acting like my hit squad.

"I hope everything works out." My stomach flip-flopped again, and I felt like I was back on the teacups ride at Disneyland.

"You do look fierce today," Mitchell said.

I turned and looked in the mirror, where I saw a scared little girl playing dress-up.

Fierce.

I bared my teeth in a growl. If I got through the day without any major malfunction, I was definitely, absolutely, positively, no doubt about it, getting a cupcake.

~

For some reason, I thought I'd be on a stationary bike, not a real one, and not pedaling back and forth in front of a green screen. At least Dalton wasn't there yet, so I got to practice my bike-riding in front of *his* stand-in guy, who looked nothing like Dalton, except for being the same height and skin color.

That bothered me. I knew I was being silly, but why had they gotten a stand-in girl who looked so very much like me that my own mother might have been tricked, but couldn't have found anyone Dalton-like for the other one? Were girls like me a dime a dozen? I felt cheap and used.

I pulled Mitchell aside and told him as much, leaving the bicycle leaning up against a wall.

He said, "I'm not quite following what you're saying. Are you angry that your stand-in looks like you, or that Dalton's doesn't?"

I could tell he was humoring me.

"Whatever. I need some corn starch or baby powder, because my inner thighs are chafing already. Can I get some bike shorts to wear under the dress at least? And is that a men's saddle on that thing? It's too narrow for my pelvis, never mind the rest of me. Is the director *trying* to break me down?"

"I'll get you some shorts, and I'll get another seat for the bike." He looked me straight in the eyes. "Those are reasonable requests, and thank you for talking to me. It's my job to take care of you, so you can do your job."

"Oh, honey, you're good. You must deal with a lot of crazy." I took a few breaths. "I don't know what came over me, but I feel the demon spirits of crazy leaving my body right now. Honestly, the seat of the bike isn't bad. A little adjustment to the angle and I'll be fine."

"You're being a good sport," he said, which made me feel ridiculous for all the emotions I was having.

229

Around us, the people with clipboards and headsets suddenly got big-eyed and quiet. Dalton Deangelo had just come out of hair and makeup.

He waved my way. "Hey, Peaches. Surprise!"

I walked across the studio toward him, caught his hand in mine, and kissed his cheek graciously. "Thank you for doing this," I breathed, acting like it had been my idea all along.

He seemed caught off guard. *Good. Let him wonder, for a change.*

CHAPTER 23

The male stand-in disappeared to go let light reflect off his surface elsewhere, and Dalton took his position near a lamp post with minimal instruction. I watched as he looked around at the lights and the camera, then made some tiny adjustments to his posture.

I thought we'd do a couple practice runs, but one of the crew snapped the black and white marker board to coordinate video and sound, and we began shooting. I chose to wear the ivory dress, which was sheer enough to offer more than the suggestion I was also wearing a pair of hot pink bra and panties. I don't know what kind of moron would leave the house looking like that, but my artistic input was of little interest to anyone, so I pulled the wide neck of the dress to one side to show the strap, and rocked the look.

I had a microphone pack strapped to my back, and we had exactly one line of dialog each. Dalton was to say, "Hey," and I was to bicycle by and say, "Hey, yourself."

Yes, the people creating the script for this commercial must have stayed up all night working on that gem. I know from watching *Mad Men* that there's an award in advertising called a Clio, and these writers were clearly in the running for one of those golden boys. (Please note: sarcasm.)

I shouldn't be so hard on the script people, but, "Hey, yourself," seemed like a shocking waste of my natural talent.

So, when the time came, I decided to improvise.

Dalton, standing by a lamp post: "Hey."

Me, trying not to run into him with the bicycle: "Hey, Mr. Sexy Pants."

The director, looking like he was about to poop in his hand and chuck it at me: "That's fine, but loop around and we'll try the line as written. Just to lock it down."

As instructed, I steered the bicycle in a circle, around all the equipment and people, and over several cords taped down with gaffer tape.

I came up on Dalton so quickly, his line sounded more startled than sexy.

Dalton: "Hey!"

Me: "Wanna see my new tattoo?"

The director, actually pulling down his pants to poop in his hand (okay, not really): "Try again!"

I looped around, enjoying the sensation of riding a bicycle. It had been too long. I definitely had to get the old bike back on the road back in Beaverdale.

Dalton: "Hello, beautiful."

Me: "You wish."

This made everyone in the warm studio laugh, which, as you might imagine, only encouraged me.

The director threw his hands up, like he was asking God to grant him the serenity to not choke the stupidity out of everyone present.

We kept going, take after take.

Dalton: "What's up, dream girl?"

Me: "Boy, I'm your worst nightmare."

More laughter.

Another loop.

Dalton: "Excuse me, miss. Which way to the Eiffel Tower?"

Me: Laughing too hard to respond, then asking Mitchell, "Are we in Paris?"

Mitchell: "With the green screen, we can be anywhere."

Another loop.

Dalton: "Hey."

Me: "Hey, yourself." (Coy smile and eyelash batting.) Okay, so the scripted lines weren't that bad after all.

Dalton: "Peaches Monroe?"

Me: "Sorry, no autographs today."

(Big laugh from the crew.)

And so it went for the next hour. I must have burned at least one cupcake pedaling in all those circles, so I increased my promised reward to a total of two cupcakes.

We switched to me in my underwear, and Mitchell discreetly powdered my inner thighs with something that smelled like peppermint.

The bright lights were battling with the air conditioner and winning, so being in nothing but my underwear was refreshing. After a quick hair and makeup touch-up, while the stand-ins did their job for a set change, I was back pedaling in circles and flirting with Dalton.

I'd had the opportunity to see him acting plenty, on my TV at home, but seeing him bring that intensity and energy out in person was impressive. I felt punchy toward the end of the session, but he was tireless.

We broke for lunch, and I caught the director smiling, which scared me. I found Mitchell and asked, "If frowning is good, what does smiling mean?"

"It means we'll all go home an hour early. You were great, by the way."

"Dalton was great." I peered around as we nudged in amongst the crew along the craft services table. They had big stacks of Ritz crackers, and I'd never wanted a Ritz cracker more, but I also wanted to talk to Dalton about how magnificent he was.

"Where's Dalton?" I asked.

"He's gone for the day," Mitchell said. "That was a wrap on his part."

I loaded up my plate with crackers and slices of white cheese. "A wrap. Okay." That meant he was gone—gone from my life. Our last words to each other would be for an underwear commercial. That sucked. Plus I still hadn't figured out how he knew I was fleeing a security guard in Malibu on Friday morning.

Across the room, someone laughed in a way that sounded like Keith's laugh, and my skin went clammy as I realized I hadn't thought about him once during the shoot. He'd asked me on the ride in if I wanted him to cancel his business plans for the day to keep me company for the shoot, and as I thought about his calm presence, I felt a pull, like there were magnets inside me, tuned to activate with thoughts about Keith.

"Mitchell, can you be in love with two people at once?"

"I'm gay."

"I live in a small town. I really don't know all the gay stereotypes, so give me a hint."

"Yes, silly. There are different kinds of love. You can be in love with the way someone makes you feel, but that's fleeting and dangerous. You can love someone for their good qualities, but that falls back into friendship, especially if they're not good at kissing. And you can love someone because you don't know how not to."

My mouth dropped open momentarily. When I recovered, I pulled him over to a corner and whispered, "The first one is how I feel about Dalton. He makes me feel like I'm going to fly apart, like stardust in a supernova. Then I met Keith, and he's just an amazing guy, so supportive and sensitive. Maybe too sensitive, but he's a fireball in bed, you know?"

"And do you love either of these guys?"

I put some cheese on a cracker and took a bite. Munching away, I said, "I like to keep my eyes open. Wide open. But you have to close your eyes to fall in love, I think."

He scratched his neck, looking thoughtful. "You close your eyes to kiss, so that makes sense."

"Keith's going to Milan, and I'm going back to Washington, so it doesn't matter how I feel."

"Don't say that. In life, how you feel is probably the only thing that matters."

We stared at each other in silence for a thoughtful minute. Some crumbs fell from my mouth down into my food-catchers.

I looked down, realizing I was standing in a room full of people, wearing nothing but my underwear.

So much for keeping my damn eyes open.

~

The second half of the day was less arduous. In fact, it was duller than sitting in the car while my mother ran her weekend errands. I was bored to the point where reading the fine print of my contract actually seemed fun and interesting.

After the seventh read-through of the same issue of *Vogue* while other people adjusted lights, I begged Mitchell to tell me more dating horror stories.

He told me about a blond guy named Trey who whipped his thing out while he was driving Mitchell home. This wouldn't have been so shocking, except Trey was married to a woman friend of Mitchell's, and he was a marriage counselor. After he was rebuffed by Mitchell, he claimed he had only unleashed Mr. Happy as a social experiment, just to see what might happen. Then he cried for twenty minutes, pulled over on the side of the freeway, no escape in sight.

"That's not very funny," I said.

"You wanted horror stories. Now you have to tell me one."

"I guess I could tell you about prom. You might not like me anymore after you hear the whole thing."

He nodded with approval. "You really know how to sell a story. Now tell."

I looked around at all the people standing around, looking annoyed and busy, moving lights and props. "Mitchell, are you really the assistant to the photographer, or is your job to babysit the models?"

"*Babysit* is such a strong word. Tell me the story before I die of suspense."

We moved further away from the hive of activity around the four-poster bed on set, over to a leather sofa. It was one of those brown sofas with loose cushions and plenty of distress marks—a real man's sofa. In fact, the sofa had reminded me of the story.

I told Mitchell of how I'd turned down two invitations to my senior high school prom from perfectly-decent guys, because I'd been holding out hope Adrian Storm would come to his senses and finally realize I wasn't just *a girl*, but *the girl*. Meanwhile, he'd been holding out hope that staring wistfully at Chantalle Hart would somehow lead to the two of them going to prom together, even though she'd been dating Kevin Spencer.

With only three days left until the big day, I received a proposal from Kevin Spencer's younger-by-ten-months brother, Jett Spencer. Despite the cool-ass name, Jett was by far the less desirable of the Spencer brothers, but he was about four-fifths better than going to prom solo and circle-dancing with the other solo girls, whose fathers were relieved and mothers were heartbroken.

Jett made a strong case for himself. He'd brought to school a photograph of himself in the tuxedo he'd already taken the liberty of renting, and he showed me a printout of the corsage he would buy me, as well as details of where we would pose for professional photos between the dinner and the dance. He said he had an "average" face, and that when I went off to college after graduation, I could proudly display the photo of us at prom together, and make other guys jealous, because they'd assume he had a big you-know-what.

At this point in my and Jett's conversation, which was in the cafeteria, I started to laugh, because I thought he was about to produce, from the folder on the table between us, photographic proof of his, er, size. To my relief, the next thing to come out was the receipt for a limousine rental.

There are only two limousines in all of Beaverdale—one white, and one black, both with tinted windows and their own legends. He and his brother had rented the white one, which, to our knowledge, had never been vomited in.

Jett got out of his chair, came around to my side of the table, and got down on one knee. He removed his thick-lensed glasses and said, "I'll take these off for the photos. What do you say, Peaches? Will you be my prom date?"

I looked up and noticed Adrian standing motionless with a tray of two cafeteria meals in his hands. (He started eating two lunches about mid-way through twelfth grade in an attempt to put some muscle on his skinny body.) He looked annoyed, which made me smile.

Jett took my smile to mean yes, and did that thing where you pump the air with your fist. A bunch of people cheered, and he returned to his side of the table looking a full inch taller. I didn't have the heart to say no after that, because he was a sweet guy, plus I wanted to ride in the good limo and make my mother cry happy tears.

On prom night, the limo showed up at my house, and I posed for pictures on the front lawn with Jett, and with Chantalle, and then all four of us, including Jett's brother Kevin. Chantalle pouted and said she hated me for having better cleavage, which I took as a compliment. I wore a blue dress with a sweetheart neckline, and I looked great... and yes, my mother did cry. My father sniffed a few times as well. Kyle came running out of the house with no pants on and peed on the bushes, as evidenced by three of the photographs taken that night. (I'll be sure to bring those out with pride at *his* prom one day.)

The whole evening started off perfect. I didn't spill food on my dress, and I didn't even say anything to embarrass myself. I guess I was partly distracted by the corset-style strapless bra I was wearing, and my constant fear of a wardrobe malfunction that did not happen.

Jett was a dream date, always making sure I had a beverage, and dancing to all the songs I liked. At my suggestion, we went over and joined the circle of solo girls toward the end of the night, and Jett tore up the dance floor in his sharp tuxedo, to the delight of all the girls. He was getting so much attention from all of them, that I found myself getting envious. The way some of them were pawing him... you'd think they'd never seen a geek in a white tux jacket before.

The night drew to a close, and we proceeded to the Spencer residence, where I had permission to stay until two o'clock in the morning. My parents had assumed the parental Spencers would be in the house, but they hadn't actually *asked*, so I hadn't needed to lie.

As you may have guessed by the fact I'd given birth to a child already, I was no virgin. (I didn't share with Mitchell the secret-baby-having details.) I wasn't holding out anything for anyone, especially since Adrian never even showed up to the prom.

To my absolute delight, Jett made a case for us having sex that night. I'd already decided hours earlier, but I did enjoy being in the role of the girl who wanted to be talked into it.

237

We were sitting in his family's recreation room, which had a pool table, two of those old stand-up video arcade games from the eighties, and a deluxe bar with a sink and a beer fridge. We were drinking beer from cans, poured into glasses. Jett had been quite particular about pouring the beer to get the right amount of foam.

We sat next to each other on the sofa, our knees touching. He said, "I feel like such a jerk, putting all this pressure on you. I feel like one of those guys in those videos we saw at school."

I laughed and sipped my beer, then wiped the foam off my upper lip. "No way. Those guys are all, 'I saw you dancing like a dirty slut. I know you want it. I'm gonna give it to you.'"

Jett laughed, but looked uncomfortable.

I tipped up the glass and finished the beer. It was my second one since we'd gotten there. Chantalle and Kevin were upstairs. I had to be home in an hour.

In a move I have to describe as possibly my classiest one to date, I stood up, kicked off my shoes, reached up under my pretty blue prom dress, and pulled my panties down and off. I rolled them up and stuck them in the toe of my shoe, then I sat back down in the corner of the sofa.

"Jett, I have to be home in an hour. I can tell by the way you dance that you're a sex machine, so why don't you climb on and start rocking my world right now."

For a second, I thought he was going to run away. His face blanched, and he was already a pale guy. He took off his white jacket slowly and set it on the round, glass coffee table alongside the two empty beer glasses. He retrieved his wallet from his back pocket, pulled out a condom packet, then leaned over and clicked off the halogen lamp standing beside the couch.

I swung one leg up onto the couch, hiked my dress up, and prepared to be boarded. I heard some balloon-animal noises, and then Jett clambered up on me. After some fumbling around in the dark, he moaned.

I pulled his head down to mine and kissed him. He moaned again, moving in a thrusting motion with his hips.

What was I feeling in my intimate area? Nothing. Absolutely nothing.

So I lay there for several minutes, which I can assure you feels like eternity when you think something's gone wrong with your vagina and it's now completely numb.

Mitchell interrupted my story at this point, waving his hand excitedly. "He was in your butt."

"Ew, no! I'd notice that. You're so bad."

"He was rubbing in between your thighs."

"Not even. I might have enjoyed that. He was sexing up the couch cushions. And, by the way he was going to town on them, I had to wonder if it was even the first time."

"No!"

"Yes. He stopped kissing me and started french-kissing the throw pillows."

Mitchell smacked my arm. "No he didn't, you fibber."

I continued, "I sensed that he was getting close to, you know, closing the deal with the sofa. So, I started to fake having an orgasm. Heavy breathing, moaning, thrashing around in ecstasy. Keep in mind I'd never actually had one before with a guy, so I was doing the movie version."

"That's so sad."

"Not really. You see, he shifted his position on the couch, so his hip bone was, you know, in a very nice place. After a few minutes, my cries became real."

"Shut up."

"We came together. Just like that. Gasping and sweating in each other's arms, me in my hiked-up prom dress and him with his rented trousers down around his ankles, his bow-tie slightly askew."

Mitchell fanned his face. "I'm a little turned on right now."

"I reached down and pulled him out of the crack in the cushions, so he wouldn't realize what had happened, and you know what?"

"What?"

"He *did* have a really big one, as it turned out."

Mitchell pointed his finger at me. "That was a good story, but it wasn't a horror story."

"The story's not over yet."

He leaned in.

"So all four of us run out to the limousine, because both of us girls have to be home by two o'clock. We get in the back of the limo, and Chantalle's being awfully quiet. I ask her what's wrong, and she opens her mouth and barfs all over me. This gross, watery barf that smells like wine, and it's in my cleavage, and I can feel it dribbling down inside my dress. So, Chantalle, who is pretty drunk, turns to Kevin and says, 'See, I told you if I swallowed your spunk I'd throw it back up again.'"

Mitchell began to hyperventilate.

I said, "So, yeah. *That happened.*"

Mitchell's jaw dropped open and he rolled forward, off the couch and onto the concrete floor of the studio, where he laughed and laughed until I begged him to stop.

Finally, he wiped the tears from his eyes and said, "That was the perfect mix of horror and humor."

"Not for me. The barf-spunk mixture got into my panties, and I had to buy pregnancy tests for the next month, because I was worried some of Kevin's swimmers had, you know, gotten in there."

"I love you, Peaches Monroe." Mitchell threw his arms around me and kissed my cheek. "I TRULY love you."

I hugged him back and smiled, because I'd been waiting a long time for a guy to say those words to me, and even from a platonic friend, it still felt good to be loved.

~

We wrapped up shooting for the day, and Mitchell wouldn't let me take a cab to Keith's, so he gave me a ride in his Miada. We stopped by a bakery along the way, where I bought a six-pack of cupcakes, including two special men's cupcakes with smokey bacon sprinkles and maple icing. Mitchell ate one of those in the car while driving, while I had a miniature vacation of the coconut variety.

I walked into Keith's apartment, all excited about the bacon cupcake. He was sitting on the sofa reading on a tablet. He looked up at me, then shook his head and turned back to his reading.

"Rough day at work?" I asked. "Having issues getting everyone ready for your departure?"

"Business is fine," he said curtly.

"So, are you having your period?"

He didn't even crack a grin.

I continued, "I thought today might be a heavy flow day for you, so I brought you home a cupcake. Let me know where your hot water bottle is and I'll get you set up."

"You were kissing Dalton Deangelo."

MIMI STRONG

CHAPTER 24

I set everything down on the kitchen counter with a thump, then got myself a glass of tap water. I called out from the kitchen, "Oh, you heard. No, I wasn't kissing him. I had to ride a bicycle past him and say one line of dialog. My thighs were rubbing together so bad on the bike, but I was a good model. No complaining, except to Mitchell."

I took a seat next to him on the sofa and passed the water his way. "Want some?"

He pushed the water back, splashing it all over my lap. I opened my mouth to let out a few choice words, but then I saw the photo on his tablet: me, kissing Dalton just outside the restaurant where we'd had brunch on Friday. Thundernuts! I'd forgotten all about that, in my hungover haze.

Keith did not look happy at all. Heavy flow day, indeed.

"I got you a bacon cupcake," I said.

"Are you just stringing me along for fun, and him, too? I actually feel sorry for the guy."

"Okay, I can explain. Dalton found me and Mitchell hitch-hiking in Malibu, for reasons that are perfectly logical and not at all illegal, and we had brunch. There were some photographers outside, and he suggested we give them a little something to get free publicity." I pointed to the short blond fellow at the edge of the image. "See, there's Mitchell. I was never alone with Dalton, not even for a second, I swear."

Keith frowned and wiggled his lips back and forth, as though goofy facial movements helped his brain process information.

"I'm sorry," I said, which is what I should have led with. *I'm sorry.* Why don't I lead off with that particular phrase more often? Pride, I suppose. I always think I can use my big mouth to talk myself out of trouble, but I should just try that whole begging-for-forgiveness thing more often.

"Now I'm the jealous one," he said, still frowning.

"Bacon cupcake?"

"I don't like how I'm feeling right now."

"If you don't like bacon, there's a pink cherry one, with those weird silver sprinkles that look like ball bearings."

He shook his head. "What time is your flight to Washington on Wednesday?"

"Nice!" I said angrily, getting up from the couch in a huff. "Real nice, Keith. Don't worry, you'll be rid of me soon enough."

He didn't say anything.

I felt the crazy coming. It swirled up around me like a toxic cloud —like the black eels that swoosh around Ursula the sea witch in *The Little Mermaid.*

I had one little in-public peck on the lips with a friend, and now Keith wanted to throw me out like yesterday's coffee grounds and banana peels? Nice. Real nice.

The crazy swirled. A big, dark, inky cloud of crazy. I curled my lips around my teeth like a mummy in a horror movie, then I grabbed the box of cupcakes and stomped to the spare bedroom and slammed the door.

The door didn't bang shut very loud, so I pulled it open and did it again, with a much more satisfying crack.

I flicked on the TV, turned it to a music channel, and cranked the volume. Sitting on the bed, I stuffed the entire bacon-maple cupcake into my mouth, pulled out my phone, and sent a message to Shayla.

Me: *The honeymoon is over! Keith Raven is a cheese-banger, and LA is hot and smelly and would you just slap some sense into me if I ever consider leaving town again?*

Shayla: *I went by Peachtree Books today. Adrian completely changed the window displays.*

Me: *Someone is going to die.*

Shayla: *The windows look nice, actually. Your father was there, building some custom shelves.*

Me: *I hate everyone and everything.*

Shayla: **Hugs.**

Me: **Goes limp. Receives hug begrudgingly.**

Shayla: *Didn't you have the commercial shoot today? How did that go?*

Me: *I guess it was okay. Tomorrow is a shorter day, and I get to sit on a trapeze thing for a bit before plunging to my death, which will be a welcome relief.*

Shayla: *Send photos.*

Me: *Anything else?*

Shayla: *The refrigerator finally broke, and the landlord got us a new one that makes ice cubes.*

Me: *OHMYGOD.*

Shayla: *I know, right?*

I shuffled off the bed and put the remaining cupcakes inside an empty dresser drawer, then got down to the serious business of discussing our new windfall, which also filtered and chilled water.

An hour later, I had simmered down, and ventured back out of the room.

Keith was in the kitchen, chopping onions and grating ginger for something that smelled interesting.

"I may have overreacted," he said.

"Apology accepted."

He gave me a crooked grin, looking very boyish with his dark hair falling down over his forehead as he peeled garlic cloves.

I asked if I could help with dinner, and he gave me some simple tasks, starting with peeling potatoes.

We made dinner together, then ate while sitting at the counter, side by side.

We were friends again, but things weren't like before. Words had been said, and doors slammed. I thought of a parable I'd once read in an advice column about anger—thoughtless words were like nails pounded into a fence, and you could remove the nails, but holes would remain, weakening the fence forever.

That night, we climbed into bed together like two roommates, he in his shorts and me in a long nightshirt. After the lights went out, I

thought about reaching for him, but after all the bike-riding and the stress plus tedium of shooting a commercial ("hurry up and wait" is the key phrase of the film industry for a reason), sleep had more appeal. I lay on my back with my hands crossed over my ribs, like how vampires sleep in movies. The room was so quiet, I swore I could hear Keith's eyes blinking, and his thoughts. Two more sleeps. Two more sleeps, and I'd be gone.

Sleep eluded me, because I couldn't shake the sensation that I could see the future, and tomorrow was going to be anything but ordinary. Out of all the props in the world, why did it have to be a trapeze?

~

Despite being cool to me the night before, Keith gave me a ride to the studio Tuesday morning, the commute almost starting to feel routine.

We arrived early, parked, and ate Egg McMuffins in the van. I was surprised Keith ate McDonalds, but he pointed out that he'd skipped the deep-fried hash brown patty.

As the time ticked down, my stomach started to flutter with performance anxiety jitters. "Does modeling ever feel normal?" I asked. "Like a regular job, where you just show up and make the required effort as you wait out the clock?"

He sighed.

"So, that's a no?" I asked.

"You could measure the amount of work a model does by only counting the clicks of the shutter—the time where light is reflecting into the camera, being recorded. Looking at the time that way, most of us have extremely short careers. Maybe an hour if we're lucky."

I gave him a sidelong look, not sure if he was joking or not. He didn't have his usual amused and light-hearted expression on. He looked serious, and he looked scared.

"You're telling me I should shut up and make the most of this opportunity," I said.

"Enjoy yourself." He kept staring straight ahead, out the window, at something beyond the industrial buildings in the area. "Like flowers in the spring, nothing beautiful is permanent."

I unbuckled my seat belt in preparation for getting out of the vehicle. My parents had me well-trained as a kid, and even as an adult, I don't feel right in a vehicle if I don't have the belt on, not even parked and eating food. Keith still had his seat belt on, too, so I guessed his parents had been the same way.

I said, "Hey, I want to take you out tonight. It's my last night in the city, and we'll go anywhere you like, my treat."

"You don't have to do that."

"I want to, and it'll give me something to look forward to during today's shoot."

"You're done around when? Three o'clock? How about I come pick you up and we go for a drive along the coast before dinner?"

"Sounds great!" I leaned over and gave him a kiss on the cheek.

"Break a leg."

"Not a good thing to say to someone who's going on a trapeze today, but thanks anyway." Grinning, I shut the door, waved goodbye, then started toward the studio.

Strangely enough, I was already at the door! Ah, that would be my beautiful stunt double/stalker. The nerve of her, walking around looking like me. Why did it bother me so much? I didn't know.

Once inside, keeping a safe distance from my double, I checked into makeup and zoned out while all of the stuff happened to my body. It's odd how quickly you can get used to something as unsettling as a stranger putting on your mascara. The makeup girl had a long shirt over her jeans, and without seeing her lower back tattoo, I couldn't figure out if she was the same girl who'd done my makeup the day before. This girl had short hair and a nose ring. Did yesterday's girl have a nose ring? Not knowing itched at me, like a scratchy tag inside a new shirt.

"My new tattoo's feeling hot," I said, reaching to my inner hip for a light scratch. "How long will it take to heal?"

She stared at me like I was a moron. "There's this website. It's called Google."

Right. No, this was not the same makeup girl from yesterday. She was nice, and this one... well, I'd have her fired if only I was more powerful. Hmm. Something to aspire to in life: having bitches fired.

I didn't have long to ponder my revenge, and I was off to wardrobe, getting stuffed into underwear. The funny thing about the bras and panties was they weren't the actual product. They were locally-made prototypes, as the line was only just going into production, mostly* overseas.

*When a company says their production is *mostly* overseas, that means it's *entirely* outsourced to another country, and you might find things like dried-out husks of scorpions inside the boxes of clothing.

The sample underwear I had on for the shoot was well made and beautiful, but not quite complete. Thank goodness for safety pins and double-sided tape.

After having strangers handle my peaches for the first part of the morning, getting on a trapeze didn't seem as unpleasant. As I did a series of simple shots leading up to the trapeze, I actually looked forward to something more challenging.

We broke for lunch, I had some yummy granola and yogurt, and got excited about the final shots.

My enthusiasm evaporated when I saw the heavy-duty winch, and exactly how high they were planning to hoist me before gently "floating" me down toward the camera. At least the trapeze was more like a kid's playground swing than a skinny bar you could grip with a closed hand, which was probably better than having a thin bar disappear in my pillowy flesh. No complaints there.

I watched as they did a test shot with the stand-in. She did look cute spinning in the air, descending like an angel, if you ignored the tractor-like noises of the winch. There was no audio on this shot, which was understandable, as you'd never hear anything over the machinery.

Mitchell walked me over to inspect the safety net, and told me to just "go limp" if I happened to fall. I made a joke about wetting myself and ruining an underwear sample. Mitchell got a serious look and told me it wouldn't be the first time for such an accident around there.

My stand-in wandered off to go reflect light elsewhere, and I got onto the swing to be hoisted up.

Now.

I've mentioned the height and I've told you about the netting. You're probably expecting me to have some hilarious malfunction and fall onto the net. Honestly, part of me expected the same thing, but it didn't happen.

What did happen was something else I found troubling.

They winched me up, and there I sat, way up high, waiting. That part of the studio was like a gymnasium, and the view from my perch was impressive. I could see every person moving around—like my own personal video game. A guy came in the door from the hallway, and I squinted to get a better look, because he had a Dalton Deangelo aura about him. Was it the stand-in from the day before? No, it couldn't be, because this guy was actually cute.

Time had flown by that day, and I wondered if Keith was already there to pick me up.

I waved, but the dark-haired guy didn't see me, because a person doesn't walk into an enormous room and scan the ceiling area for people he might know. After a minute of watching him walk around the room and talk to various people, I had no doubt it wasn't Keith, but Dalton Deangelo. I'd know that vampire swagger anywhere.

He walked up to my stand-in, who wore a white robe over underwear similar to mine. Seeing him approach her made the hair stand up on the back of my neck, despite the heat I was in, up near the rafters.

The winch continued to rumble away, blocking all sound I might want to hear.

I watched the scene below, my mouth dropping more and more open, as Dalton chatted with the not-Peaches girl, doing flirty things like sweeping the blond hair from her face.

Did he think he was talking to me? My eyes are blue, and that girl had brown eyes and a gap between her front teeth. But... he seemed to be staring more at her peaches than at her face, so perhaps he hadn't noticed. They moved closer to a wall, where his body language got extremely flirty. With one palm on the wall, he leaned in over her, their faces close enough to kiss. Unbelievable.

I nearly fell off my trapeze, but my survival instincts kicked in and I clutched the ropes. I couldn't hear anything over the roar of the equipment, but I just knew my evil double was giggling like crazy as smooth-talking Dalton fed her cheesy lines about being future old friends or stardust or whatever.

I tore my gaze off them, thoroughly annoyed, and spotted a clock on the far wall. Time had really flown by, and we were running behind, because it was already three o'clock. Keith would be arriving soon, and—

Movement below caught my eye.

Actually, Keith was already there, striding in through the side door. Striding over to where Dalton was talking to not-Peaches. Punching Dalton in the face.

NO!

I shrieked, leaning forward and nearly falling out and down to the netting.

Someone honked an air horn. I looked straight down at Mitchell, who gave me the thumbs-up, just as my trapeze began to twirl.

Another honk.

It was Mitchell, gesturing for me to arch my back as discussed.

But Keith just punched Dalton! Didn't anyone else notice?

I arched my back and tried to think angelic thoughts as I twirled and twirled, descending from the heavens.

When I reached the bottom point, they turned off the winch so everyone could talk. I jumped off the swing and landed on the net. I swore at the thing as it grabbed at me, then finally extricated myself and started running toward Keith.

Keith stood with his chest out, having a face-off with Dalton, who was squinting, one eye already swelling up. Not-Peaches, my twin, had already run off and was nowhere to be seen.

I put one hand on each of the guys' chests, trying my best to hold them apart before more damage happened to either of their faces.

"What the hell!" I yelled at both of them.

Shaking his head, Keith turned to me and said, "I came in here and saw him all over you, and I just lost it."

"He was hitting on my stand-in, not me."

Keith's forehead wrinkled. "Yeah, I figured that out just as his face threw itself at my fist."

Dalton rubbed his eye, grinning and taking a step back. "I guess I have a type," he said to both of us.

I glared at him. "You guess you *have a type*? Really? What are you even doing here?"

"I didn't get a chance to say goodbye yesterday."

"So you thought you'd come say it to whoever looks like me?"

He looked down, grinning like he was thrilled to be busted. "She has a name, you know. Justine. She says you're turning into a bit of a diva."

Keith interrupted just then, saying, "You're the diva," to Dalton. "Peaches got over you, and you can't stand it."

Dalton turned, like he was going to walk away, then twirled back and punched Keith in the face.

I screamed.

CHAPTER 25

Keith charged toward Dalton to retaliate, knocking them both to the floor.

"Not the face again!" Dalton yelled. "I'm an actor, you idiot."

Keith grumbled and panted, both of them wrestling on the floor like kids. "You punched me in the face, and I'm a model, you idiot. They could write a black eye into your stupid show. I don't have that luxury."

They rolled, over and over each other, arguing over whose face was more important.

Dalton growled, "What luxury? I can't even get a haircut without approval."

"Yeah? I can't gain five pounds or I get fired."

"Who's your manager? That's terrible. I have fifteen."

"He said five pounds was STANDARD!"

Over they rolled again, both red-faced, yet not doing much more than fighting for top position.

Dalton replied, "You should fire him and call MY GUY!"

"Ow, ow. What? Are you pulling my hair?"

Dalton rolled on top. "Say uncle!"

He was pulling Keith's hair, his hand full of it.

I looked around at our audience of two dozen or so people, all of them rapt. Three of them held up their cell phones, recording.

"Enough already!" I reached down and grabbed Dalton by the armpits and hauled him off Keith.

Keith jumped up and gave me an angry look, made even more crazy-looking by the swelling around his left eye. "I was just about to pin him," he said.

"We'll call it a draw," I said, keeping them apart with the mere power of my steely glare. "People are watching, so why don't we take this somewhere more private?"

They both nodded, so I led them down the hall and into the makeup room.

"Please stop hitting each other," I said. "Threatening bodily harm is awesome, but actually doing it is just sad. Okay?"

They both nodded like scolded puppies, then sat down on opposite ends of the long bench in the room. I sat across from them in the swivel chair. Looking down, I said, "Great. I'm in nothing but my underwear. Again."

"You look great," Dalton said, leering at me.

Keith jumped up, whipped his T-shirt off, and tucked it over top of me like an apron.

"Thank you," I said sweetly to him.

To Dalton, I said, "I appreciate you coming by, but we've got one shot left, and they're going to be banging at that door in a minute. You do nothing but cause chaos in my life."

"It was Alexis," he said. "That's how I knew you were in Malibu that day."

"Oh." Mystery solved, sort of. Alexis was the daughter of the porn star actress Dalton ran away from home with a few years back. She was also a giant pain, always lurking around and taking photos when you didn't want her to. Just thinking about her gave me the urge to check the closets in the makeup room.

Dalton explained, "She's trying to get out of the paparazzi stuff and do some private investigation work."

"You had her following me?" I looked around for something to throw at Dalton, but all I saw was a bowl of fruit. Good enough! I picked up a banana and a grapefruit and chucked them at him. "You creeper."

"She wasn't following you." He caught the fruit easily and started peeling the banana. "Bruised. Yuck." He tossed it into the trash bin.

"She has a scanner and she listens into some frequencies for leads on photos, just to pay the bills in the meantime. She raced out on a security lead and saw you, sleeping on the chair of some rich oil sheik's vacation home, and she called me."

"She could have at least woken me up and given me a little warning."

He began peeling the grapefruit. "You're not exactly her favorite person. You reamed her out pretty hard at that coffee shop in your town. Made her re-examine her life. People don't appreciate so much honesty at once."

I held up my hand, because I'd had about enough on the topic of Alexis. She didn't deserve another word.

Dalton glanced warily over at Keith, who was sitting shirtless and being very patient, then he said, "Peaches, I want you to spend your last night in town at my place."

Keith blinked at me. "Is this happening?" He blinked again, his eyebrows high. "Are you... ?"

Mitchell tapped at the open door, his face pinched in apology. "I'm really sorry to interrupt..." He waved his hand at the three of us —two of us partially undressed. "All of *this*. But we really need, like, two more takes of that last shot. Three, tops."

I stood, handed the T-shirt back to Keith, and said, "I have to do my job."

In unison, both of them said, "I'll wait."

I walked out of the room with as much dignity as I could muster, praying they weren't looking at my nearly-bare butt.

Following Mitchell down the hallway, my stomach hurt from all the stress.

Out of the side of his mouth, Mitchell said, "Two guys. Aren't you lucky."

I snorted. "So lucky. I bet the videos are already online, right?"

"Nope. Everyone here is bound by certain terms. A couple people forgot themselves and started recording, but everything's been deleted. I saw to it. That's why I was only listening in at your change room door for the tail end of that exchange."

"That's a relief."

"Easy to do your job when you care so much."

I stopped walking, just short of entering the big studio space. "Mitchell, you are one of the coolest people I've ever met. I cannot thank you enough for everything. Or can I? What can I do for you? I could write a letter of recommendation."

He patted my hand, the sheen of his eyes betraying emotion. His voice thick, he said, "It's just nice to be appreciated. Send me a postcard when you get home."

I gave him a hug.

"Thank you for not leaving me with that security guard woman," he said.

"How did she get you tied up? Isn't that illegal? She wasn't a cop or anything."

He pulled away from me, blinking and smiling. "I know, right?"

"But seriously, if you can think of anything, let me know. And of course you have a place to stay if you're ever in my part of Washington."

"We'd better get this shot, or we'll be back here tomorrow, and saying goodbye one more time will feel even more awkward."

"Good point."

I hustled my way back over to the trapeze and climbed on. "Thank you, you're gorgeous," I called out to my stand-in, who was sitting on a folding chair nearby.

She gave me a limp wave in return. What was her name?

I ransacked my memory banks.

"Thank you, Justine!" (Big grin. Nailed it!)

She gave me a second half-hearted wave. Oh well, at least I tried.

Up I went, over the roar of the winch, and I began to twirl. I arched my back and imagined the beautiful evening I was going to have. I could hardly wait.

I reached the bottom, and the director said, "Loving that Mona Lisa smile. Keep it up. Another take. Bring her up, boys!"

Up I went again, a peaceful smile on my face the whole time. My last night in LA would certainly be memorable.

We did one more take, and doubt crept in, but by the time my toes hit the netting, I was sure.

I barely waited for them to call it a wrap, and I was off.

I stepped into the change room. Both of the guys sat holding ice packs to their eyes.

Seated across from them, I broke the news gently. "Dalton, I value our friendship, and I appreciate your offer, but I've already made plans with Keith. Justine is still in the building, and if you'd like to ask her out, you have my blessing."

"She's no Peaches."

"Maybe she's stardust from the next galaxy over."

He turned to Keith and shook his hand. "Take care of Peaches, and call my manager, and also fuck you."

They were both grinning, teeth bared like animals. "I sure will, and thanks for the suggestion, and fuck you, too."

Dalton got up, swept his hand through his hair as we briefly made eye contact, then he left.

I looked over at Keith, who seemed stunned. I joined him on the bench and rested my head on his shoulder. He wrapped his arm around me and kissed the top of my head.

"You had me fooled," he said. "I damn near walked out of here right after you left."

"You deserve someone better than me, but in the meantime, you're stuck with me for one more night. We're each other's rebounds, and we have one last night to unbreak each other's hearts."

He was quiet, and when I looked up, he was smiling. We sat there for a few minutes without talking. I let my breathing relax and deepen. What I didn't tell Keith was how tempted I'd been. To my shame, I'd considered the other offer. Dalton had a way of throwing me off balance, and I'd liked it, the way kids love twirling on carousels and getting dizzy. Part of me wanted another night of that carousel ride (on a pony named Lionheart, no less), but then Keith had literally given me the shirt off his back. He'd covered me with his T-shirt so I wouldn't be exposed.

There is no such thing as a *small* gesture; gestures can realign lines of fate.

Because of Keith's gesture, and a hundred other sweet things he'd done for me, I got dressed and left the studio that day with him.

I looked around the parking lot for the green van, which should have been easy to spot. Keith led me to a little sports car, an Alfa Romeo.

"What's this?" I asked.

He rubbed his eyebrow, which was red and swelling from being punched, and put on a pair of sunglasses. "Nice car, right? Borrowed from a friend. The owner of the restaurant I took you to the first night. He really liked you, and insisted I show you off in proper style."

"See? I *knew* I made the right choice. Dalton's car is boring."

Keith laughed and held open the passenger door for me. I settled in and put on my big sunglasses for the ride.

We drove through the city, me pretending to be cool behind my sunglasses, but gawking around to see if anyone was looking at me. The car was flashy enough that we got a few looks, but nobody was staring. It was LA, after all.

We drove up along the coastline on a sun-soaked road locals call the PCH—that's the Pacific Coast Highway to Washingtonians such as myself. On one side, there's nothing but blue water, beaches, and surfers. On the other side, you see mountains dotted with mansions, every one with a spectacular view.

One last night.

As I admired the scenery, I felt homesick for the lush woods of Washington, seeing familiar faces everywhere I went, and even the misty rain.

~

After the drive, we had dinner at Keith's friend's restaurant again, where my money was no good. We danced, alone on the dance floor, lost in our own world.

Then we went back to Keith's place for our final night together. Keith showed me so much affection, my heart healed and then broke all over again, because I was leaving in the morning.

We lay nestled together under the top sheet, and he practiced his Italian phrases on me. I was exhausted from the day and drifting in and out of sleep. He murmured things that sounded intimate and personal—things that sounded like Italian for love.

I fell asleep in his arms, and when I woke up, I was alone.

~

Morning had come quickly, and my first thought was that I would miss the light. Keith's apartment got fantastic morning light through the blinds if you didn't pull the blackout curtains.

I got up and gathered the clothes I hadn't packed in my travel bag the night before.

Even though I was probably a completely different person than I was nine days earlier, I planned to wear the exact same outfit I'd arrived wearing, because it was comfortable for traveling, and feeling good is important. I pulled on my black leggings, a pair of Keds, and a red shirtdress with a black belt.

I found Keith in the kitchen, making blueberry pancakes.

"Early flight," he said.

"Wouldn't feel so early if someone hadn't kept me up so late."

"You weren't complaining last night, unless that's what those moans were."

I took a seat on one of the stools at the counter and tried not to get emotional. Mitchell had already sent me a text message wishing me a good flight, which made me miss him already.

"I'm going to take a cab to the airport," I said.

Keith peered over at me, but didn't say anything.

"Because I hate goodbyes," I explained.

"Peaches, nobody likes goodbyes. Everybody hates them. My parents are already driving me crazy, and I don't leave for a few more days."

"You'll do great in Milan. I can feel it."

"You could change your flight and stay here a bit longer."

I grinned, fighting back the emotion choking me. "If we try to top last night, somebody's going to break something. I need to leave right now, for the health and safety of both of us."

He chuckled and served up the pancakes, alongside fried eggs and stunning toast made of marbled dark rye and sourdough. Then he sat beside me, and we both ate, barely making a dent in all the food. I would miss this. Sharing a meal with him. Everything about this borrowed relationship felt so good, but it was a loaner, like the Alfa Romeo. A rebound.

I looked up the phone number for a cab and made the call, despite Keith's protests.

Five minutes later, the driver was there, and Keith insisted on hauling my luggage out. My suitcase was packed tight, and I had two shopping bags as well, with my haul from the boutique. I had a third bag, with Mitchell's roommate's dress, and I would be dropping it off at the dry cleaner's on my way to the airport. Yes, everything was going according to plan. So, why did the movements of that morning feel so wrong?

"Maybe goodbyes shouldn't be so serious," I said to Keith. We both stood beside the cab as the driver waited patiently inside.

Another cab pulled up behind it, and the older woman I'd seen near the courtyard pool stepped out. It was eight in the morning, and she wore a black dress and spike heels. She gave me a wave and an embarrassed smile as she entered the courtyard.

"Walk of shame?" Keith said.

"I'd say so. Good for her."

"Yeah! Good for her."

"Peaches, I want to tell you something."

I shifted back a few steps. "I should go."

He took my hands so I couldn't slip away. "I used to struggle with my addiction, but I found my cure in the truth. As long as I always tell the truth, and take care of myself, I'm not tempted to start using again."

"I can't imagine you doing drugs. I keep forgetting, because you're just so... you."

"Everything ends eventually," he said, gazing down at me, his gold-brown eyes serious. "I'll get older, whether I have birthdays or not. This career won't last, and the next one won't either. But maybe things that are brief are better, and brighter, and sharper." He took my hands and held them to his chest. "I feel you, in here. Like a diamond."

My eyes burned, and I gritted my teeth. "I feel you, too, and... I don't know what to say."

"Bright and sharp," he said, and he leaned down to kiss me.

My whole body was trembling, even my lips.

I pulled away after the kiss and fumbled with the door handle of the cab. Keith reached down and pulled the door open easily.

I got in the car, before my shaking legs collapsed.

Keith closed the door, tapped the roof of the car twice, and the driver put the car in gear.

We drove away. I raised my hand and watched out the back window as Keith waved back. I watched him until we reached the end of the street and rounded the corner.

Why did the driver have to drive so fast? What was the hurry? I turned back around and frowned at the back of his head.

Sharper and brighter.

Like a diamond.

I heard Keith's words echo in my mind.

Home, I told myself. *Think about home.*

MIMI STRONG

CHAPTER 26

I'm pretty sure I saw Gwyneth Paltrow at the dry cleaner when I was dropping off Luscious Hilda Mae Sparkles' dress. This skinny blond lady in granny boots and black leggings was chatting with the woman at the cash register when I came in.

I looked around at the array of autographed glossies lining the walls and tried not to get paranoid about my taxi abandoning me.

The skinny lady turned around, gave me an apologetic smile, then turned back to finish putting her wallet back in her purse.

Holy porkchops, that's Gwyneth Freaking Paltrow. The room started to swirl. My mouth dried up, and my heart started pounding like crazy.

She finished and started to leave, but I was blocking the door.

"I'm a big fan!" I said, which wasn't even true. I mean, I like Gwyneth, but someone gave me her latest vegan cookbook as a joke gift. I wasn't a *big fan*, not really.

She gave me a gracious smile—almost regal—and walked out with her dry-cleaned pantsuit over one arm.

Such is life in Los Angeles.

I dropped off the dress, pre-paid, and returned to the waiting taxi. The whole way to the airport, I mused over my reaction to Ms. Paltrow (assuming it was her).

I would have thought that the whole experience with Dalton Deangelo would have changed me more, made me less starstruck when I met other celebrities. But, apparently, a brief affair with one famous person hadn't inoculated me against other celebrities. I was, after everything that had happened over the last few weeks, not that different after all.

Or was I?

There were moments, like when I walked through the crowd at the airport and didn't care that people were staring at the big girl in the red shirtdress—moments where I felt something harder over my entire surface, like that skin Jell-O gets after a few days in the fridge.

~

Seated on the airplane, I nodded my head to the right and gazed wistfully out the window. There was nothing to see but pavement, but I liked the idea of how I thought I might look to a casual observer—like the girl at the end of a movie who has grown in some way and is an adult now, which you can tell because she does something different from how she did it at the beginning of her tale.

We got in the air, and the flight attendant offered me a beverage. I'd had a Ginger Ale on the flight down, which was my third flight ever. This was my fourth flight, and I was different now, so I ordered a Bloody Mary. I'd never had one before, but people in movies order them on airplanes, and the words just came out of my mouth.

The flight attendant nodded curtly and came back with the tomato-juice-based drink. "Matches your outfit," she said.

I paid, and she walked away, without having asked to see my ID. The nerve!

The girl sitting next to me said, "That smells so good."

"You should get one. Call the attendant back, my treat."

She laughed and looked pointedly down at her stomach, quite clearly swollen with a baby.

A chill went through my body. "How long?" I asked.

"Two weeks."

"And they let you fly?"

Her lip started to tremble, then she put on a big, fake smile. "Short flight. Even if I went into labor..." She trailed off, as if she didn't have the energy to finish the thought, to tell the lie that everything would be fine, no matter what.

She looked young—about as young as Amy, the sixteen-year-old girl who'd been my employee until recently.

I pulled out my phone and looked for a good photo of Kyle to show her.

"This is my son," I said, showing her a picture of him pretending to eat two slices of pizza at the same time.

"Wow," she said, looking back over at me.

"I was fifteen when I had him."

She nodded, her eyes getting wet before she blinked them clear. Her words burst out of her. "I'm scared. I don't like pain."

I patted her on the knee. "Nobody likes goodbyes, or labor pain. And it's okay to be scared. I was, too. But I had a good doctor, and my parents were beside me the whole time. We're so lucky to live in a time of hospitals, and medicine, and epidurals."

Her chest rose with a deep breath I could hear, even over the whooshing white noise of the airplane.

"What about down there?" she asked, looking embarrassed. "Did everything go back to where it had been?"

"Yes, and everything works fine. No complaints."

"Were you scared during labor?"

My skin started to tingle all over. I grabbed my Bloody Mary and shot it back.

"No," I lied, smiling. "Your body kicks in with all the right hormones at the right time, and maybe there are a few moments where you get tired or frustrated, but you'll know what to do. Everything's going to be fine."

Her face relaxed and she leaned her head back against the armrest.

I pulled a magazine out of the pocket in the seat in front of me and pretended to be engrossed in an article about natural fibers being trendy come autumn.

I felt bad about lying to the girl, but I also knew telling her the truth wouldn't help either of us.

~

Me.

That night.

It's Friday, and my stomach's been acting up all day, but Mom and Dad are out of town I am ready to party! And by party, I mean I am going to order pizza with the money they left for groceries, and I'm going to eat it in the formal sitting room, where Dad and I aren't allowed to eat.

I have it all planned out. I'll put down one of my bedsheets like a drop sheet for spilled crumbs. I won't even need to vacuum.

I wish Shayla was here, but it's her loss, and I sure hope her babysitting money is worth it.

The pizza guy arrives, and I pay him for the pizza, plus two dollars for a tip. The look on his face tells me two dollars is on the cheap side, so I dig around in my pockets and hand over my loose change, which is humiliating for both of us. My guts are killing me with first-day period cramps. I'm sweating so much from pain, the change in my hands is wet, and he makes a face.

After he walks away, I lock the door, throw the pizza on the coffee table, and run up to the main bathroom, which I then murder with an epic poo.

I walk back downstairs, feeling pounds lighter and thinking my problems are over. I open the box and the smell of the double-pepperoni pizza nearly puts me off, but I push myself to take a few bites, thinking I'll feel better any minute. I'm usually hungry for salty, greasy food when Aunt Flo comes to visit, but I'm strangely disinterested tonight.

I turn on the TV and begin my planned marathon session of re-watching the entire first season of *Veronica Mars*.

My guts are really killing me by the second episode, and I'm pretty sure it's punishment for eating pizza in the formal sitting room. My mother has hired a gypsy to put a curse on the room, and now I will pay, in pain.

This idea of a curse gets less funny over the next few hours, as I toss and turn on the sheet-covered sofa, unable to get comfortable. My lower back hurts like someone's kicking me in the kidneys with pointy boots.

These are the worst period cramps I've ever had, and the weirdest part of all is that I haven't started bleeding yet. I go to the bathroom to check, and my tampon has only watery stuff in it.

My ankles are swollen like crazy, either from the salty pepperoni or my mother's gypsy curse. All this from eating pizza in the living room. Can you imagine what would have befallen me if I'd touched the dandelion wine? My head would have just split right open.

It's only ten o'clock, too early for bed, so I lie down on my parents' big bed, still wearing my clothes. They have a zillion pillows, which I use to make a comfy nest for myself.

I wake up to the sound of myself whimpering. The house is dark and quiet. I'm curled up, and my hands are balled up in fists. I punch the bed a few times, but the sharp pain in my back is relentless. Did I herniate one of my discs today during my epic, naked, interpretive dancing? It doesn't seem so hilarious anymore, all the hip wiggling and towel snapping.

Still whimpering, I slide off my parents' bed and start to crawl toward their en suite bathroom on my hands and knees. Technically, I'm not allowed to use this bathroom, unless it's an emergency. I'm getting an urge to push, though, so I think it's an emergency.

The phone rings. I know it's my parents calling to check up on me. The ring just has that sound, and nobody else would call the land line at this time of night.

The pushing feeling has faded to more of a general ache, and my back feels better now, strangely. Maybe I just needed to get some crawling exercise.

I shuffle to the bedside table and pick up the ringing phone.

My father says, "Peaches? Is that you?"

Oh, right. I forgot to say hello.

"Yessssss," I say.

"Are you drunk? What the hell's going on? Are you having a party?"

I groan. "No, Dad. I was just having a nap."

"Why were you having a nap?"

A sharp pain sends a tremor through my body, and I feel heat between my legs. Moisture. I put my hand on the crotch of my sweatpants. I did not just piss myself, did I? How embarrassing.

"Uhh. I think I have, like, a stomach thing."

"Oh." He does not sound like he's buying it.

I shuffle into the en suite bathroom, praying I didn't get any of the carpet wet.

"What's really going on?" he asks.

"I have the worst period cramps of all time, if you must know. And I just made a mess, okay? Aren't you glad you have a daughter? Because I'm sure happy to be a woman on days like today."

"Did you take a Midol?"

"Dad, I—" The pain in my back returns, and I curl up on my side on the tile floor in the bathroom, panting.

He says, "You should take a Midol before the pain gets really bad. Pain-killers work better if you take them right at the beginning."

My voice pitches up like a squeak. "Okay."

"And try taking a hot bath," he says, repeating what my mother is saying in the background.

"Yup."

"Peaches?"

I can barely breathe, let alone speak, but I gasp out, "Yes?"

"If there's ever anything you're scared to tell me, don't be scared. I love you, and your mother loves you, and nothing will ever change that. If you promise to always tell us things, we promise to not be angry. Okay?"

"Okay."

"Now, you're really at home right now? You didn't have the calls forwarded?"

"Yes, I'm at home."

"Did you take any drugs tonight?"

"Just Midol."

"Okay, sweetie. We love you and we miss you already. Do you want a souvenir from Arizona?"

"Nope." What I do want is to get off the phone so I can try to get some relief on the toilet, or maybe draw a bath, like he suggested.

"Are you sure?"

"No souvenir. Love you! Bye."

I click the button to end the call, then strip off all my clothes during a pain-free flash. On the toilet, I have a small pee, but nothing else. My vagina seems to be leaking fluid now, so... I guess that's just another weird puberty thing people don't talk about. I can't comprehend all this. It's too weird.

I start running water into the tub, and then I climb in. I'm not even naked. I still have my socks on, and my bra. This makes me laugh.

I look down at my stomach, and the way the water is over my body, it looks like my body is moving even when it isn't, with ripples moving across my belly.

I close my eyes.

I sleep.

The phone rings.

Nobody answers it.

I hear a car with a loud stereo drive by outside.

The water drips into the tub rhythmically. Drip, drip, drip. I drift.

I'm awake again.

I will just push and push until I feel better. I'm on my back, one leg hanging over the edge of the tub.

The pain is worse than before.

Something terrible is happening to me.

I'm going to die here.

I need to drain the water before I drown, but I don't want to.

The phone is ringing.

Someone is at the front door.

I just want to sleep, escape the pain.

I try to take off my wet socks so I can be comfortable, but I can't reach with my hands, and it's too hard.

Why is everything so...

Am I awake?

Someone is banging on the door downstairs.

It's the pizza man. No, it's not.

I roll onto my side. I don't want to hurt anymore.

There's a crash.

I should be scared, but I'm not.

The phone is still ringing, and I know it's my father. I know his ring.

He won't let anything bad happen to me.

~

269

The airplane dropped from the sky, the engines roaring as we came in for the landing. The pregnant girl next to me was holding my hand and praying.

Pray for me, too, I thought. *Pray for us all.*

The wheels went RZZZZT on the pavement, the plane bounced like a car losing control, and then my seat felt more upright again. We slowed.

I let out a nervous laugh and turned to the girl. "See, everything's fine."

She released my fingers and looked around like someone waking from a nap. "My first time flying," she said.

I nodded like an old pro of four flights. "You'll get used to the landings."

~

We got off the plane, and I hugged my new-yet-nameless friend goodbye. I gathered my luggage and set out for the taxis to take me to the bus station.

Beaverdale is too small to have its own airport.

The night the EMT guys found me barely conscious and in labor, I heard them talking about a helicopter, and how they might need to transfer me elsewhere for an emergency C-section. I was delirious with pain, and I had pre-eclampsia, so my blood pressure was sky-high. Everything seemed like it was happening to someone else— someone on TV—so I wasn't at all worried. I struggled to keep my eyes open just to see what would happen next.

We drove to the hospital, siren on the whole way. The siren is louder inside the ambulance than you'd think, which only made me respect the calm EMTs more.

The next part happened quickly, with me barely getting transferred off one rolling bed to another, and there was an entire human being coming out of me.

They took him away, and I began to wail and wail, inconsolably. I didn't know I was pregnant, and now I was so sure I'd messed up this little human who deserved so much better than me. I was so sure he was going to have everything wrong. When they brought him back into the room, bundled up in a pale yellow blanket, I thought they'd brought me someone else's child.

He was so perfect, so precious.

And I couldn't look at him.

I couldn't hold him, because I was too ashamed. The nurses would take better care of him, and they didn't argue. They just took him away, checked my vitals, and whispered outside my door.

I stopped talking to everyone there, except for yes and no answers. I didn't want to look anyone in the eyes. I wanted to die.

My parents arrived at the hospital in the morning, having come straight home as fast as they could. They didn't say anything except that they loved me. I rolled over and said I was tired. They took turns staying in the room, so I was never alone.

For that, I will always be grateful. For their love, their forgiveness, and for never leaving my side.

~

By the time the bus pulled into the Beaverdale depot, I felt like those hobbits at the end of the Lord of the Rings. There is nothing glamorous about traveling, unless you own a private jet that can land on a regular driveway, but I don't think those have been invented yet.

The plan had been for my father to give me a ride home, since Shayla, my usual taxi, would be working. To my surprise, I stepped into the bus terminal and saw three familiar faces between the potted ficus trees. My mother held up a hand-made sign covered in stickers, reading *Welcome Home*. Kyle was holding a Mylar balloon shaped in a heart. His little orange T-shirt had Team Peaches written on the front with those standard block letters you get at T-Shirt Bonanza. My father looked embarrassed, but his expression turned to happiness as soon as he spotted me.

My mother called out in a stage voice, "Isn't that Peaches Monroe? The world-famous superstar?"

I ran over to them quickly, my rolling suitcase wheels unable to handle the speed, the bag rocking back and forth with a thwap-thwap-thwap. I dropped everything and grabbed all three of them in a hug. Kyle wrestled free, so I had to chase him around the potted

271

trees, threatening him with big, sloppy kisses as he squealed and squealed.

I nabbed him finally and spun around with him in my arms. "I missed you so much!"

He squirmed out of my arms and used his chin to point over to my suitcase. It was a gesture I'd seen my father make a thousand times. "What did you bring me?"

We walked back over to my parents, then proceeded out to the car, still talking.

"What makes you think I brought you something?" I asked, teasing.

"Mom said."

"You don't believe everything Mom says, do you? She puts vegetables in the chocolate cake."

My mother elbowed me. "Libel and slander."

My father cleared his throat. "Technically, it's either libel or slander, but not both. It's more of an accusation, but given what I've seen happen to zucchini in our kitchen, not a baseless one."

We climbed into the car, both of us kids in the back. I gave Kyle the package from inside one of my shopping bags, and he tore through the wrapping.

It was a science kit I'd picked up at LAX, with over three hundred separate pieces to delight him and drive my parents crazy. We spent the short car ride to my house arguing over whether or not the package could be opened in the car, or if doing so violated my father's rules for in-car conduct.

At my house, my father brought my bags into the house, and all three of them came in. My mother tidied up the living room (making some very big eyes over the ashtray full of evidence of Shayla's recent downward spiral), then she karate-chopped the pillows. My father checked that the railing on the staircase was still secure (he'd fixed it two months earlier) and looked around for other hazards. Kyle went straight for the new fridge, as though he had a special psychic sense for new things, and started filling cups with ice cubes and water, much of it ending up on the floor.

Half an hour later, I'd shooed them away, and I went up to my bedroom to rearrange my walk-in closet to make room for my new designer clothes.

My parents had invited me to the house for dinner, but I'd declined, saying I was tired, even though I wasn't *that* tired.

I tied the heart-shaped Mylar balloon to a dresser drawer, so it could bob around in my room until the helium leaked away.

Whacking the balloon with my finger and watching it rock in the air, I had to laugh. I'd missed Kyle so damn much while I was out of town, but forty minutes with him was more than enough.

I used to feel guilty about that, back when I'd come home from college for a visit and spend more time partying with my friends than seeing my family. I don't feel bad about that anymore, though, because self-torture gets old, and life is hard enough without being your own worst enemy.

It's easy to doubt yourself.

Every time I've been asked about my pregnancy, my memory shifts. My father says the clues had been there all along, just like in a great detective novel. According to him, I'd wrinkled my nose at certain foods the same way my mother had during her pregnancies. He hadn't noticed the weight gain—not exactly, but he had been bothered by my louder footsteps on the staircase. He says that when I was on the phone that night, my moans had sounded exactly like my mother's when she went into labor with me. Everything clicked in that brilliant brain of his, and he just *knew* what was happening. He'd even guessed I was in the en suite and instructed the EMTs to check there for me.

I've thought about those same clues a million times. There was a blouse I'd thrown away in disgust because it made me look pregnant, and when I say I was still getting my period throughout, what I should say is I wasn't, and I didn't care. My mind was hazy, and whenever I thought about my period... I changed the topic. But I must have known. On some level. I stopped going over to Toby's house, and offered him no explanation. We'd been having fun, so why had I stopped? I think sometimes that another person lives inside me, and keeps my secrets from me. I'm not ill, like one of those people with multiple personalities, but I think I have secret closets in my head, where I put things I don't want to think about, and the door is clearly marked: *Deny, deny, deny.*

~

My phone was ringing. In yet another classy Peaches move, I'd fallen asleep on the floor of my walk-in closet, on a pile of towels.

The call was coming from an unknown number in California.

"Hello," I said chirpily, finding it odd the underwear company would call after ten o'clock at night.

A male voice: "Happy to be home again?"

"Who is this?"

"It's Keith. Don't tell me you've forgotten all about me already. Way to kill a guy's self-esteem," he joked.

"I deleted your phone contact so I wouldn't be tempted to drunk dial you."

There was a pause.

"Keith?"

"I guess I shouldn't have called," he said.

I sat up and pulled down a shawl to cover my arms, so I wouldn't feel cold and sound cold. "I'm glad you called."

"Long distance relationships don't work. I'm not trying for one, but I've been thinking about you all day. Did you see your little boy?"

I wrapped the shawl tighter against the goose bumps on my forearms. "Yes, he came with my parents to pick me up. He gave me a balloon, and then he drove me crazy. My mother has the patience of a saint."

"Are you going back to your bookstore tomorrow?"

"Afraid so. There aren't a lot of modeling jobs here in the Beav."

"Really? I've always heard that the hot spots for the fashion industry are Milan, New York, and Beaverdale."

I laughed and looked down at the chipped nail polish on my toes. Already the veneer of LA was peeling away.

"Keith, I really admire you."

"Yeah?"

"You're flying off to Italy, starting this amazing career, and you're not even scared."

"I'm terrified, if you must know. I just hide it under a big smile and a spray tan."

"You'll be fine," I said, and I meant it.

We talked for another hour, both of us having to plug in our phones to keep going. I could have stayed on the line until dawn, but I heard Shayla come in the front door and call my name.

I said goodbye to Keith, and he told me to "take care." When I ended the call, I wondered if that was the end for us. I started downstairs to greet Shayla, then paused just long enough to program Keith's phone number back into my contacts list, just in case.

I ran down the stairs and straight into my roommate's arms. She put her hand over my mouth and pretended to stage-kiss me, both of us swaying back and forth laughing our butts off.

I was home.

Even as we laughed and play-wrestled, I felt something sharp and bright in my chest, where heartbreak had been. Keith hadn't left a scar or a wound, but something else. Our shared experience lived on, near my heart. Tiny and brilliant, like a diamond.

Maybe I had changed, or maybe I had just gotten older, the way Keith had when he finally gave in to birthdays. They call this process *growing up*, and I think I know why. With every new experience, your view of the world broadens, and your own life starts to look smaller, because you're *up* above things, like a plane flying over.

CHAPTER 27

Thursday morning, I walked out the door of my house with my Pop Tart in one hand and my cell phone in the other. Mitchell sent me some funny photos from LA and told me about a wacky photo shoot they were doing that day, with some half-naked girl and a hundred white rabbits.

I didn't believe him about the rabbits until he sent me a photo.

Mitchell: *They're multiplying! I swear. I just re-counted and there are 105 now.*

Me: *I'm so mad that I didn't get any bunnies.*

Mitchell: *Shoot me now. I was holding one for a close-up and it pooped little chocolate balls right in my hand.*

Me: *Chocolate?*

Mitchell: *Yes! I'll gather them in a basket and mail some to you.*

I walked by my neighbor, Mr. Galloway, who called out, "Can't wait to see your new photos!"

Stopping near his rose bushes, I pretended to be offended. "Mr. G! You do know it's an underwear campaign, right? That means I'll be in my skivvies."

His cheeks reddened, and he pulled his glasses off his long, fine nose and cleaned them on his shirt, flummoxed for a minute.

"Just teasing," I said, laughing. "I hope everyone sees them, because they're going to be gorgeous. I'll autograph yours."

"As long as you have a nice smile in the pictures, because I swear that's the only part I'll look at."

I started backing away, aware of time slipping by. "Did you get rid of your problem? Your rat?"

277

He shook his head. "I took away all the food, except I forgot the bananas on the table. Wouldn't you know, he got the bananas."

"Maybe it's a monkey."

Mr. Galloway waved goodbye, signaling he was finished with this particular topic, and off I went.

~

With my mocha in hand, I opened the door to Peachtree Books. The shop smelled different.

I started to feel irritated, then angry. Someone had moved the round pedestal table, and it wasn't aligned with the chandelier anymore, which meant that a tall man browsing one side would hit his head. He would hit his head and then stare at the *store manager* (that's me) with a very litigious-looking scowl. I could practically see it happening, like a clairvoyant.

"Stupid Adrian," I growled, and I set to work putting everything right again.

~

My new coworker Adrian didn't return any of my text messages on Thursday. I suppose my tone may have been too scary for him. That, and me calling him a cheese-banger. I didn't say anything about him talking about my high school crush on him, or his highly inappropriate dick pic (never mind that I started it with my nip pic), but I did give him the excoriating he deserved over messing with my system at the bookstore.

On Friday, I started creating a binder of Do's and Don'ts for the store. Actually, it was more of a collection of Do's, Don'ts, Absolutely Never's, and Death Will Befall You If's.

The day went by quickly, and I closed up the shop at six, as per the new schedule. We had been open later hours on Friday through most of summer, with Amy working the later shift, but now she was gone and apparently Adrian was doing Friday shifts at Chloe's, making pies, so we were just closed at six.

I snuck out quickly and kept my head down to avoid eye contact with any potential customers on their way in for some evening shopping.

Someone called out my name, so I started walking faster. Then he started chasing after me, his footfalls approaching rapidly.

I turned around, prepared to go back in and open the store for someone's literary emergency.

The man chasing me down was middle aged, with a brown mustache and long hair tied back in a ponytail. At first I thought he was a regular customer, because seeing Vern, Dalton Deangelo's butler, didn't make any sense in Beaverdale.

"Sorry to be any trouble, but where would you buy towels here in town?" he asked.

"At the mall, I guess. Why?"

"There's a mall?"

"Yes, with a K-Mart. Beaverdale isn't that small." I stared into Vern's cool, professional face. "No offense, Vern, but why are you here?"

His calm veneer cracked as his eye twitched. "Mr. Deangelo didn't tell you?"

"Vern, tell me you've quit working for that Hollywood phoney and you've moved to Washington for a slice of the small town life. Tell me you've joined three book clubs and you're thinking of getting a mountain bike. Tell me he's not here, in this town, where I live."

"He's not here."

I hugged Vern and kissed his cheek, to his surprise and dismay.

Vern explained, "I'm preparing the cabin for his arrival."

"Tell him I won't see him. We're through. Tell him don't bother coming to Beaverdale for me."

Vern shuffled his feet, his eyes cast down. "He's not coming here for you. He needs somewhere to hide, and I'll admit I suggested coming here because I do enjoy the town so much."

I shook my head. "He's hiding? Now what has he done?"

"It's quite unfair, really. He hasn't done anything. I'm afraid it's something rather troublesome from his past. I suppose you could read it along with everyone else in today's papers, or tomorrow's. Apparently, Mr. Deangelo bears a striking resemblance to a young man in some adult films."

My insides grew heavy from the weight of the news.

We stood there a few more minutes, as Vern described how everything had happened so quickly, starting Monday morning. As his lips moved, words came out and fell on my unhearing ears, because my body was focused on pumping out panic sweat and adrenaline.

Dalton had told me his secret, about how his parents had been in adult films, and how when he grew up and ran away from home, he'd been in a couple himself, despite being underage. That was all before he changed his name and started fresh. He told me his story, then he had me sign a Non-Disclosure Agreement, promising I wouldn't divulge any of his secrets.

But then I'd gotten really hurt by him, and...

Did he suspect me of being the one who leaked the information? Was he going to sue me? Did people do that?

Oh, no.

In the last week, I'd been pretty angry with him, and I'd had at least two nights of heavy drinking. Everyone who knows me would agree my mouth is the biggest thing on me.

I couldn't remember blabbing about Dalton's seedy porn-star past, but I didn't remember getting a tattoo, either. Did I...?

Vern was still talking, saying, "Most people aren't annoyed by sounds from nature. Even the most shrill of bird calls is still a welcome antidote to city life and big trucks with air brakes... and there's a goat that comes with the cabin, but I don't expect I'll be milking her, though who can say, really."

I nodded. "Right. Who knows?"

"Goats are the ones with the weird little eyes, right? Do they have hooves, or feet?"

"Everything has feet." *(How am I having this conversation right now? How are my lips moving and saying these things?)*

He said, "I suppose hooves and feet aren't mutually exclusive. So, which way to the mall?"

I pointed down the hill. "Five blocks. Take the east entrance or you'll have to walk in through the food court, and have cheese popcorn smell in your nose the whole time."

Vern thanked me, then turned and went on his way, in a manner I would describe as *merry*.

I started walking home, mulling over the news of the day.

Vern didn't seem upset at all about Dalton's secret getting out. He'd been disappointed with life in Beaverdale the previous time he was there, until I gave him a few pointers about making an effort, and now he acted like an eager transplant.

Had Vern released Dalton's secrets to the media? He'd always seemed so loyal.

Who knew, besides me and Vern? I didn't know who else Dalton had confided in, besides his manager and legal team. Could one of them have slipped up? Delicious secrets were difficult to keep.

That awful girl, Alexis, knew, but they were making friends with each other now. And besides, she'd known for years.

So, why now?

More importantly, without Keith around to keep me busy, how was I going to stay away from that charming liar, Dalton-whatever-his-real-name-was?

~

Shayla took me out that night to drink and get my mind off all things Dalton-related.

We started with dinner and sangria at DeNirro's, where I was happy to note they'd changed the decor back to the red-checked tablecloths.

I took that as a positive omen that things were going to work out.

Then a framed print spontaneously fell off the wall as I was sitting down. Shayla said I bumped the artwork with my chair, but I swore I had a foot to spare. The glass broke when it hit the floor, and a small piece flew out and nicked my ankle. I pressed a paper napkin between my crossed ankles and didn't say anything, because the staff was already horrified and apologetic.

I took that as a negative omen that my life was going to get way more disastrous.

After a pitcher of sangria, though, I didn't really care.

I just wanted to dance.

We finished our pasta, sucked the last of the sangria off the ice cubes, and wobbled our way down the street to Cougar Town.*

*The bar is actually called Kaleidoscope, but who can say that when they're partying? Also, it's full of older women in leopard print dresses, so maybe management needs to open their eyes and embrace reality with a new, more appropriate name.

The place wasn't too full yet, because the night was still young, even if the regular patrons sitting at the bar were not.

We hit the bathroom to sling on extra makeup before we lost hand-eye coordination, then found a choice table and ordered a round of drinks. Soon, we were joined by some friends, including Golden, her brother Garrett, and Chantalle, who was dating Garrett.

Shayla and I hit the dance floor for a few songs, and when we came back to the table, Adrian was on my chair, taking up all the space with his ridiculously tall, muscular body. His blond hair was styled to point up, making him another ridiculous inch taller.

I poked him in the chest with one finger. "You messed up my bookstore. I spent the last two days fixing everything!"

He grinned, as if he hadn't heard me over the music and thought I was complimenting him.

I grabbed a chair from a nearby table and dragged it over. Everyone was talking. I had plenty of things to say, but couldn't get a word in. The drinks were really going to my head, and I found myself caring less and less every minute.

At one point, I tried to contribute something to the conversation, only to be interrupted by Adrian saying, "One time, in LA..."

He grinned, and they all laughed. I hadn't been talking about LA that much, had I? They were all envious jerks, that was it. Oh, they patted me on the shoulder and said they were kidding, and to go ahead and say what I was going to say about my trip to LA, but I wasn't having any of it.

I told them all how stupid and annoy they were, with swear words, then I grabbed my purse to leave.

The world was blurry, and chairs kept getting in my way as I pushed my way toward the exit. When did Cougar Town get so big inside? I found an exit sign and pushed the metal bar below, only to find myself on another planet.

Wait, no, it was just the alley side, where I'd never been before. Two people were kissing over by the dumpster. My eyes adjusted to the weak light of the alley. Oh, gross, they were doing more than kissing.

I turned around to go back in the way I'd come out, but the door had no handle. Instead of doing the logical thing, and walking around to the front, or to the taxi stand to get a lift home, I banged on the door and swore at it.

The door opened, and Adrian walked out, looking concerned and sweet.

"There you are," he said. "We were worried about you."

He let the door close behind him.

"You weren't worried. They were all making fun of me, and you were, too. Jealous buttholes."

Twenty feet away, the gross couple was making grunting and panting sounds, only adding more charm to the moment.

"I was just teasing," he said. "Your friends love you. They're all dealing with your success as best they can. Trust me, I've been through this myself, when I was on the way up."

I stared up into his face, at his eyes, which were still beautiful even though I couldn't see their blue color in the yellow light of the alley.

I remembered the last text message he'd sent me, before the photo, and before I got back in town and started sending him my rant list items.

"Did you really know in high school that I liked you?" I asked.

"On some level, I think I did. But denial can be a powerful thing."

I laughed, my voice ringing through the alley. "I think I know a thing or two about denial."

"Why are you so upset tonight? Shayla said your boyfriend Dalton is coming here to visit. Shouldn't you be happy?"

"We're not together. I need to stay away from him."

Adrian blinked down at me silently.

"Can you help me?" I asked.

"How?"

I reached my hands up and clasped him behind the neck. He didn't want to budge, and he was so much taller, even with me on my toes. I pushed him back against the door and pulled at his neck harder, until he was leaning down, his lips coming closer and closer.

His mouth touched mine. He tasted like beer.

Hot buttered noodles, I'm kissing Adrian Storm.

~

The End of Starlight, Peaches Monroe #2
To be continued in #3, Starfire.

MIMI STRONG
www.mimistrong.com

Made in the USA
Lexington, KY
11 June 2015